By Dean Murray

Hunted

Dean Murray

Copyright © 2013 by Dean Murray

Published by Fir'shan Publishing

ISBN 978-1-9393631-9-0

www.FirshanPublishing.com

First Edition

For Mom and Dad

One book just doesn't seem like enough.

Chapter 1

I had a headache again, but that was pretty much the case all of the time. I was almost used to my brain trying to work its way out through my ears, so that couldn't have been the reason I opened my stupid mouth.

I'd hated Janessa for a long time and managed to keep my mouth shut, so I was pretty sure that wasn't the reason either. Maybe it wasn't either reason, maybe it was both of them together combined with a couple of other things that were so small that I didn't even realize they were bothering me, but I wanted to get up from my table and go tear Janessa's hair out by the roots.

Normally I'm not even the slightest bit violent. Unlike my sister, Cindi, I've pretty much made it through school by keeping my head down and ignoring other people as much as possible. You'd think in a school with a student body approaching five thousand that it would be easy to get lost in the crowd, but I'd had to actively work at staying anonymous. It was almost like there were so many kids attending our school that anybody could find a clique without even having to try.

Janessa and her friends talked crap about pretty much everyone in the school most days, but today it was getting to me like it never had before. Maybe it was the way that she was leading a smear campaign against Jackson, one of the new guys who had just moved into school. It wasn't that she didn't like him, she was doing it to make sure that none of the other girls would date him.

Once she finished sucking her current boyfriend dry then she'd be able to move in and redeem Jackson's social image by dating him. It was beyond shallow, but she'd invented a kind of social cold storage for future boyfriends. Given how oblivious I was to most things in school, if I knew about it then everyone else in the school did too.

Janessa was bad, but the people who let her get away with it were nearly as terrible, and the whole thing was making my headache even worse than normal.

"...and I was like seriously? Not only can I do a better back handspring than you, I'm going to ace our history test, at which point you're going to turn over your spot on the homecoming committee to me."

Janessa's voice was like an icepick shoved into my brain. It didn't seem to matter what I did or how I sat, I could still hear her as well as if she were sitting right next to me instead of at the next table over.

"...I know, right? She's still complaining that I had to have cheated somehow. She totally can't deal with the fact that not only am I hotter and more talented than her, I'm also smarter."

I couldn't help the snort of disbelief that made its way out of me. Maybe if I'd kept my head safely buried in my book I would have been able to pretend like it hadn't been in response to Janessa, but I looked up at the same time and she locked gazes with me.

"Did I say something funny, chubs?"

My fists clenched tight at the despised nickname, but I didn't actually want to get into a yelling match with her so I dropped my eyes back down to my book and hoped that she'd just let it go.

"That's right, you lame nerd. Next time don't forget your place."

Seventeen years of life had conditioned me to let the comment go, to turn the other cheek and just be glad that I had less than two years left in this hellhole, but this time I found myself looking back up and glaring at her.

"Yeah, you said something funny. You're kind of forgettable so I can't quote it exactly for you, but I think it boiled down to the fact that you tried to use the words 'talented' and 'smart' in a sentence that included you as the subject."

She was on her feet now, which should have been an alarming development, but somehow I was standing and instead of backing away from her, I was actually moving towards her too.

"You're forgetting who you're talking to, chubs. You're getting above yourself and I'm glad that it gets to be me that puts you in your place."

I could see it in her eyes. Normally Janessa and the rest of the cheerleaders, my sister included, ruled the school with an iron fist, but she was scared—not that I'd hurt her, but that I'd say what everyone else had to be thinking.

"You didn't ace your history test, you paid Richard Parsons a hundred bucks to steal the answer key for you and everyone knows it."

Janessa yelled something about me spying on her as she threw herself at me, but somehow I managed to give as good as I was getting. The neckline to her cheerleading outfit ripped with a satisfying sound that brought excited whistles from some of the bystanders who'd gathered around us within seconds of the fight starting.

She slapped me hard enough that I saw stars, but it wasn't enough to stop me. I punched her in the eye, which hurt my hand a lot more than I'd expected it to, but the blow nearly knocked her on her butt. A second later she scratched me on the arm, so I tackled her and scratched her across the face at which point two of the football players who'd been watching decided that they'd better break us up before somebody lost an eye.

Janessa was yelling that she was going to kick my head in for ruining her outfit as the guys pulled me off of her, but I was suddenly less worried about her than I was about just how much trouble I was going to be in with the administration. The assistant principal had already made it to the study hall and he looked even more pissed off than normal.

It turned out that he was pissed off, but I got the feeling that his ire wasn't directed at me as much as it was at Janessa. He read us both the riot act and then sent her home to get some new clothes and me to the school psychiatrist's office. Mrs. Bauer left me cooling in one of the hard plastic chairs outside her office for nearly two hours before opening her door and gesturing me inside.

"Okay, Adri, what gives?"

I shrugged as I sat down on one of the battered wooden chairs in front of her desk. "What do you mean?"

"I've been reading your record and this is the first time that you've gotten into any kind of problem at all. Your grades are above average, but nothing spectacular and until today I couldn't even put your face and name together.

You're not the kind of girl who ends up in my office for having a knock-down-drag-out fight with one of the cheerleaders."

"I don't know. I guess I'm just getting tired of the way that Janessa and her friends lead such a huge double life."

"They are cheerleaders, sweetie, it's practically a job requirement." She waved my protest away. "I'm not saying that it's right, but it's hardly like it's a new development, so it can't be the root problem behind today's little outburst."

I shrugged. "I really don't know. It was just one of those things, I guess. She was talking about how she aced her history test but the whole school knows that she cheated on it."

Mrs. Bauer shook her head. "I know this is hard to believe, but I spend more time actually talking to the kids in this school than anyone else here. By the time that 'everyone' knows something I've usually known it for at least a couple of days. I hadn't heard anything about this before you yelled it in study hall, and neither had any of the half dozen other kids who've been in my office in the last two hours."

She leaned back and rubbed her eyes like she wished that she'd been able to go home when school ended rather than having to stay after and deal with one more problem kid.

"You're related to Cindi Paige, aren't you?"

"Yeah, so?"

"So Cindi is on the cheerleading team, and from what I've been hearing, she and Janessa are rivals. They are both sophomores and Janessa having won a spot as a flyer has to have rubbed Cindi the wrong way. Isn't it possible that you did all of this as a way of helping Cindi out, of taking her rival down a couple of notches for her?"

I didn't mean to laugh, it just kind of exploded out of me.

"You obviously aren't as well informed as you think you are. Cindi and I hardly talk to each other. If I was going to get into a fight for someone, I can pretty much guarantee that it wouldn't be for Cindi."

"Are you sure, Adri? Maybe you don't even remember Cindi telling you about her suspicions that Janessa had cheated, maybe you didn't set out to start a fight with Janessa, it just kind of happened."

I shook my head. "That part is right, I didn't mean to start a fight with her, but this honestly has nothing to do with Cindi or anyone else."

Mrs. Bauer closed her eyes for a couple of seconds and then sighed. "I can't make you tell me the truth, but *I* would be lying if I said that I wasn't disappointed. I have dozens of kids come through my door every day who are basically beyond help. I do what I can, but after more than twenty years doing this I've learned that it ultimately comes down to whether or not the kids I'm working with want to be helped. I can give the ones who want to change the tools that they need, but there's not a darn thing I can do for the kids who are determined not to change."

I felt like she was waiting for me to respond, but I didn't know what she was after so I just shrugged.

"Adri, whenever a new kid comes through my door with a record like yours I usually get excited because those are the kinds of kids who generally just need a little help to get back on track. You need to think about your life and what you're doing with it because right now you're coming across as one of the kids I can't help."

She dashed off a note and handed it to me without looking. "You're going to get in-school detention at the very least, but I'm recommending that the administration not come down too hard on you this time. You know where the door is."

A few seconds later I was standing outside of her office a little bewildered at just how quickly she'd gone from interested and supportive to cold and uncaring. I looked up and down the empty hall and wondered if I dared go home now, but the sound of someone clearing their throat brought me around to find that Cindi had been sitting in a chair waiting for me.

"So you got in your first fight, huh?"

"No need to look so smug about it, Cindi."

She shrugged and picked up the stylish black messenger bag that Mom and Dad had finally purchased for her a month ago just so that she'd give them a few minutes of peace. It had taken two months of her begging and I'd spent the entire time hating the fact that she was making them buy her yet another expensive accessory that she didn't need.

"I wouldn't say that I'm smug, more like I'm just astonished that something finally brought you out of your shell enough to notice other people."

"Very funny. What are you doing here anyways?"

"I figured that there wasn't any reason to let a good catastrophe go to waste. I called and told Mom that you'd been in a fight and that I'd stay to walk you home. She agreed, which meant that I got to stay here and talk to my friends for nearly as long as if I'd had practice today. Thanks for that, by the way."

I wanted to hit her on the arm as hard as I could, but I settled for just frowning at her. It only took a second for the frown to slip though as I realized just how much more violent I'd become lately.

"I was serious, by the way, Adri. I don't think that you hit Janessa for me or anything, but it's actually worked out pretty well. Her uniform is basically ruined. I mean, she could still wear it, but I don't think anybody would be watching the game."

Cindi's expression was so mischievous that it drew a smile out of me despite my best efforts.

My smile made her smile in turn and then she pushed open the main door.

"Janessa could always use one of the loaner uniforms, but Miss Winters is kind of pissed off at her for all of her drama over the last couple of weeks, so she's going to be out of commission for at least a few days until she gets a new top ordered. Which means...I get to be the one at the top of the third pyramid!"

"Um, congratulations, I guess?"

"You guess? This is the hugest opportunity ever. I'm only guaranteed the spot for tomorrow's game, but if I do a good job there's no telling what might happen. I might manage to bump Janessa out entirely."

I shook my head at her. "I still can't explain your fascination with flying. The idea of being thrown twenty feet into the air and just trusting that someone on the ground is really going to catch me doesn't sound fun at all."

"You should try it sometime, Adri."

I snorted. Actually I was snorting a lot lately. I needed to watch that. I wasn't exactly gunning for a boyfriend or anything, but I didn't want to end up being repulsive to everyone around me.

"I'm not exactly flyer material, in case you haven't noticed. Janessa was quick to remind me today, just in case anyone else had forgotten that stupid nickname you gave me."

Cindi didn't look repentant very often, but she looked sorry this time. "I'm really sorry about that. I should never have given it to you in the first place, and I definitely should have made sure that I never used it around anyone from school. It doesn't actually apply any more though."

"What do you mean?"

"Gosh, sometimes I seriously question the fact that we're the same gender. Do you mean you really haven't noticed how much weight you've lost lately?"

"I haven't lost any weight, Cindi. You're still the skinny one in the family."

"Seriously? Have you looked at yourself lately? Your clothes are all practically falling off of you now. Honestly, that's probably part of why Janessa came at you like that. She's pretty self-conscious about her body and you're pretty much the same size as her now. You should come work out with the squad, you'd totally be flyer material in like a month."

I turned and grabbed Cindi's arm, pulling her around so that she had to face me. "Is this some kind of joke?"

"What the freak? You're turning into a total head-case lately. No, it isn't a joke. Seriously, look at yourself in the mirror sometime, you've totally thinned down."

Cindi was a lot of things—not the least of which was a spoiled brat—but she'd never lied to me when it mattered, so I let her go, somewhat mollified.

"That doesn't make any sense. I haven't changed anything. I'm not eating any differently, I'm not exercising, there's no reason for me to be losing any weight."

Cindi shrugged. "Well, I guess you're just lucky then because you're definitely losing weight lately."

We started walking again and I once again wished that we lived somewhere else. We were well past the hottest part of the day, but even now the humidity made any kind of exercise unpleasant. I could already feel a trickle of perspiration running down between my shoulder blades and it wouldn't evaporate until we made it home and got into the air-conditioned and de-humidified air inside.

Another month or two and the temperatures would drop, but we'd be lucky if we got all of a full week of nice weather before the snow and extreme cold arrived. Living in Minnesota meant you constantly had to worry about either heatstroke or frostbite, which would have sucked badly enough all by itself, but we lived close enough to the school that Cindi and I had to walk there and back all winter through the worst of the cold. If the temperatures dropped far enough sometimes Dad would run us into school before he had to leave for work, but that just meant we had to hang out at school for the better part of an hour before classes started.

As much as I hated the heat, I hated the bitter cold even more, so I decided I should be appreciating the weather today rather than just dreading the rest of the walk home. I knew that Mom was going to freak out once I got home, so I tried to think about something other than the events from school, but I couldn't seem to get Mrs. Bauer's words out of my mind.

We were nearly home before I broke the traditional silence in which Cindi and I usually made the trip.

"Were you the one who told me that Janessa cheated on her history exam?"

Cindi looked at me oddly. "We never talk about the squad. I mean, we hardly talk at all as it is, but we never talk about the other cheerleaders because you think that they're all a bunch of stuck-up idiots."

"I know that, I'm just trying to figure out where I first heard that she'd cheated. Maybe you were talking to someone on the phone and I just overheard your conversation."

I got another odd look as Cindi shook her head at me. "My phone has been broken for almost two weeks, you know that. I've been restricted to just texting people with my iPod since I dropped it in the parking lot while doing stunts with the other girls. Besides, I never even considered that Janessa might have cheated. I just figured she'd conned some poor sap into helping her study for it."

"I'm pretty sure that she really did cheat. The way that she attacked me was crazy. It was about more than just the fact that she doesn't like me."

Cindi shrugged. "You're probably right. Cheating would be more Janessa's speed than any form of studying, even studying with a nerd-assist."

"So where did I hear it then if not from you?"

"I don't know, Adri. I didn't think that you really talked to anyone else. Maybe you dreamed it."

It was like she'd reached out and slapped me. I'd been less shocked when Janessa had hit me. I gasped, but Cindi just rolled her eyes at me and kept walking. I thought about trying to explain my reaction to her, but it was just too crazy to try to put in words.

I *had* dreamed it, and now that she'd raised the possibility, even in jest, it was like a set of floodgates had opened up. I'd been having a ton of really weird, specific dreams about people lately, and almost every dream was about someone I knew.

I didn't have an explanation, but if there really was something going on inside my head other than just run-of-the-mill dreams, then I needed to figure out a way to keep the dreams from ruining my waking world. If I didn't keep the two separate then I was going to end up in all kinds of trouble. People wouldn't just ignore a girl who spent time inside of their minds.

HUNTED

If they really believed that I was capable of knowing their deepest secrets then I'd be lucky to make it out of high school alive and sane.

Chapter 2

Mom came unglued on me when I finally made it home. She was going on and on about suspensions and me being grounded. It was looking pretty bad right up until the shiny red timer on the fridge went off. That was the signal reminding her that she needed to do something with the photos that were being developed in her darkroom, or her cave, as we jokingly called it. She said our conversation wasn't over as she disappeared into the specially-designed rotating door that prevented light from getting inside the room, but I knew I was safe now. As long as Cindi didn't stir things up, Mom probably wouldn't even remember that I'd been in trouble.

Once Mom got buried in a photography project it was pretty much guaranteed that she would ignore anything less catastrophic than the house burning down, so I only needed to worry about Dad now.

HUNTED

Mom had the beginnings of dinner laid out on the counter, but past experience had shown that if we just waited for her to finish it up we might not eat for hours still. Cindi and I washed our hands and started grilling the chicken and cutting up the green peppers so that the food wouldn't go to waste. It looked like Mom was planning on tacos, but sometimes she took us by surprise. Once the chicken was started cooking I pulled out Grandma's recipe book and double-checked to make sure that we actually had all of the ingredients on hand.

It looked like we were safe, so Cindi and I fell into our normal rhythm of cooking interspersed with breaks to study whenever we were waiting on something. It was actually nice. We'd been filling in for Mom so long now that we didn't need to talk about what we were doing when it came to a meal like tacos. It meant that we could be together and yet still have some space inside our own heads.

I had to hand it to Cindi. She was a cheerleader and all, but she did work hard to keep her grades up. In fact she was probably doing better than I was. It was another reason to hate her. She was skinny and pretty and smart and I was just me. I didn't really hate her though. She was my sister and I was proud of her, even if I wished from time to time that the talents and looks had been split up more evenly between us.

Dad got home early, which is to say about the time most normal dads got off of work. He didn't say anything about my fight as he walked through the door, which gave me some hope that maybe Mom had forgotten to call and tell him about the incident.

He kissed Cindi and me each on the forehead and took a deep breath. "Those tacos smell really good, girls, thank you for cooking again tonight. How's your homework coming?"

Cindi smiled up at him with a warmth and brightness that exceeded anything she displayed even out on the football field. If she ever figured out how to bottle that expression she'd be very rich and dads all over the world would suddenly be wondering why they'd purchased their little girls a sports car and twenty-thousand dollars' worth of new clothes.

Dad had built up a little bit of resistance over the years, but even he struggled not to give in when Cindi really poured it on.

"Homework is fine, but I have really good news. I'm going to get to be the top of the third pyramid for the game tomorrow night."

That earned her a frown from both of us. Dad was frowning because despite having agreed and signed something like half a dozen liability waivers, he was still not completely onboard with the idea of his baby girl being thirty feet up in the air with nothing but a couple of irresponsible teenage girls between her and a serious injury.

I on the other hand scowled at her because she was getting unacceptably close to bringing up my fight with Janessa. She made a 'calm down' gesture at me when Dad bent back down to pick up his briefcase, which mollified me somewhat.

"What about you, Adri? How are your studies coming?"

Pretty poorly to be honest, given that I had missed the last hour of school and therefore my chemistry class, but I wasn't about to tell him that.

"I'm doing okay. I'll be glad for this semester to be over though."

This time it was me he frowned at, but his expression wasn't so much disapproving as it was worried. "Don't wish your life away, Adri. Someday you'll look back at high school and wish you'd enjoyed life. Trust me, things only get more complicated and hectic the older you get."

I shrugged in response, which was about as safe of a route to go as possible. His smile seemed to say that he knew exactly what I was thinking, but he let things rest there.

"How long has your mom been in her cave?"

Cindi checked the antique metal clock on the kitchen wall. "Half hour, forty-five minutes maybe."

Dad nodded and headed down to Mom's cave. His voice floated up the staircase from the basement so we could hear him despite the distance. "Nikki, the girls have dinner ready to go. Are you where you can stop and join us?"

I heard something bang into something else and then a muttered oath from Mom. "John, you're home? I wasn't expecting you for another half hour at least. I'm right in the middle of something. You and the girls will have to start dinner without me, I guess."

I heard a longsuffering sigh out of my dad and then he came back into the kitchen and helped me set the table. Dinner went about like normal. Cindi dominated the conversation while Dad and I watched in bemusement at the way she managed to talk nonstop about so many different things without ever seeming to have to pause for food.

I was actually starting to relax by the end of the meal. My headache even disappeared right up until Dad leaned back in his chair and patted his stomach. "The tacos were excellent, girls, thank you very much for stepping into the breach once again. Cindi, would you mind doing the dishes tonight while I talk with Adri?"

It felt like my head was going to explode. I didn't hear much else for the next few minutes, but all too soon I found myself sitting in the tiny guest bedroom that doubled as my dad's office. Cindi and I had been begging Mom and Dad to let one of us move into the guest bedroom so that we didn't have to share a room any more, but it was one of the few things that Mom had held firm on. She kept telling us that Dad needed a space of his own just like she had her darkroom and had refused to budge despite an epic amount of pleading from Cindi.

"The school called your mom today, Adri. You were in a fight. What happened?"

"I...well, there was a girl in school who was lying and I knew she was lying so I kind of made a disbelieving noise and then things kind of escalated from there. She called me chubs, so I insulted her back and then I told everyone in study hall that she'd cheated on her history test."

Dad looked tired a lot of the time lately. He was working longer hours than ever and it showed in the set of his shoulders and how bloodshot his eyes always were. He rubbed his eyes and stared at the ceiling for several seconds.

"I'm not sure what to say to you, Adri. I always thought that only having girls would mean that I wouldn't have to worry about having these particular kinds of talks with any of my kids."

I felt sorry, for the first time all day. The assistant principal, the psychiatrist, Mom, they all mostly just yelled at me or at the very least scolded me, but I'd known that their unhappiness came from how I was impacting their lives. Dad was different, and I knew it without him having to even open his mouth. He was worried about how my actions were going to impact *me*.

"I'm sorry, Dad. I don't know what I was thinking. It just kind of happened."

Dad looked back down from the ceiling and took my hand between both of his. "I have some questions for you, but I don't want answers right now. I want you to think about them and then come back to me with the answers later."

My headache was stronger than ever. Tears started pooling in my eyes, but I managed a nod, which seemed to satisfy him.

"The first question is who you think was the bully in this situation. The second question I'd like you to think about is some of the ways that the situation could have spiraled out of control and gone oh so much worse than it did, and the last question is whether or not fighting was justified and if so, why."

"You're not going to tell me that fighting is never justified?"

Dad shook his head. "Your teachers and mother are probably going to tell you that there's no such thing as a justifiable fight, but I don't agree with them. I'm not saying that your fight with this girl at school was that kind of fight—maybe it was, maybe it wasn't—but some fights are justified."

"Okay, Daddy. I'll think about your questions."

I stood up to go help Cindi finish up with the dishes, but he stopped me with a gesture. "I'm sorry, Adri, but you need to have some kind of consequence for what happened today. I'd take away your phone, but you hardly use it, so it wouldn't be the same kind of punishment for you that it is for Cindi. Instead I'm going to say that you need to deep-clean the house. I want you to finish up a room every other day between now and whenever you have a set of answers for my questions."

I opened my mouth to answer his questions right then and there, but he held up a hand.

"If you have good answers to my question then I may shorten your punishment, but if I feel like you haven't really given them any thought then I'll be adding to it."

I didn't like it. The normal teenage response would have been to yell and scream in an attempt to convince him that the pain of sticking to his guns was much greater than he'd expected, but I couldn't bring myself to explode into those kinds of theatrics. Dad already had enough to worry about what with Cindi starting to really take an interest in boys and Mom spending ninety percent of every day lost in some other world where her art actually mattered.

"Okay, Dad. I'll think about it and I'll start cleaning the kitchen tonight."

"You can wait to start until tomorrow, sweetie. How bad off is your arm?"

I'd forgotten that Janessa had scratched me. The school nurse had patched me up while I'd been waiting in the office.

"It's okay. It probably won't even scar up or anything."

Dad pulled me onto his lap and wrapped his arms around me in a fierce hug. "I'm just very glad that you're okay and that things didn't end up worse than a scratch on the arm. I love your mother, and I love Cindi, but you feel things more deeply than either of the two of them and that makes you special to me."

It was hard to talk past the sudden lump in my throat, but I nodded. "I love you too, Dad. I'm sorry if I was stupid about everything today."

"It's okay. We're not going to talk about it anymore until you have had a chance to think about those questions. The important thing will be what you learn from today's events."

The rest of the night passed by in a blur. Cindi was faster than normal, so the dishes were already done by the time I left Dad's office.

Dad fired up his work laptop and logged back into work for the rest of the night. He paused for a few minutes when Mom came out from her cave to eat, but she just wolfed down her food and then fidgeted like a little kid until Dad gave her a hug and sent her back to her darkroom.

Cindi finished up her homework and then spent most of the rest of the evening texting people on her iPod. I stared at my textbook for another hour or so, but I didn't really make any progress on my chemistry homework.

I finally just put everything away and got ready for bed. Dad looked up absently at me when I padded into his office to give him a hug good night.

"You're going to bed already?"

"Yeah, I haven't been sleeping very well lately. I thought maybe I'd just turn in early tonight and see if it helps."

"Your headaches are still bothering you, aren't they?"

It was like Dad had developed some kind of weird sixth sense to compensate for the fact that Mom was so oblivious to everything going on around her.

"They seem to be getting a little better. They don't bother me as much as they did."

It was a lie, maybe even more than just a white lie. The headaches were worse than before. I was just getting better at ignoring them lately. Well, better most days at least.

"Well, I'm glad to hear that they are a little better, but if they are still bothering you next week I think you should ask your mother to take you to the doctor. She can take me into work on Tuesday or Wednesday so that she has the car to drive you to the clinic."

"I'll be fine, Dad. It's just a little headache from time to time."

"I'm serious, Adri. I want a promise out of you that you'll be responsible enough to ask for help before things get worse."

Right. I had to be the responsible one because Mom certainly wouldn't be. I hated when Dad made me promise him something. It was pretty much the one thing guaranteed to get Cindi or me either one to do what he wanted. Unfortunately he knew it, so he wasn't averse to using promises to get his way whenever he thought we weren't taking care of ourselves or that we were going to get into trouble.

"Okay, Dad. If things don't start getting better soon then I'll go see a doctor."

I kissed Dad on the cheek and then went into the small room I shared with Cindi. We actually had bunk beds—black metal monstrosities—of all things, so I climbed up to the top bunk and closed my eyes.

"You're really going to sleep already, Adri?"

"Yeah. It's been kind of a long day."

"Okay, I'll just put my iPod on silent then. Good night."

"Good night, Cindi."

I fell asleep instantly. It didn't make any sense, but once I was dreaming it was actually easier to remember some of the other dreams that I'd been having recently. Remembering didn't particularly help because they were still so odd.

Mostly it was just a collage of images involving people I knew—Richard Parsons, Janessa, even a couple of my teachers, which luckily wasn't as gross as it otherwise could have been. Tonight was different though. I wasn't at school or anywhere else I knew, and I wasn't dreaming about anyone familiar.

HUNTED

I was standing in the top of a partially-constructed skyscraper. The steel skeleton had been assembled and most of the floor and exterior wall had been finished for the floor I was on, but if I looked up I could see open sky above me in some parts.

There was movement a little ways ahead of me. Part of me said that I should just steer clear, that dreams in abandoned buildings never end well, but I crept forward anyway. There was a small man sitting on the very edge of the floor I was on. His legs dangled out into thin air, but he didn't seem worried that he might fall.

He was obviously intent on watching something below us, so I took a couple of steps forward until I could see over the edge of the building too. What I saw was odd, even for a dream. We were somehow both really high up and only a few feet from the ground all at once. When I looked straight ahead at the buildings around us, we were even with the very tops of most of them, and they were all dozens if not hundreds of stories tall, but when I looked down at the ground it seemed like it was close enough that I could just hop down from the building without any risk of injury.

I shook my head and closed my eyes, but when I opened them back up everything was still the same. Down below, on the street, someone walked into view and I suddenly realized what else was wrong about the scene.

There was only one person visible down there. We weren't in some kind of ghost town—the buildings all looked well-maintained, the streets were still in working order—but there wasn't anyone else down there. I'd never been to New York or Tokyo, but it just didn't look right to have a city as big as this be completely deserted.

The man looked up at us and my heart skipped a beat. He looked familiar somehow, not like I knew him, but like he was related to someone important to me. Only he didn't actually look like anyone I knew.

It would have just been one of those things that you dismiss as a weird coincidence, but my heart was still going a mile a minute. It was like it was trying to tell me that whoever this guy looked like was the reason that I'd never been particularly interested in any of the guys my own age. It wasn't that I was gay or asexual, I'd just been saving my emotions and attention for this one person whom I still didn't know, but whom I finally had the tiniest of links to.

I came within a second of throwing myself off of the building so that I could stop the man below us and ask him where I knew him from, but something stopped me at the last moment. I'd heard people say that if you hit the ground in a dream that you'd die without waking up. I'd never believed it before now, but there was something about this dream, weird though it was, that made it feel as real as anything I'd ever experienced with my eyes open.

Instead of jumping, I turned to the man a few feet away from me and asked what I thought was a non-threatening question.

"Who is that and is there a way for me to get down there in time to talk to him before he disappears?"

The man practically jumped out of his own skin. It was like he'd been on a hair trigger, but he'd been expecting the threat to arrive from a different quarter.

He went from sitting to standing without ever actually having seemed to move, but that was the least alarming of the changes. Between one second and the next his face changed. He went from looking like a non-threatening, elderly Native American to something out of a nightmare. His teeth lengthened and got sharper at the same time that his face got broader and sprouted fur.

The change happened so fast that I blinked and missed most of it, but before my words had even died in the air I was standing only a few feet away from some kind of wolf-man monster who looked like he was about to rip my head off.

"How did you get here? How did you find me?"

I opened my mouth to respond, but he grabbed me by the throat and slammed me into a steel girder so hard that I saw stars.

The sheer terror I was feeling was messing with my senses. I was trying to talk around the panic surging up from my gut, but all I could think about was the way that it felt like a prickly wind was pushing me back against the structural member at the same time that his hand pinned me against it.

We stood there staring at each other for what felt like an eternity and then suddenly the entire building rang like a gong. Still holding me several feet off of the ground, the monster walked back over to the edge of the building and looked down. I was just able to see the man we'd been watching—at least I assumed it was the man we'd been watching.

He'd transformed into a beast that was almost a mirror image of the one that had me by the throat and seemed to be climbing up the outside of the building. It was hard to be sure, he still seemed to only be a few feet below us, but now the ground looked to be quite a ways below him.

"You can't be him, not if he's coming after us, but you're inarguably here so I guess I'm not as unique as I always thought." My captor looked back down at the beast that was climbing towards us and shook his head. "I don't know who you are, but this is the only warning I'll provide. You need to stay away from me. I'll let you go this time. Go ahead and jump out. I'm not holding you here now."

HUNTED

It was like he was a raving lunatic. Nothing he was saying made any sense. How could I possibly jump anywhere when he was still holding me by the throat? The sheer ludicrous nature of what I was experiencing finally got to me. I opened my mouth as he relaxed his grip slightly and instead of a scream of terror, laughter bubbled out of me.

Seriously, a talking wolf-man was holding me by the throat and telling me to jump. My subconscious had gone ape-crap crazy this time.

"I will not be mocked."

The words wouldn't have caused me to even bat an eye, but his fist tightened around my throat to the point where his claws started to dig into the back of my neck. The glee washed out of me, instantly replaced with the terror that the situation called for.

"I just wanted to know who he was."

It came out barely more than a whisper, but he didn't seem to have any problems hearing me.

"Trust me, you'll be much better off if you never see Kaleb again in your entire life."

The crash of splintering glass as Kaleb climbed up the outside of the building was getting closer. My captor closed his eyes for the briefest of seconds and then sighed.

"I wish we had more time to talk. If you're what I think you are, then you need some guidance, but we simply don't have time. I'm going to be hard-pressed to get out myself now.

We've burned up too much time talking while Kaleb has approached."

I opened my mouth, not because I had a question to ask him, but because it seemed like the situation called for a whole host of questions. He shook his head at me.

"There's no time. Just remember that this place isn't safe. You'd be far better off if you simply stayed away. Think of home, of those you love."

Before I could even process what he'd just said he pivoted with a strength that exceeded even what I would have expected out of such a massive body and threw me towards a nearby wall.

I'd been on rollercoasters that created less g-forces than what he generated. Time slowed to a crawl as I flipped end over end towards a pair of steel girders. I started to black out, my vision narrowed down to a tiny tunnel, but his last words were echoing in my head. If I was going to die then it was only right that my last thoughts be of my dad, my mom, and Cindi.

I hit the massive beams with enough force to shatter every bone in my body. I felt them all break as my body wrapped itself around the one on the right and then my head impacted with the one on the left.

I woke up with my heart pounding, positive that I was about to die. Some of the other dreams I'd had, dreams that had seemed more vivid when I'd been asleep, were already fading away from my memory, but the dream with the two wolf-men was still as strong as when it had happened.

I still couldn't explain it, but somehow I knew that what had happened was in its own way as real as anything else I'd ever experienced. My dreams were real, and despite the fact that trying to find Kaleb might get me killed, I still had an almost unstoppable urge to go back to the unfinished building and see if I could talk to him.

Chapter 3

I'd lost track of how many days it had been since my fight with Janessa, but it seemed like it shouldn't still be such a big deal among the rest of the student body. I'd spent so many years trying to stay safely anonymous only to have it ruined in the course of five minutes.

There was probably a life lesson in there somewhere, but I was having a hard time getting past the fact that everyone in the school seemed to know me and they'd split themselves firmly into two camps. On the one hand there were the rich and popular kids, all of whom seemed united in their hatred of me. For the most part they didn't seem to like Janessa any more than I did, but as nearly as I could tell they were all weighing in on her side because I'd upset the natural order of things. Nerds and loners like me were supposed to bow down to their kind of people, not get into fights with them, especially not fights in which the nerd came out more or less on top.

The other camp consisted of all of the nerds, drama geeks, loners and anyone else who didn't either fit in with the popular crowd or regularly abase themselves in the hopes of being able to work their way into the A-list kids.

I wasn't particularly liked by most of these kids either, but they were just super excited that somebody had finally stood up to Janessa. Apparently she was a monster to just about everyone in the school who wasn't at least as rich and cool as she was. I'd known she was bad, but I hadn't realized she was *that* bad.

It was all kind of dizzying, especially given that I'd never managed to learn the names of most of the people who were now either shooting me nasty looks or patting me on the back and giving me high-fives as I walked through the hall.

I kept hoping that it would all die down. I'd wanted to just serve out my detention and then go back to being anonymous, but a day or two after I got in trouble the administration finally got around to investigating my accusation that Janessa had been cheating on her history exam. From what I'd been able to gather secondhand, it sounded like Richard Parsons pretty much cracked as soon as they got him in a room by himself. He backed up everything I'd said, which had caused the principal to check Janessa's locker.

She probably would have gotten away with a mere slap on the wrist except they found hundreds of dollars' worth of drugs in her locker. She'd been suspended within hours of that little discovery and her parents had shoved her into rehab so fast that nobody had even known what happened to her until some of the cheerleaders had gone over to her house to find out why she'd been missing practice.

News that Janessa was out for at least the next six weeks had rushed through the school like wildfire and had further sealed my infamy. For all that I hadn't anticipated any of the events that had occurred as a result of Janessa and I trying to rip each other's heads off, the thing that really took me by surprise was how hard it all was on Cindi.

Although we'd never been rich, Cindi's looks and status as a cheerleader put her firmly in the popular camp at school. Her friends were exactly the people who'd once largely ignored me but who now hated me.

I expected her to just go with the flow. She and I hadn't ever been particularly close. It was hard to be friendly with someone who was better than you in practically every way. The logical thing for her to do would have been to at least give me a cold shoulder when we were at school, but if anything she was going out of her way lately to try and include me.

I'd been suspicious at first that she was just trying to get me around her friends so that they could make my life miserable, but the first time that one of them had tried, she'd put them in their place so fast that everyone's jaws had just kind of hit the floor and stayed there until lunch ended.

Given my druthers I would have just avoided the other cheerleaders and waited for everything to blow over, but Cindi reaching out to me like that meant that I had to at least make an effort to hang out with her and her friends. Honestly I couldn't have cared less about the friends, but I didn't want to let Cindi's peace offering go to waste.

We'd had some absolutely spectacular fights in the past. Things got a little better once we were both in high school, but I still felt a lot of the time like there was something missing in our relationship. Sisters should be closer than what we'd managed so far in our lives.

I'd never talked to Cindi about that in so many words, but that was how I felt, which helped explain how I ended up out at the football field after school, sitting on the tired old metal bleachers at the fifty-yard line, rather than back home cleaning the house.

The cheerleaders were having tryouts tomorrow to fill Janessa's spot, which meant that Cindi and three other girls were busy leading two dozen hopefuls through the practice cheers that the tryouts would be based on.

It was actually pretty painful to watch, but not for the reasons that I'd expected. I'd expected to be bored out of my mind watching a group of girls perform the same few cheers over, and over, and over again while I tried to work on my homework.

Instead I found myself unable to study for other reasons. The girls trying out were simply awful. They were obviously trying and Cindi and her friend were doing their best, but none of the girls seemed to be able to get the routines down, especially the last one that they were supposed to be learning.

It didn't make any sense. I've never been one of those people who are able to remember a string of movements well enough to actually perform anything, but this routine was super easy. I'd already memorized it despite the fact that I was only halfway paying attention.

As the allotted time for the practice started to wind down I could tell that a lot of the girls were getting frustrated by their inability to master the routine. Alice Backman—at least I thought that was her name—finally threw down her blue and white pompoms and stalked over in my direction to get her books off of the bleachers.

Cindi started in our direction too, obviously wanting to reassure Alice, but she'd been on the other side of the group so it was going to take her a minute to get here.

"I'm never going to get this last one. It's just too hard. I thought maybe that I could come and memorize all of them enough that I could practice them on my own later, but this last one is just too complex. I can't remember more than just the first five or six movements."

"I could write it down for you if you wanted. I mean so that you could have it to study later tonight."

Alice gave me an incredulous look. "Is this your way of making me look bad? Write down a bunch of random stuff so that I'll go practice the wrong routine and look like an idiot? Is that why you came today? Just so you could make someone else's life difficult?"

I'd already turned to a blank piece of paper and had written down the first three parts of the routine, but now my pen stuttered to a halt. Apparently Alice didn't approve of me getting into it with Janessa. It was actually a bit odd. Alice was trying out for a spot on the team that never would have opened up if Janessa hadn't gotten kicked off, but apparently that didn't matter enough for her to cut me any slack.

"Actually I'm only here because of my sister, Cindi. We usually walk home together and I thought I'd just sit here and study while I waited for her. I was just trying to help, but if you don't want any help it's no skin off of my nose."

"She's really your sister? I'd heard rumors, but it's kind of hard to believe. You know, given how cool and pretty she is and how, well, you know, ordinary you are."

I wanted to say something spiteful, like maybe point out that she was the girl out there least likely to make it on the squad because she bungled every third piece of the routine, but I gritted my teeth and finished writing down the first half of the routine.

"Yeah, that's about what I thought. You're all big and bad when it comes to picking on Janessa when she's vulnerable and strung out, but you totally back down when somebody stands up to you."

That did it. I ripped the sheet of paper I was writing on out of my notebook and balled it up before throwing it at her feet.

"Here you go, it's only the first half of the routine, but based on what I saw out there you're probably not going to even make it through that. Don't say I didn't try to help though. I've always tried to be nice to anyone with special needs."

I'd taken things too far and I knew it, but I was just so tired of people picking on me. The fact that she was here trying out for the cheer squad didn't make her better than me, it didn't give her license to be mean.

Alice stepped towards me like she was about to attack me too, but Cindi arrived and cleared her throat.

"Hi, girls. What's going on?"

Alice bent down to pick up the paper at her feet and then turned towards Cindi with a sugary-sweet smile on her face. "Your sister just tried to sabotage my chances to get on the team by writing down the wrong routine and giving it to me. I really think you should ask her to leave so that she doesn't cause any more problems."

Right, like me leaving three minutes early would make the slightest bit of difference to Alice or any of the other girls.

Cindi took the piece of paper without saying anything and smoothed it out against her leg, running her hand along the paper and down the blue material of her skirt. She read down through it and then stopped and read it again, slower this time. Once she was done she handed it back to me.

"Adri, can you finish this?"

"So I can help *her*? Not very likely."

I got a head shake and a frown. "Please just do it for me?"

I rolled my eyes and then jotted down the rest of the routine and passed the piece of paper back to Cindi.

Cindi scanned down through my additions and then turned to Alice. "I think you owe Adri an apology. This is the exact routine we were just trying to teach you."

"Really? Are you in on it with her or something? Is this about that time I forgot to invite you out to Crater Lake?"

Cindi sighed and handed Alice the paper. "Go check it with one of the other girls if you want. Or don't, it doesn't really matter to me, but practice is over so I'm done here."

Alice opened her mouth like she was going to argue with Cindi, but my little sister just gave her the kind of look most of the cheerleaders gave me and after a second or two Alice grabbed her backpack and walked back to where the other cheerleaders were answering last-minute questions from the other hopefuls.

Cindi watched her leave and then turned back to me. "How did you do that, Adri? I didn't think you were paying that much attention."

"I wasn't. I don't know, I guess the routines just stuck with me. It's not like they're difficult. Honestly I don't know why Alice and the others were having such a hard time remembering the moves. Actually doing the moves is probably tougher, but memorizing something like this should be child's play, even for them."

Cindi was looking at me like I'd just grown another arm or something. "Adri, that's the hardest routine the squad does. Miss Winters wasn't actually expecting any of those girls to get all of the routine, she just wanted to see how far they would be able to get. It took me two weeks to get that routine down. The entire squad struggled with this one. For days we did nothing but practice this routine every waking moment we could find and then dream about it while we slept."

I shrugged, but I knew that the motion wasn't very convincing. I wanted to tell her that I didn't know what was going on, that it was all some kind of fluke, but I didn't want to lie to her. She'd actually just hit the nail right on the head. I hadn't even remembered where my knowledge of the routine had come from until right then.

She'd dreamed about the routine, all of the cheerleaders had. They'd spent their nights working through the routine and I'd somehow shared at least some of their dreams. I should have remembered sooner than I had, but none of it had stuck with my conscious mind until something triggered an association between the practice sessions and the real world.

"Will you try something for me?"

The request took me by surprise. Cindi was usually so self-contained that it was rare for her to ask me for anything.

"Maybe. What do you need?"

"Can you try to do the routine for me? The hard one, the one that you wrote down?"

I shook my head. "No way. I'm not making a fool of myself, especially not in front of someone like Alice."

"What about if it's just me? No, wait, that won't work, you'll never believe me. What about if it's just me and Sheree?"

I didn't understand why she thought someone else needed to watch me trip over my own feet as I tried to perform a routine I'd never practiced, but she'd picked the one and only girl in the school that everyone liked.

Sheree Fieros was so incredibly nice that you couldn't even hold the fact that she was pretty and talented against her. I couldn't imagine Sheree making fun of anyone. She was the kind of girl who once I finished up my routine would tell me how well I'd done, and she'd really mean it, even though we'd both know that I'd done a terrible job.

"Cindi, I don't get why you want me to do this."

"Please, Adri. We'll go around the corner of the school and it will just be the three of us. I hardly ever ask anything from you but I'm asking for you to do this now. For me, as your sister."

I opened my mouth to tell her that I wasn't going to do it, but I couldn't get the words out. I'd been wanting for us to be closer, but that kind of thing didn't happen without taking some risks.

"Okay, but only for you and Sheree."

Cindi's grin was like sunshine and kittens wrapped into a fluffy blanket. "Great! I'll go get Sheree and we'll meet you on the other side of the school, back around in that section with all of the trees."

Still wondering why I'd agreed, I picked up my things and started towards the designated spot. I was setting myself up to fail. Just because I'd spent a few nights inside the heads of a bunch of cheerleaders didn't mean that I could do this. Memorizing a sequence of moves was one thing, actually performing them was something else entirely.

I'd nearly talked myself into backing out when Sheree and Cindi arrived.

"Adri, I'm so glad that you're thinking about trying out. I can't blame you for being a little nervous. I was totally nervous when I tried out last year. If it hadn't been for my mom pushing me I don't know if I could have gotten up the courage to try out."

I shot Cindi a questioning look, but she made an encouraging motion and I decided not to make a fuss about the fact that she'd told Sheree that I was going to try out when I actually had no intention of doing any such thing.

"So I just start?"

Sheree nodded brightly at me. "Yeah, you should probably go ahead and assume beginning position just so that it's like it will be tomorrow, but then just go for it."

I started to ask her what the beginning position was, but realized that I already knew. Apparently my dream education was good for at least a little more than just memorizing the sequence of moves in the routine. I placed my feet together, toes even, and then looked forward with my fists on my hips and my elbows straight out from my body.

I probably would have stood there forever without moving, but all of a sudden Cindi called out, "Ready!"

I found myself responding with the "Okay!" that all of the girls in my dreams had called out at the start of each routine. Reflexes that I hadn't even realized I had suddenly took over and I started waving my arms around and moving my feet in time to music in my head that matched up to exactly what the girls performed to.

It was one of the most bizarre experiences of my life. I'd never practiced this routine before, but I *remembered* practicing it dozens or maybe even hundreds of times. If I tried to think about what I was doing then my movements got clumsy and halting, but if I just let the routine flow out of me, then everything was smooth and snappy.

I threw myself into the last spin and then looked up to meet the eyes of a satisfied Cindi and an astonished Sheree.

"Wow, Adri. That was really, really good. I don't think you have anything to be nervous about. There are still a few rough spots in there, but you were head and shoulders better than anyone else we had out there today."

I would have dismissed Sheree's compliment, but even now she still looked too shocked for it to just be something she was saying out of simple politeness. Sheree shook her head and then turned to Cindi.

"How long have the two of you been practicing that? I'm totally amazed. Cheerleading barely leaves me time to finish my studies and sleep at night. I don't know how I'd ever fit in the time to teach anyone else the routines."

Cindi just smiled and shrugged. "I can't take any credit, Adri's a natural. How about if we do it one more time, Adri, only this time you and I can do it in formation just like it will be tomorrow."

There it was, the insinuation that I'd be trying out for Janessa's spot on the team. I almost told Cindi no, but Sheree practically jumped out of her sneakers.

"That's a good idea. Cindi, you should start it off again. I'll watch and this time I'll be ready so I can critique both of you."

Cindi took up a spot to the right of me and once again when she yelled out "Ready!" I responded and launched into the routine that I'd never in a million years imagined that I'd be performing. It was easier this time. I didn't try to fight my reflexes. Instead I just shut my brain down and let my body take over.

At one point Cindi and I were facing each other and I returned her smile almost in spite of myself. I was actually having fun, which lasted right up until I came around on the final spin and saw the other two cheerleaders who'd been helping Cindi and Sheree.

Having observers, especially those particular observers, made me nervous enough that I messed up the next move and stumbled into Cindi. We ended the routine tangled up in a knot on the ground. Sheree was there instantly, helping the two of us up.

"You guys were really rocking it there right up until the end. It was like watching a pair of twins out there, I was super impressed! Adri, you're as good as if you'd been on the team since the start of the school year." Sheree clapped her hands over her mouth and squealed in excitement. "Oh my gosh, I just realized what I said. Miss Winters is going to be so happy. We all thought we'd have to get a new girl up to speed but instead you'll be able to just pick things right up. This is so great!"

The other two cheerleaders didn't look very happy to find out that Cindi's nerdy older sister was cheerleader material, and a couple of the girls who'd been hoping to make it on the team themselves had wandered around the edge of the school just in time to catch the end of Sheree's outburst.

I opened my mouth to tell everyone that they didn't need to worry, that I wasn't planning on showing up for tryouts tomorrow, but Cindi stepped on my foot and then innocently asked Sheree what time it was.

"Oh, no. It's after five. I'm sorry, girls, but I've got to get home right away or my mom is going to freak out. I'll see you both tomorrow!"

That last bit was yelled back over her shoulder as she took off towards the parking lot. It was like Sheree leaving was a signal. Everyone else turned and went their separate ways, leaving me alone with Cindi, who seemed desperately determined to have me join the cheerleading team.

Chapter 4

We made it almost exactly halfway home before Cindi started begging me to join the team. "Please, Adri. It would be so much better if you were on the team with me."

"Why? I don't see why it matters to you. I would have thought you'd feel like I was stealing your thunder if I did something like that."

Cindi looked at the ground for a couple of seconds before responding. "I used to know what I wanted, but lately I feel like I'm just kind of drifting. I thought maybe the problem was Janessa—she'd actually been giving me a lot of crap for a while before the two of you got in that fight. I think she'd figured out that I was the one who was probably going to replace her if she couldn't keep everything together."

I almost stumbled. It was hard to imagine Cindi as anything other than the self-assured golden child. A Cindi with doubts and social problems was something new, something I wasn't quite sure how to handle.

"Why didn't you say anything? I didn't even know that she was being mean to you."

Cindi shrugged. "I don't know. I guess I felt bad. Half the reason she was being nasty to you was probably just because you're my sister, so I didn't want to say anything and give you another reason to hate me."

"I wouldn't have hated you."

"Maybe not, but it's not like we've ever been very close. I didn't want to risk giving you something else to hold against me."

My throat tightened up. "I'm sorry that we've never been as close as we should have. I think that's probably my fault. It's hard not to be jealous of you. I mean look at you, you're practically perfect. You're smart, you get good grades, you're pretty and skinny and you're a cheerleader who pretty much everyone likes. It's hard to compete with that."

Cindi gave me an unhappy look. "Why does it have to be a competition? You're practically as skinny as I am these days and you care a lot less about what other people think than I do. Not only that, you're a lot closer to Dad than I am. I think he's still trying to figure out how he had a daughter who ended up as a cheerleader. He tries, but he has a lot harder of a time relating to me than he does to you."

I opened my mouth to protest that Dad loved her just as much as he loved me, but she just kept going. "Do you know that you're the reason that I get good grades? Back before I even started kindergarten I saw how much of a big deal Dad made of you when you'd bring your report card home. I decided right then and there that I wanted to be smart like you."

I kicked the ground. "I'm not sure who the joke is on there. It turns out that I'm not smart at all."

Cindi shook her head. "You don't get good grades any more, but that isn't because you're not smart, it's because you stopped caring. You're still smart, you've just been as lost in your own way as I've been in mine for the last couple of years."

"I'd like to be closer too. I…well, I've been thinking a lot lately that there was something missing in our relationship. That's actually why I went to that stupid practice with you. I've never wanted to be a cheerleader."

"I know you haven't, but this is a chance for us to spend more time together. That's how we'd get to be better friends. You come do this with me and I'll do something you like to do with you and over time we'll grow to be as close as we both feel like we should be."

I sighed and then shrugged. "Let me think about it a little. This would be something totally out of my comfort zone."

Cindi rolled her eyes at me. "It can't be that far out of your comfort zone, not if you spent enough hours to learn that routine. I'm still not sure when you found the time to practice without me finding out, but I'm super impressed."

I managed a wan smile. If Cindi and I had been better friends maybe I'd have tried to tell her about my dreams, but as it was I was pretty sure she just wouldn't believe me.

I was still on cleaning duty as a punishment, but when we got home Cindi volunteered to do all of the cooking by herself so that I could get my chores done. It was a nice gesture. I knew she had an ulterior motive behind the offer, but it was still a nice thing for her to have done.

There was a note on the fridge from Mom when we got home telling us that she'd been planning on making lasagna, but that she wouldn't be home until late because she was having dinner with a gallery owner that had expressed some interest in her work.

With just two of us in the house things were pretty quiet, but it was a silence that was more companionable than normal. I called Dad when the lasagna was twenty minutes from being done to see if he would be home to eat with us, but I only got his voicemail, which Cindi and I took as a good sign. Usually if he didn't take one of our calls it was because he was on the road and hadn't heard his phone.

We were right. Dad walked through the door five minutes before seven, gave both of us hugs, and then the three of us sat down to eat.

Dad asked us how our days had gone and Cindi started to tell him about my performance at the end of practice, but I kicked her under the table and she cut off midsentence with a hurt look. Dinner went by pretty quickly after that. Dad loaded the dishwasher up and then retreated to his study to finish up some of the work that he hadn't been able to get to during the course of the day.

He looked so worn out that I almost couldn't bring myself to go in and bother him with my problems, but I knew he'd rather be bothered than out of the loop so I took a deep breath and stuck my head inside of his office.

"Hi, Dad. I know you're busy, but could we talk for a few minutes?"

"Of course, come on in, Adri. Is this about your punishment?"

"Actually it's not, but now that you mention it I have been thinking about your questions and I think that I have some answers for you."

Dad gestured at the tiny chair stationed at the side of his desk. "Well, which do you want to start with?"

"Your questions, I think."

He smiled at me like he knew that I was trying to avoid getting into the real reason we were talking and then waved for me to proceed.

"First you asked who I thought was the bully in my fight."

"What did you decide?"

"I think that we both were, at least a little. She was calling me names and she was the one who got in my face first, but by telling everyone there that she'd cheated on her test I put her in a position where she felt like she had to do something to protect her image. I guess you could say that I escalated things."

Dad nodded. "I think you've done the situation justice. So how do you think the fight could have gotten out of control?"

"I don't know, I guess there are a lot of different ways. When I scratched her I could have missed her cheek and gotten her eye instead."

"She had friends there, right, Adri?"

"Yeah, why?"

"These days friends don't always just stand by and let a fight be settled between two people. I've read about plenty of incidents, especially in cities like ours, where an entire group of kids jump one kid after the fight starts. Those situations don't usually end very well, sweetie. Usually the loser ends up in the hospital, at the very least."

My mouth opened and closed a few times as I tried to process what he'd just said. I'd seen some of the same kinds of headlines online, but somehow none of that had crossed my mind, either at the time of the fight or in the days since.

"I guess you're right, that would have been pretty bad."

Dad sighed. "You being hospitalized or even dead would have been pretty much the worst-case scenario, but there are other things that could have happened that wouldn't have been very much fun. To be honest, I half expected that Janessa's parents would try to get the police or lawyers involved."

My stomach knotted up like it was trying to digest a rock. We couldn't afford a lawyer. I didn't know a ton about our finances, but I knew that despite the long hours Dad worked that there wasn't a ton of money to spare and lawyers were super expensive.

"I'm sorry, Dad. I didn't think about that either."

"I know, sweetie. You wouldn't have purposefully done anything to hurt your family, but you need to understand that your actions can have much bigger consequences than you realize."

I felt like crying, but he really wasn't mad at me. He waited while I pulled myself back together a little bit.

"So what about my third question? When is fighting okay and was your fight with Janessa justified?"

"You said the other day that sometimes fighting is okay, but now all I can think about is all of the ways that things could have gone really wrong."

"The consequences can be pretty serious, but sometimes the consequences of not fighting can be even more serious."

"Like if someone else might be killed or hospitalized if I didn't fight."

"Yes, like that. Fighting is always a last resort; it's always something you should consider only when fighting a bully and only when the consequences of not fighting are at least as bad as the potential consequences of fighting."

I nodded and stood up to leave but Dad grabbed my hand and pulled me back down into my chair. "You had something to ask me, and we also haven't talked about your punishment."

"I did a pretty bad job answering your questions, so I'm guessing my punishment is going to continue for the foreseeable future, which makes the question I came in here with a pointless one."

Dad shook his head. "I actually thought that you did an okay job with my questions. I think that there are plenty of adults who haven't thought things through to the degree that you have now. Not only that, I feel like you now understand the gravity of any decision to get into a fight. I think your punishment can come to an end, which means that you can go ahead and ask me your other question."

"I...well, Cindi thinks that I should try out for the cheerleading squad tomorrow."

Dad's eyes got a little bigger like I'd just completely blindsided him. "That's what Cindi thinks. What do you think?"

"I'm not sure. If I knew that I wouldn't be able to make the team then it would just be a matter of whether I was willing to go make a fool out of myself at the tryouts. I'm pretty sure I can make the team though, so if I go try out then I'm looking at making a huge change. I'll have to go to practices and games and I'll have a lot less time to do my homework."

Dad shook his head. "The act of trying out doesn't mean that you are committing to join the team. You still have a decision to make after that, so the real question you should be asking yourself is whether the things you lose by going to the practice are greater than the things you gain."

"So I would gain the opportunity to be on the team, and I would lose two hours of my life?"

"At the most basic level, yes, but there might be other considerations as well. Based on how excited Cindi was about telling me something before you kicked her under the table, I'm guessing that Cindi loves the idea of having you on the team with her."

"I guess you're right. My going to the tryouts would probably gain me brownie points with Cindi, but isn't it a waste of time to go do something just for the possibility of being on the team if I'm not really interested in joining?"

"Yes, if you're positive that you don't want to be on the team, but you don't seem like you really know what you want to do yet."

"Yeah. I think I'm worried what people will think. I've always thought that most of the cheerleaders were stupid and shallow. If I'm a cheerleader then everyone is going to think the same thing about me."

"Is that your only concern?"

"No. I'm the reason that this spot on the team is open. How is it going to look if I get Janessa's place on the team after getting her kicked off in the first place?"

"I'm not going to lie, Adri, it's going to look pretty bad. On the other hand, if you spend your whole life making decisions solely based on what other people will think, you'll have a very unhappy life and people will still end up disapproving of your choices."

I nodded and stood back up. This time Dad didn't stop me. "Thanks, Dad. You've got some good points. I'll at least go try out tomorrow and then I can make a decision from there."

"You're welcome, Adri. Have a good night's sleep if I'm still working when you turn in."

Cindi was predictably thrilled when I told her I would at least go try out. I kept telling her that I still wasn't positive that I'd be joining the team, but she didn't seem concerned. In Cindi's world, once you got an offer to join the cheerleading team there wasn't any way you would not join.

We talked about random stuff until it was time to get ready for bed and then almost before I knew it our light was off and I was trying to go to sleep.

It seemed like my eyes had only been closed for a second before I started dreaming. I could tell that this wasn't just a normal dream because there were things that were off about it and I noticed them rather than just accepting that the flawed version of reality I was seeing was accurate.

I was in a house that was bigger than any house I'd ever been inside before, but it still somehow gave the feeling of being cramped and confining. It took me a couple of seconds to figure out how a room that was almost two stories tall could feel so small, but it seemed to be something a bit like the visual distortion that I'd seen when I'd looked down from the tower in the dream with the wolf-men. When I looked directly at a wall or the ceiling, it was obvious that the room was huge, but out of the corner of my eye everything seemed to move in closer. When I looked away and focused on the windows, the walls angled in towards me and the ceiling sloped down to the point where it felt like it was going to collapse and crush me.

I walked over to the window and pushed aside the massive curtains that kept the room in a perpetual twilight, only to recoil at the sheer brightness of the sun. I wasn't looking directly at it, but the light was still so strong that it made my eyes tear up and shut despite my best efforts to keep them open.

It was another piece of reality that wasn't quite right, another sign that I was in someone else's dream rather than my own. I let the curtains swing shut again and then once my eyes had readjusted to the darkness I looked down and found in surprise that I was wearing Cindi's cheerleading uniform.

I wondered idly if it was possible for me to change aspects of my surroundings inside someone else's dream. It seemed easiest to start with my clothes, so I tried to visualize myself in jeans and a normal top. My clothing flickered for a second, becoming embarrassingly translucent for a heartbeat before I gave up and allowed the cheerleading uniform to snap back into place.

I'd been so absorbed in my efforts to swap out my clothing that I didn't hear the footsteps when they first started up. They were alarmingly close by the time they registered. My pulse skyrocketed as I remembered the two wolf-men. I wasn't completely safe here, but I didn't know how to leave someone's dream once I got sucked into it.

I thought about running, but I didn't know how to get out of the house or even if it was possible to get very far away from the person who was dreaming. I vacillated for too long and then *she* stepped into the room.

From the neck down she looked like a normal person, a little too skinny to be healthy maybe, but still pretty much like anyone else. Her face though was disturbingly indistinct, almost like a wax model that someone had left out in the sun for a moment or two too long.

"Who are you?"

Her voice had a hissing nature to it that I was pretty sure wouldn't be possible outside of a dream and it gave off a sense of great age which didn't match her young-looking body. I opened my mouth to answer her and then thought better of it. I already knew that I could be in danger while dreaming, the last thing I wanted was to give her the information she'd need to track me down in the real world.

"I'm sorry, I'm not sure how I got here."

"That's not what I asked you."

"I know, but you're kind of scary, no offense. I'd like to keep my identity a secret."

One second she was all of the way on the other side of the room and the next she had ahold of my throat and had slammed me up against the wall. Her movements had been inhumanly fast, but I got the feeling that it wasn't a dream thing. She was actually that fast in real life too, just like the wolf-man who'd warned me to stay away from Kaleb. I had a split second to wonder if everyone I ran into in the dream world was some kind of supernatural creepy-crawly, and then her hand started squeezing.

I managed to choke out something to the effect that I couldn't breathe, but she just smiled. "I don't need you to talk to get the information I want out of you."

I'd been able to get a little bit of air in and out until then, but as she finished talking she tightened her fist even more and suddenly I couldn't get anything in. I started hitting her, kicking with my feet and hammering on her arm with my fists, but it was like kicking a tree, there was absolutely no give to her.

I was in a full panic now, but even so I knew that the dark, smoky tendrils extending out from her head and face weren't a figment of my imagination. I tried to break away, clawing at her face, but she simply whipped her head back out of the way and then threw me against the wall with enough force that a black veil slowly slid over my face as unconsciousness claimed me.

As everything else disappeared the tendrils touched my face and then slid under my skin, seeking a way into my mind. I tried to fight back, tried to push the tendrils back out of my mind, but my strength evaporated, leaving me with nothing but the certainty that she was about to loot my mind, that no secret I'd ever had would be safe from her probing fingers.

Chapter 5

Maybe Cindi was onto something when she said that I was losing a lot of weight lately. When I looked at myself in the mirror I didn't see it, but when I put on my old workout clothes they practically slid off of me.

Cindi had offered to let me wear some of her shorts and a tank top, which I'd reluctantly tried on. They didn't look anywhere near as good on me as they did on her, but they actually didn't make me look too repulsive so I agreed to wear them. It was that or risk exposing myself mid-routine as my shorts fell down around my ankles.

I changed back into my normal school clothes, packed Cindi's workout clothes into my backpack and then walked to school with Cindi. Cindi spent the whole trip gushing over how excited she was that I was going to be on the team, which was nice, but it made for a more jarring transition when I got to school and found that now the *whole* school disliked me.

HUNTED

The cheerleaders and popular kids had never stopped hating me, but now that rumors had started flying around the school about me trying out, the nerds and geeks seemed to have decided that I'd betrayed them too. Honestly, it was enough to send my headache into overdrive, which then reminded me of the dreams that had made their appearance at the same time as the headache.

My recollections of the dreams were still pretty hazy, but once I started thinking about them I remembered the encounter with the wax-faced woman and I started shaking. At one point I thought I was going to puke. Apparently I went white as a sheet too because Mr. Jenkins, my English teacher, sent me to the bathroom.

I was still freaking out when the bell rang to announce that English was over and it was time to go to history. I stood up to go, more because I knew I couldn't afford to be late than because I'd pulled myself together, and nearly broke down into tears. I still felt jumpy, like there was someone standing just behind me, always barely out of sight no matter how quickly I might turn and look for them. I kept telling myself that it was just a dream, that I'd survived, but I knew that wasn't true. My dreams lately were more than just dreams and I was in danger—it just didn't seem to be immediate danger.

Cindi found me less than a minute after the bell rang.

"Adri, are you in here?"

"Cindi, is that you?"

I let her help me over to the sink. I probably would have collapsed if I hadn't had *something* to lean against while she grabbed some paper towels and got them wet.

"You're going to be okay, Adri. It's just nerves, it's perfectly natural, especially when you're trying to get something that you really, really want. I literally puked before my first game, but it's obvious that you've practiced a ton, so you're going to be okay. Don't let this tryout get inside your head like this. You'll go out there on the field and the routine will just kind of take over and the next thing you know it will all be over and you'll be on the team. Trust me; I'm not going to let anything bad happen to you."

I opened my mouth to tell Cindi about the dreams, to tell her that I was worried about something much worse than some silly tryouts, but the words just wouldn't come. Cindi and I were closer than we'd been a few weeks ago, but I still didn't know if she'd be able to deal with the revelation that her sister was some kind of psychic freak. Instead of telling her the truth I just took a deep breath and nodded.

She was right, if not quite in the way that she meant. The dreams were important, but they weren't as immediate as my actual everyday life. I had people who cared about me and who would do everything they could to protect me and keep me safe. That was the important thing.

I couldn't let my dreams start controlling my waking world or I'd go crazy. I had to live in the real world and I'd deal with the consequences of the dreams as they happened.

Mr. Jenkins took quite a bit of reassuring when I went back for my books, but eventually I convinced him that it hadn't been anything more than nerves and he let me go on to history. The rest of the day passed more or less like the first half of school had, and then before I knew it I was changing into my shorts and hurrying out onto the field with the rest of the girls who were trying out.

It was a relief to be out of the locker room. The other girls had all pretty much turned against me too, and I heard a lot of whispering going on that I was pretty sure was them saying nasty things about me. The football field was marginally better even if it did mean that I had an audience now.

All of the current cheerleaders were there, as was Miss Winters, their coach, but I was surprised at some of the other people who were sitting in the bleachers. Amber Bondie was there with her camera, obviously hoping to capture something worth going into the yearbook, and behind her was a collection of nerds and geeks who were pretending not to watch as a couple of the cheerleaders demonstrated routines to some of the hopefuls who still weren't confident that they had all of the movements down.

Beyond the geeks, sitting at the very top of the bleachers was a handful of popular kids who were playing on their phones and looking extremely bored, but all of that faded into the background because there was one figure who stood out from the rest. Jackson Ayer, the Jackson who Janessa had been so busy trying to turn into a social pariah, stood off to the side of the bleachers talking to Sheree Fieros.

My stomach clenched back up. Out of all the people who could have attended, why had *Jackson* decided to come watch us? It wasn't just that he was gorgeous, tall with broad shoulders and wavy dark hair, there was something about him that just pulled my eyes towards him whenever he was around.

Normally I hardly noticed guys other than to wish that they'd hurry up and mature to the point where they were capable of carrying on a conversation that didn't revolve around sports or video games, but Jackson was different somehow. It was like the idea of dating Jackson filled a hole in my life that I didn't even know existed when he wasn't around. I couldn't really explain it, but it was a little bit the same as the way that I kept feeling that Cindi and I should be closer than we actually were. I've never believed in soul mates or anything, but being around Jackson was almost enough to convince me otherwise.

Jackson abruptly looked up from his conversation with Sheree and caught me watching the two of them, but he just smiled and waved, which caused my cheeks to heat. I awkwardly waved back to him and Sheree and then pretended to be interested in what was happening on the other end of the field.

Cindi had been involved in a conversation with Miss Winters, but she noticed me as I started stretching, so she said her goodbyes to her coach and hurried over a few seconds later.

"Remember, you've got this. Just relax and let all of that practicing take over."

I nodded jerkily and gave her my best smile. "I'll give it my best."

Cindi squeezed my arm in a suitably sisterly fashion and then walked over to a clump of cheerleaders. I'd been stretching for nearly five minutes before I realized that the stretches I was using were from the stretching regimen that the squad used to warm up before games, a regimen that I'd never bothered learning, but which I'd absorbed via my dreams just like I'd absorbed their routines.

I was idly wondering what else I'd learned that I hadn't stumbled onto yet when Miss Winters turned to those of us on the field who were trying out and wished us all luck. A few seconds after that Cindi and the rest of the cheerleaders positioned themselves around us and the first cheer started.

I hadn't practiced since the night before, so I started out worried that I wouldn't be able to repeat my earlier performance, but the routine came naturally. We progressed on to the second cheer and then the music came on for the final routine, and just like Cindi had promised, my mind shut down and I just moved to the beat.

When the music stopped it was all I could do to keep my legs from collapsing rather than holding the ending pose for three seconds like we were supposed to. It wasn't exhaustion, at least it wasn't just exhaustion. It was more just relief at having made it through the tryout without making an idiot of myself.

Miss Winters released us all from the field, but asked us to hang around for a few minutes while she deliberated with her squad. Since Cindi was off huddled up with the rest of the team, there wasn't anyone for me to talk to, so I walked off of the field and then just kind of stood there by myself.

Now that the initial rush of having made it through tryouts was past I was left with the question of whether I'd join the team if Miss Winters did indeed pick me as her first choice. As much as I wanted to spend more time with Cindi, the nasty looks I was getting from most of the rest of the cheerleaders was a pretty good indication that they were prepared to make my life extremely difficult if I joined the team.

I'd pretty much decided against joining the team when someone gently touched my arm. I turned and found myself looking into a pair of deep blue eyes. Jackson smiled at me and then cleared his throat.

"I just wanted to say that I thought you did really awesome out there."

I was blushing again, but it wasn't like I could run away and hide when he was standing right here talking to me.

"Thanks. I didn't think I'd be nervous, but it turned out I was pretty freaked out by the time I made it onto the field."

Jackson shrugged. "It didn't show. Don't tell the other girls, but I thought you were the best one out there. I didn't know that you were interested in being a cheerleader. Have you tried out before?"

I shook my head. "This is the first time. Honestly I'm not even sure if I can handle the time commitment if I join."

I got another smile, and this one made my heart beat even faster somehow. "Well, I'm pretty sure that you'll make the team, so all I can say is that I hope you decide to join. Miss Winters just announced that she wants to start doing some coed stunts, so she's looking for some guys to join the team. Maybe we'll be on the team together."

Did it make me a fraud if I joined the team solely because I was hoping to spend some time with Jackson? Probably, but I didn't care. If Miss Winters gave me a chance to be a cheerleader then I was going to say yes and I was going to put up with whatever crap the rest of the girls put me through.

I wanted Jackson like I'd never wanted anything or anyone else before.

Chapter 6

As I ran out onto the springy green grass of our school's football field I had a split second to wish one last time that my first football game had been an away game. Dream-assisted learning or not, I was still pretty sure that I was going to screw up in some kind of spectacular fashion. At an away game there would have been fewer witnesses, but in the grand scheme of things it probably wouldn't have made much of a difference. The other cheerleaders were going to make sure the entire school knew exactly how badly I did regardless of how many witnesses actually saw my mistakes. At least Miss Winters had put me on the back row for all of the routines.

I'd only been able to attend two official practices before the night of the next game, but Cindi seemed confident that everything would be okay. Dad had shelled out a painfully large amount of money to get my uniforms both ordered and overnighted to our house, which had almost been enough to make me reconsider my decision to join the team, but he'd waved away my concerns and promised to be in the stands for at least my first game.

Most of the other girls were doing handsprings or flips, but I wasn't about to do anything that complicated. I just ran, waved my pom-poms and then let out a quiet sigh of relief when it was time to line up with the other girls so that the football team could run between us.

Miss Winters hadn't gone any further than just assigning everyone to one side or the other for the good luck tunnel, but we might as well have had assigned spots. We basically lined up according to status inside of the squad. The leaders were all closest to the entrance, with the rest of us filling in the spots according to seniority in the squad, which meant that I was at the absolute end.

I'd known that going in, but I hadn't expected for Cindi to come over and stand by me. She glanced over at me just before the starting quarterback ran past us, and I realized that seeing her smile had turned my smile from the plastic expression that I'd had drilled into me over the last couple of days to something genuine and radiant.

I'd expected for things to get better with Cindi after I joined the team, but I hadn't expected them to get this much better. I finally felt like we were headed toward being as close as

I'd always wished we were. Cindi had helped me a lot over the last few days. She'd covered everything from doing my hair up with a blue velvet ribbon for the game, to showing me half a dozen other things that she'd said would make my first game less traumatic.

Watching over the shoulder of other cheerleaders as they'd dreamed had apparently taught me the cheers, but it hadn't been any help when it came to all of the other aspects of being a cheerleader. I would have been utterly lost without Cindi's help, especially since the rest of the girls on the squad still seemed to hate me.

It seemed to take forever for the football team to run through the good luck tunnel, but then finally the last blue-and-white helmeted figure was past me. I turned to run over to our normal spot on the sidelines and found myself face to chest with Jackson.

He looked incredibly gorgeous in the blue-on-white uniforms that Miss Winters had picked out for the male cheerleaders. I was still honestly more than a little blown away that Jackson was on the team. Not that he'd made it, but that he'd tried out in the first place.

I didn't have any room to talk, but the guys we'd had try out for the cheer squad were mostly nerds. I generally got along with nerds better than with most other kinds of people, but once I'd realized that the guys on the team were going to be catching Cindi as she did a backflip off of the top of the pyramid I'd suddenly become a lot more concerned about how strong they were than how smart they were.

Jackson was the shining exception in the group. Miss Winters had eventually selected five other guys, two per pyramid, but it was Jackson who was already taking the lead in practices. He was even talking about getting the other guys into the weight rooms a few times a week so that they could bulk up.

I tried to stop before running into Jackson, but I was moving too fast. If it had been one of the other girls I would have knocked them flat, but Jackson simply put his hands around my waist before I collided into him, and then picked me up so that I was looking down at him with my feet pointing straight up in the air.

I'd seen Jackson practice this particular lift with a couple of the other, smaller girls but I'd never expected to find myself performing it with him. My hands found his shoulders out of reflexes I didn't even know I had, and I pushed against him in an effort to take some of my weight off of his arms.

I had a split second to feel my stomach knot up from being so high up in the air, and then I felt my skirt slide down towards my stomach, revealing the tight little shorts that were part of the skirt. Cindi was a flyer, and she had a good point that it wasn't like anyone was actually seeing our underwear, but the shorts were still more revealing than anything I normally wore.

As Jackson brought me gently back down to the ground I could feel a blush breaking out all over my face, and I honestly wasn't sure whether it was because of my skirt having slid down or because I was making a spectacle of myself in other ways. He'd just saved me from the humiliation of bouncing off of him and falling down, but the last thing I wanted to be doing right now was to be performing the kinds of tricks that would make people notice me.

"Sorry, Adri. It was the only thing I could think of to make it look like you'd planned on running the opposite direction from everyone else."

My cheeks got even hotter as I realized he was right. Somehow I'd gotten turned around and I'd been headed towards the visitor's side of the field. I'd almost been doubly embarrassed and only quick thinking on Jackson's part had saved me from looking like a complete idiot.

"Thanks, Jackson. I guess I'm even more nervous than I realized."

I got a smile in response as we both ran to our assigned spots and started into the first cheer. The game went by more quickly than I'd expected it to. We yelled and jumped and kicked and almost faster than I could believe it, I looked up to find that there was less than a minute left in the first half.

My nerves had settled down during the first half of the game, I'd even pretty much forgotten about my near miss with Jackson earlier. I was just starting to worry about our halftime routine when I heard screams of outrage from the fans on our side of the field.

A couple of the other girls were disciplined enough not to turn and look, but I wasn't one of them, not that it did me a lot of good. The only thing I could see was a group of blue and white uniforms gathered around someone else, also in our uniform, who was on the ground curled up in pain.

I looked at some of the other cheerleaders, hoping for a clue as to what was going on, but all I could tell was that most of them looked really worried. Our coach and a couple of EMT's hauled our guy off of the field on a stretcher a few seconds later, and then the last few seconds of the clock ran down and it was halftime.

The butterflies in my stomach seemed to have put on a couple of pounds each. Somebody I knew had just been hurt, maybe seriously, and I was about to go out and do a dance that I'd only actually practiced in real life five or six times. I wanted to puke, but instead I just forced my face back into the squad-approved smile and ran back out onto the field with the rest of the girls.

I'd been doing my best not to notice anyone in the crowd, but this time I was looking slightly more to the right and I saw my dad sitting on the third row up.

Once again my smile transformed into something more genuine. Our team was actually pretty good and the bleachers usually filled up more than half an hour before the game even started. For Dad to have garnered a spot that close to the front he had to have arrived nearly an hour before the game was scheduled to start.

Dad hated football. The only reason he was here was to see my first game, just like he'd made sure to see Cindi's first game when she made it on the squad. I knew that Dad had hours of work still that needed to be done tonight, but he didn't look like he was resentful at having to be at the game rather than at home working. He was drumming his fingers against his legs like maybe he wasn't sure what to do without a keyboard in front of him, but he was smiling, and when he saw that I was smiling back at him his grin got even wider.

A second later the music for the routine started up and I threw myself into the dance with even more abandon than normal. It didn't matter whether I messed this performance up. The other girls on the squad and all of the kids at school would probably make me miserable if I did, but that just didn't seem important against the fact that my dad cared enough about me to come watch in spite of all of the other things he was supposed to be doing.

As luck would have it, everything went smoothly and five minutes later we were all running back off of the field to make way for the drill team. Cindi was one of our best dancers so she was at the front of the squad and was one of the first to make it back to where Miss Winters was waiting for us. She handed me my water bottle as I made it over to our end of the bleachers.

"Good job out there, Adri."

"Thanks, Cindi. I kept expecting to screw up."

She smiled and shook her head. "I knew you would do just fine. Did you see Dad up in the stands?"

"Yes. Not until halftime, but I saw him then. I take it that Mom didn't come?"

Cindi's mouth compressed to a disapproving line. "No. At least I haven't seen her yet tonight. It's not like it's a surprise though."

It seemed for a second like Cindi was going to say something else, but then Miss Winters clapped twice to get everyone's attention and we all gathered around to get our marching orders for the second half of the game.

I'd barely been able to keep up with what *I* was supposed to be doing out on the sidelines, I hadn't had any time or attention to keep up with the game, but apparently the game was a mix of good and bad. Miss Winters double-checked that we were all there and then took a deep breath.

"Okay, girls, as you all know we're up by two touchdowns, but this has been a high-scoring game and now that Victor Stalking is out with an injury, things could get ugly. I want you all to give it everything you've got. Hopefully if we can get the crowd really excited it will help the backup quarterback score some points."

She looked down at her clipboard and then rattled off a string of formations that she wanted us to work into the last half of the game. We all nodded and each put a pom-pom into the middle of the group. I screamed "Go Wolves" with everyone else as I double-checked that the board with the cheers on it was still resting inconspicuously against our end of the bleachers.

Miss Winters knew that nobody would be able to remember all of the cheers she'd just queued up for us, so she used the white board to remind us all during the actual game. I'd sort of expected more of a pep talk from Miss Winters, but the drill team looked like they were almost done with their number and it turned out that Cindi and a few of the other girls had been assigned to go help the mascots throw t-shirts into the crowd.

Just before Cindi rushed out on the field she grabbed my arm. "You've got about five minutes before our next routine. It would be a good idea to stretch out anything that's feeling tight. You don't want to start cooling down and then pull something, it happened to a couple of girls at the start of the season."

A stubborn piece of me thought about trying to go find my dad, but I knew that even if I did find him I wouldn't really have enough time to talk to him. Besides, Cindi was just trying to help out and it would be stupid of me to ruin how well things were going between us now. She wasn't actually being bossy, she just knew more about what was going on than I did.

I grabbed Cindi's yoga mat and rolled it out on the grass so that I wouldn't get my uniform dirty. A couple of the other girls were doing the same thing, but nobody said hello or even smiled at me. I'd pretty much expected to be ignored by everyone but Cindi and Sheree for the first few weeks at least, but that didn't make it any easier.

I looked around, hoping to find Sheree so that I could walk over and talk to her once I was done stretching, but she was standing over behind Miss Winters. She was talking to Jackson again.

I took a deep breath in place of the sigh of disappointment that I otherwise would have let slip out, and closed my eyes as I wrapped my hands around my ankles and leaned forward to stretch out my hamstrings.

"Do you want me to put a little pressure on your back so that you get a deeper stretch?"

I recognized Jackson's voice even before I opened my eyes to confirm that it was him, and that he was really talking to me instead of someone else.

"Um, thanks, but I'm going to pass. Miss Winters seems pretty against assisted stretching like that. It's not that I don't trust you, but I'm such a klutz that I'd probably end up injuring myself somehow and have to sit out the next three games."

Jackson's shrug was so laid-back that I was pretty sure I hadn't offended him. "I don't think you're giving yourself enough credit. You're really not any more klutzy than any of the other girls, but that's okay. Do you mind if I join you?"

I realized he had a mat in his left hand, which I hadn't noticed before because I'd been too busy staring at his face while trying not to look like I was staring. I nodded and he unrolled his mat and sat down next to me. About the time he started stretching out his quads I managed to process what he'd just said.

"That's nice of you to say, but I am the girl who just about ran over you earlier tonight. Thanks, by the way, for figuring out a way to make me look like less of an idiot."

He waved away my thanks. "Don't worry about it. It was actually kind of fun to stunt with you. You're pretty good considering that you haven't done any of that kind of stuff before. You tensed up the right amount without getting so tense that you forgot to help me out. We should practice that kind of stuff together. I'm stuck with whomever Miss Winters assigns me to for the pyramids and the like, but nobody said that we can't do some stunting together at other times, like we did today."

It was like there was a little fairy somewhere who was trying to make my life more difficult than it had to be. I'd never been even the slightest bit interested in any other boys before now, but there was something about Jackson that changed all of that for me. I wanted to get to know him, I *really* wanted to get to know him. If he'd asked me if I wanted to go to dinner and a movie I would have said yes in a heartbeat, but this was something else entirely.

Just agreeing to join the cheer squad had been a stretch for me. Stunting was way beyond anything that I was comfortable with. I much preferred to keep my feet safely on the ground, but as scared as I was of putting myself so completely in his hands, the physical danger wasn't even as worrisome as the social consequences.

I looked around to confirm that we were far enough away from everyone else that nobody was likely to overhear and then shrugged.

"That sounds both terrifying and fun, but I'm not sure it's a very good idea. Most of the other girls already resent me for getting Janessa kicked off of the squad and then taking her place. It doesn't matter to them that I didn't plan for any of this to happen; they still think that I'm basically pond scum."

Jackson shook his head. "I don't think any of them would call you pond scum…"

"Right, but only because they'd be calling me something worse. If I start stunting with you then everyone is going to think that I'm gunning to take over as a flyer. That has trouble written all over it."

"What if I told you that you'd make a better flyer than one of the other girls?"

"Sorry, as much as I think that stunting with you could be fun, assuming I can get past the sheer terror of it all, I still wouldn't be interested in taking someone else's spot."

Jackson brought his right arm across his chest, stretching out his shoulder and back, and it was all I could do to tear my eyes away from the way that his white uniform hugged the muscles along his side. He practically had wings and the material of his shirt was thin enough for me to see just how much definition all of that muscle had.

"You're very unusual for a cheerleader, Adri. Do you know that?"

"If by unusual you mean that I don't belong here in the slightest, then yes, I knew that. Even if I hadn't known that coming in, I would have figured it out pretty quickly given the way that all of the other girls on the squad are treating me."

Jackson rolled his eyes at me. "That wasn't what I was talking about. How many of the girls on the team do you think would show you the same kind of consideration you're so determined to show them?"

"I don't know—half maybe?"

"Not even close. Sheree definitely, and maybe Cindi, but if you weren't her sister there wouldn't be any kind of guarantee there with her either."

I bristled. "Cindi is a nice person."

Jackson held his hands up as though surrendering. "I'm sorry, I didn't mean to insult your sister. You're right, she's very nice. I was just trying to point out how unusual it is for anyone to forgo something they want because of how it might impact someone else."

I let my eyebrow rise. "That's a pretty cynical view of humanity. Is that the way you operate too? Do you just ride roughshod over anyone between you and what you want?"

"I said that most people do that, not all. You're obviously an exception to that rule, and I can say definitively that I'm not like anyone else you know." Jackson waved his arm out towards the field. "What do you think is going to happen with the game?"

"I don't know. Miss Winters seemed a little worried. I mean, it's a big deal to lose your starting quarterback, right?"

"It can be, but a lot of people are in for a big surprise tonight. Tristan is really good. I've seen him practice a couple of times and he's fast and accurate. If he wasn't a sophomore and he was twenty or thirty pounds heavier then he'd probably be the starting quarterback instead of Victor."

"That's good then, I guess?"

My response earned me another smile. I would have called it mocking, but there didn't seem to actually be any spite to it.

"You don't actually know anything about football, do you?"

"Not really."

Jackson shrugged. "I suppose that most of the other cheerleaders probably didn't start out knowing much about football either. You should learn though, it's actually a pretty cool sport."

There was an element of longing there that I hadn't been expecting. That didn't make any sense though. Jackson was plenty built, if he loved football as much as I thought he did, he should be playing football instead of watching from the sidelines like this.

"Why don't you play?"

Jackson started like I'd caught him off guard, like he hadn't been expecting me to be quite so observant.

"I wish I could, but my...mother doesn't approve. She thinks it would take away from my studies and distract me from other things that she thinks are more important than football."

"That doesn't make any sense. I mean she let you join the cheer squad, right? Helping us out is at least as big of a time commitment as being on the football team."

"Yeah you've got a pretty good point there. Partly it is because we move around so much. I couldn't have played here because I missed the tryouts. Mostly though, she just hates football. Even me being able to join the spirit squad wouldn't have happened normally. Things just kind of lined up perfectly last week for me to be able to try out and for her to say yes when Miss Winters picked me."

There was something there that I wasn't sure how to classify. It wasn't quite vulnerability, but it was a close cousin. I opened my mouth to say something harmless, but the words that came out weren't what I'd been planning on.

"Well, I'm glad that things worked out. I have a suspicion that you'll probably have to save me from making an idiot out of myself at least once or twice a game."

"Somehow I don't think you're going to struggle anywhere nearly as bad as that, but I'll gladly help out as often as you need me to. Let me know if you change your mind about practicing some stunts."

He leaned in closer so that I could hear him despite the fact that his voice had gone soft.

"It could just be our secret."

Jackson winked at me and then stood and walked away as he rolled up his mat. I felt like my head was spinning. I'd been worried that I was being too forward when I'd told him that I was glad he'd made the team.

In no world I'd even read about did a guy dripping as much hotness as Jackson ever want to get to know a chubby basket case like me. I was pretty sure I'd fallen asleep while stretching. I had to be dreaming, there was no other way to explain it.

Chapter 7

The rest of the game flew by in a blur. I managed to hit all of my marks and I didn't drop either of the girls I was supposed to spot for the stunting routines. All in all, if that had been the final result of the evening, I would have felt pretty good about my debut appearance on the squad.

After my mind-blowing conversation with Jackson I figured that the night was probably out of any other big surprises. It turned out I was wrong, it just took a little while for the rest of the surprises to shake out.

Things calmed down on the cheer front, mostly because Miss Winters was so enthralled in the game that she stopped feeding us cheers as quickly as what she'd done for the first part of the game. Apparently she was a hardcore fan and the game was even more exciting than I'd expected after Jackson's tip about Tristan.

If anything Jackson had undersold just how good Tristan was, which was lucky because we lost one of the offensive linemen on our first possession. Even with the tiny amount that I knew about football, I still could see the difference in the game after that happened.

From what I overheard from the other girls, the first half of the game had been all about offense with neither team's defense being able to slow down the other side's offense very well. Victor apparently had enjoyed tons of time in the pocket before being forced to make a throw. Tristan was under almost constant pressure, but it hardly seemed to faze him.

I watched in awe as the football exploded out of his hand and arrowed towards his receivers. Each and every snap was a race between whether or not Tristan could get the ball out of his hands before the other team tore through his crumbling offensive line and sacked him, and Tristan was winning nearly every snap.

Tristan and the rest of the offense worked their way down the field in a series of short hops and then scored and it was the defense's turn. Miss Winters came back to herself enough to signal for a couple of cheers, so I missed most everything until we had possession of the ball again, but our defense managed to stop the other team and then it was time for Tristan to come back out.

We didn't manage to stop them from scoring after that, but their defense was even less effective against Tristan and our guys, so we ended the game up by three touchdowns, which caused the crowd to go absolutely crazy.

I half expected everyone to pull down the goal posts or something, but they just ran out to centerfield and jumped around and screamed for half an hour. The players were just as crazy. Most of the cheerleaders were dating someone from the football team and within thirty seconds of the game ending most of the squad was riding around on their boyfriends' shoulders.

At first I tried to fight my way through the crowd, but it only took a couple of seconds to realize that I was wasting my time so I gave up and just let the press of people carry me further onto the field.

I'd never experienced anything similar before that. Grown men were acting like high-school kids. It felt like one of those intense TV moments. When I was little I'd been unhappy because it never seemed like real life was as good as TV. As I'd gotten older it had sunk in more fully that TV was pretend, that it wasn't fair to expect reality to compete with fantasy. This left me wondering though. This was reality, but it had an almost unbelievable excitement to it, the kind of energy that before I'd always thought could only be found in Hollywood productions.

I wanted to just throw myself into the moment along with everyone else, but for all that I was there in the middle of all of those people, I still didn't feel like I was a part of whatever was going on. I was experiencing the same events, but I wasn't experiencing it the same way that all of them were, I wasn't feeling the same things as them.

It was a depressing realization. I'd always known that I was a bit of an outsider, but usually it didn't bother me so much. Usually I didn't feel like I was missing out on anything important, but there was something there on that field that made me wonder if I'd been wrong all of these years, if there was something important missing from my life.

The football team started jumping up and down and the next thing I knew I was in the middle of a giant mosh pit. I expected for the adults to calm things down, to back up and create enough space for those of us who didn't want to be trampled to get out, but incredibly they just started jumping and shoving their way in tighter and tighter.

I tried to move with the crowd, jumping at the same time as everyone else, but I was just too small and it was only a matter of time before someone knocked me over. I actually made it longer than I expected to, but then I went to jump as someone stepped on my foot and someone else bumped into me from the side and the next thing I knew I was headed towards the ground.

I was going to get hurt. There wasn't any two ways about it, the mob was packed too tightly and everyone was twice my size. I closed my eyes, not because it was the smart thing to do, but because I couldn't bear to see what was about to happen.

Instead of hitting the ground and being trampled, I found my descent arrested as someone grabbed me from behind and then set me back on my feet.

"We need to get you out of here before something unfortunate happens."

Jackson's voice cut through all of the noise like it didn't even exist. I started to shake my head, started to tell him that there wasn't any way out, but he'd already pulled me tight against his chest and stomach with his left hand and was pushing people out of the way with his right hand.

I slid back around behind him, holding onto his waist for balance as he used both hands to open a way up out of the crowd for us. I knew Jackson was strong, but he was straight-arming guys out of our way who were even bigger than he was. The trip out to the edges of the crowd seemed to take forever, but sooner than I wanted to, I found myself in the clear and having to let go of his waist.

I looked up at Jackson and my face heated up again. "Thanks for getting me out of there. I guess I was more right than I realized when I said that you were going to have to save me a couple of times tonight."

"I'm just glad that I was close enough to lend a hand."

"Me too. I'm sorry I pulled you away from the celebration though."

Jackson shook his head. "I wasn't in there to celebrate."

It was an odd comment, one that begged the question of why he'd been out there in the middle of the mosh pit, but I couldn't bring myself to ask it. Out there in the center of all those people I'd felt like I was alone, but I hadn't been alone, not really. I could tell from the way that Jackson looked back at the crowd that he hadn't been any more at home there than I had been. Jackson was more of a kindred spirit than I'd realized.

Before I could open my mouth and say something stupid someone wrapped their arms around me from the side.

"Adri! I'm so glad you're okay. I saw you get caught up in the crowd and worried that you'd get crushed."

"I'm okay, Dad. It was a close thing but Jackson stopped me from falling and then got me out of the mosh pit."

My dad looked over at Jackson and then nodded. "Thank you, Jackson. I've never seen this kind of response at a high-school football game."

"You're welcome, Mr. Paige. I'm just glad that I was close enough to help."

There was a couple of seconds of that awkward silence that always seems to take place whenever two people from different aspects of your world meet and then Jackson shrugged.

"If you guys are all okay then I'd probably better be headed home. My mom will be wondering what the holdup is."

I turned and watched Jackson walk away from us for a second and then remembered that Cindi had been out on the field too when the spectators had all rushed centerfield.

"Dad, what about Cindi?"

"I'm fine."

I turned and realized that Cindi had walked up to us while I'd been watching Jackson. She was all flushed and sweaty, but otherwise looked no worse for wear. Cindi was even shorter and lighter than me, so I was having a hard time believing that she'd escaped the mosh pit without injury. My disbelief lasted only as long as it took me to notice the football player standing just inches behind her.

"Dad, Adri, this is Tristan. Tristan, this is my dad and my sister Adri. Tristan kept everyone from crushing me when things got crazy out there."

I'd been terrified the entire time I'd been stuck in the crowd. I hadn't really stopped shaking until Jackson had dragged me out to safety. Cindi and Tristan on the other hand looked like they'd been having the time of their lives.

I looked back at my father and realized that he felt the same way that Jackson and I felt. He was as much of an outsider as I was. He'd only come here because of Cindi and me, which made me love him all the more.

"It sounds like I owe you my thanks, Tristan. I was almost sure that my little girls weren't going to make it out of that mess."

"Yeah, I guess we all got a little carried away. Just as everyone started jumping around I looked down and realized that Cindi was going to get crushed, so I got a couple of the other guys on the team to help me get her out."

My dad nodded. "Well, I'm indeed grateful. It looks like your adoring public is waiting for you though. I wouldn't want us to keep you from them."

I followed Dad's gaze and realized he was right. Most of the spectators were still screaming in the center of the field, but there was a group of about ten people of various ages who were standing just out of earshot looking like they really wanted to talk to Tristan. I was actually surprised that they hadn't already mobbed him, but something—maybe my dad's manner—was keeping them at a distance.

"You're right, I better go hobnob with the fans. It was nice to meet you, Mr. Paige."

Cindi watched Tristan walk away with a glimmer in her eye that I was pretty sure my dad noticed too. He watched her watching Tristan for several seconds and then cleared his throat.

"You were both amazing out there tonight. I never would have guessed that you'd do a lift like that, Adri."

I blushed again. "It wasn't actually planned. I was headed the wrong direction and then when I practically ran Jackson over he just threw me into that lift so that I wouldn't look like quite as much of a spastic idiot."

We had Cindi's attention now. "Where's Mom?"

Dad frowned. "I'm sorry, girls. I tried to get her to come with me tonight. I reminded her a couple of times during the day that you were both performing tonight, but when it came time to leave she said that she had some prints that she was in the middle of developing. I had hoped that she'd arrive still before the game ended, but I guess it wasn't to be."

"Yeah, most things with Mom aren't to be lately."

My jaw dropped at Cindi's tone, but it looked like Dad had made as many excuses as he was willing to make for Mom tonight because he didn't respond to his youngest daughter's venom, at least not directly.

"Do the two of you want a ride home or were you planning on just walking?"

Cindi shook her head. The unhappiness that had graced her face just a second ago had already vanished. "It's going to be at least another half hour by the time we talk to Miss

Winters and get all of our stuff together. You go ahead without us, Dad."

I nodded. "Cindi is right. Thank you for coming tonight, but you probably have a lot of work waiting for you at home."

I could see the battle going on inside of his head. On the one hand were his work commitments, on the other was living up to what he thought was his fatherly duty.

"Are you both sure? I can stay if you don't want to walk. It is dark outside already."

Cindi's smile was a perfect study in innocence. "Really, Dad. We'll be fine. Besides, the odds are pretty good that one of the other girls on the squad will give us a ride later anyways."

I gave Cindi a confused look, but she gave me a covert 'calm down' signal. Dad looked back and forth between us for a couple of seconds and then nodded.

"Okay, I'll head out now then, but if you two change your minds or can't get one of the other girls to drop you off then just call me. I'll happily drive back over here and pick you up."

Cindi and I gave Dad hugs and then hurried over to where Miss Winters was standing. There were only a couple of other girls there at that point, but our making it over there triggered some kind of critical mass. More and more girls showed up over the next couple of minutes at a faster and faster rate until everyone was there waiting for the post-game critique.

"You girls all did really well. I'm proud of you all and the way you helped keep the team in the game. I'm sure you're all exhausted by now, so I won't keep you for a lengthy discussion, but this may not be the last time we see everyone rush the field like that. If it happens again when you're out on the field like that then the best thing to do is just stay in the front of the crowd and then circle back around after everyone stops moving forward."

We all put a hand into the center again, yelled "Go Wolves" and then everyone started splitting up. Based on Cindi having told Dad to go home without us I'd been expecting a much longer analysis. I picked up the bag with my things and then followed Cindi, only she didn't ask one of the other girls for a ride, and she didn't head towards the front of the school and the road home.

I caught up with her on the forty-yard line and she was so excited she practically beamed. "If the fans rush the field again I'm going to do exactly what I did tonight."

I shook my head at her in amazement and then slapped one of the lucky mosquitoes that hadn't succumbed to the pesticide that the city sprayed on all of the stationary bodies of water in an effort to keep us all from being eaten alive.

"You do realize that things could have ended up a lot worse, don't you? If Tristan hadn't been there when everyone started moshing you probably would have been hurt pretty badly."

Cindi frowned at me. "Seriously, did you not feel the energy out there tonight? This is the kind of thing that made me want to be a cheerleader in the first place. Besides, it wasn't just luck that put me close enough to Tristan for him to save me. I've been trying to catch his eye for weeks now."

I had to fight the urge to roll my eyes at her. Cindi seemed to crush on a different guy every week. She wasn't shy or anything so it was pretty incredible that she hadn't really had a boyfriend yet, but things never seemed to work out. Usually the timing was off. By the time the boy realized that she was interested in him, she'd generally moved on to someone else. I was pretty sure that her saying she'd been pursuing Tristan for weeks was a gross exaggeration.

Cindi looked at me and it was almost like she read my mind. "I'm serious, Adri. I really like Tristan. I stopped talking to you about this kind of stuff because you always roll your eyes like you did just now."

"I didn't roll my eyes at you!"

"Yes, you did. It's okay, I know I've been flighty in the past, but this time things are different."

I took a deep breath and tried to put my skepticism to one side. "Okay, what do you want me to do? Is there some way I can help?"

Cindi's smile was back and I knew I'd made the right decision. Even if she lost interest in Tristan tomorrow, whatever she wanted me to do right now would be worthwhile if it made her that happy.

"I knew that the meeting with Miss Winters would be short, they always are."

She looked at me and took in my expression of astonishment with a giggle. "I've been staying late after every game for weeks. At first it was because I wanted to talk to the other girls on the squad, but lately it has been because it gives me a chance to talk to Tristan."

"How do you find time to do any homework around all of the cheerleading and boy-chasing?"

"It's not easy, let me tell you."

This time I did roll my eyes at her. "Okay, so what do you want out of me?"

"Just come with me to talk to him. We usually exchange a word or two after every game, but today was different. I think he would have stayed there talking to me for an hour if Dad hadn't sent him away."

Whatever response I would have come up with was preempted by the return of the football team to the field. Most of the rest of the squad was still hanging out on the bleachers, so it wasn't like we were the only two girls who'd stayed to talk to the players, but I still felt pretty conspicuous. Cindi didn't seem to share any of my misgivings.

I was still trying to pick Tristan out of a sea of white uniforms, but Cindi was already angling us down a slightly different trajectory. As the football team started dispersing I was able to finally find Tristan. Cindi had done a surprisingly good job picking our route. We were going to walk within a couple of feet of him, but it didn't look like we'd planned that, it just looked like we'd happened by him on the way towards the parking lot. Cindi was even better at this guy-chasing thing than I'd realized.

"Hey, Tristan. Thanks again for getting me out of that mosh pit."

Tristan turned and bestowed a confident smile on both of us. "Hey, no problem, it was actually kind of good." He leaned forward so that he could whisper. "I'm not really into that kind of thing so you gave me a reason to get out without all of the other guys thinking I was wussing out or something."

"I feel the same way. I'm totally not into that kind of thing either."

I had to stop myself from saying something. Cindi had just finished telling me that she loved being in the mosh pit. I didn't like the way that she was pretending to be someone different than she was, but it wasn't like she'd thank me for pointing that out right now.

"You girls headed home?"

"Yeah, you?"

"There's this big victory celebration over on Crater Lake. Hey, you two should come with us."

I could see the wheels turning in Cindi's head. She wanted to come up with a way to go to the party, but we both knew that there was no way that Dad was going to buy off on that, not on a school night. It only took her a second to come to the realization that there wasn't any way for her to manage it short of sneaking out.

"That would be cool, but we're probably going to have to pass this time around."

Tristan shrugged. "It won't be the same without you, but that's okay, maybe next time."

He looked the two of us over and I was pretty sure that his gaze stopped and rested on me for an extra second or two. He was probably wishing that I'd kept walking or something so that he could just talk to Cindi by himself.

"I've got plenty of time before I need to head off to the lake. You two want a ride home?"

I was impressed that Cindi managed not to squeal in excitement. It was starting to look like this might be the crush that actually went somewhere for once.

Chapter 8

Between finding out that Cindi had the hots for Tristan, the stress of cheering at my first game, and the thrill of being saved by Jackson, I went to bed without even considering that I might have another of the crazy dreams that had been plaguing me lately.

I was tired enough that I dropped off to sleep almost as soon as my head hit the pillow. My dreams started off normal. I was in the middle of finding out that I'd forgotten to study for a test in my history class when the classroom suddenly changed.

It took me a second to figure out what was different. At first it was just a subtle change in the amount of light in the room, but it continued to grow as I tapped my pencil on my desk. It wasn't just that there was more light in the room, the light seemed to almost be coming out of the people.

It was eerie enough that I looked around the room in an effort to see if anything else had changed. I almost missed it, but the corner furthest from the door was slightly blurry. It was like I was looking at it through a dirty pane of glass.

That was one oddity too much and I realized that this had to be another dream. I pinched myself to try to confirm my suspicion, but contrary to what I was expecting the pinch hurt.

I hadn't taken my eyes off of the corner for nearly a full minute now and I distantly heard my teacher asking me if everything was okay. I was desperately scouring my memories. I didn't think that I remembered getting ready for school that morning, but it was hard to be sure. Every morning at my house was pretty much identical to every other morning.

"Adriana, is everything okay?"

I looked away from the corner to answer my teacher and I realized that the desk was in a different place than it had been when I'd entered the class. It had to be a dream, but it felt too real. I needed more time; I needed a second to think without everyone badgering me.

I opened my mouth to respond and realized that everyone had stopped moving. I'd wanted time, wanted people to *stop* and they had. I was surrounded by a classroom full of other kids, but it looked like a wax museum.

The way that everyone had frozen in place was creepy, but the silence bothered me even more. It felt wrong to be in a classroom, surrounded by people, and not hear a single sound other than my own breathing.

I looked back up to the corner of the room where I'd noticed the odd light distortion, but it was gone. The corner looked just like it should, but I could still feel a presence in the room that I couldn't explain. I turned in my chair, looking for the source of my unease.

I found it in the empty desk two rows over from me. It was shaped differently now, more like a person, but still almost impossible to see. That wasn't the only change. It was less like a dirty pane of glass now and more like the disturbance in the air that you can see on a cold day when you look along a dark wall that the sun has been shining on for a few hours.

The distortion moved slightly and I somehow knew it was staring at me.

"I can see you. I know that you are there."

The words came out evenly and with more confidence than I actually felt. I'd had scores of safe, normal dreams, but both times that I'd run into something odd like this before I'd been sure I was going to die. I had an uneasy feeling that this was going to be another one of the dangerous dreams.

Nothing happened for a couple of seconds and then the air flickered and the tiny Native American man from my skyscraper dream came into view.

"How did you pull me out of my rest?"

It wasn't until I heard how tired his voice was that I realized how worn down he looked. The bags under his eyes and the odd color to his skin would have been concerning all by themselves, but there were bandages visible just past his sleeves and at his collar too. He'd obviously been in some kind of massive accident, or possibly a fight.

Honestly he looked like he should still be in a hospital, but that wasn't the most unsettling thing of all. I could see some kind of golden light leaking out of him. It was pretty faint where he was uninjured and it was super strong in a couple of spots on his chest, which I was pretty sure meant that he'd taken some serious injuries there.

"I don't know. Lately things just happen when I dream. I don't have any control over it."

He frowned at me. "It's not safe for you to be doing this. These injuries weren't sustained in the real world; they were sustained in dreams just like this one. You can be killed in a dream just as easily as in the real world, more easily in some ways."

I hadn't forgotten the way that he'd tried to kill me the last time I'd seen him. He didn't look particularly threatening now, but I knew that there was some kind of monster hiding inside of him.

"It's not like I have a choice about this or anything. It just happens."

His color looked like it was getting worse.

"You're angry that I threw you into the wall the last time we spoke."

"Yeah, that's a safe bet. Also I'm a little confused as to why you're all chummy this time around after being so scary the last time."

"I wasn't trying to hurt you. It wasn't safe for you there; I was trying to send you back to your own mind."

"By killing me?"

"By shocking you, by weakening your grip on that reality in the hopes that you would naturally fall back into your own reality."

There was something else there he wasn't telling me. "You weren't positive it was going to work, were you?"

Was it my imagination or was his breathing becoming more shallow? I was almost positive that something had changed there.

"No, I wasn't. It's become obvious to me that your gift works differently than mine. At the time it was only a suspicion, but I've been searching for you since our last encounter and haven't been able to sense even the slightest trace of your dreams. That's never happened before."

"So you did something that you knew might kill me?"

"I had no choice. If Kaleb had found you he would have killed you. I nearly didn't escape myself. You would have had no chance of staying out of his clutches."

"So teach me. You say that our powers are different, but there must be some commonality between them."

"You're wearing your own form, I can see that much, but that doesn't mean that you're as harmless as you appear."

I looked down at myself. I'd never even considered that I might be able to look like someone else while I was dreaming.

"I don't understand."

The light leaking out of his chest seemed to be getting stronger. It was oddly beautiful, but I suspected that it meant he was getting weaker, that his real body had started bleeding again.

"I can usually tell when someone is trying to project something other than their real form. There is a haziness about them."

"That's how I knew you were there earlier. It looked like an empty corner, but there was a weird kind of distortion in the air."

"Indeed. It's a sign that your gift is strong, potentially stronger even than mine. You need training. Tell me your name and where you live. I'll come to you as soon as I'm healed enough to travel."

I shook my head. "I'm not telling you anything of the sort. You're some kind of monster and I'd be stupid to just blindly trust you. Teach me what you can now and the next time we meet you can teach me a little more."

"I'd be just as much of a fool to teach you what I knew without first verifying that you are not more than you seem to be. There's not even any guarantee that we'll run into each other again."

I wasn't normally very good about standing up for myself, but this was different. The stakes this time were huge.

"I'm not telling you where I live."

"Give me a name then. Trust is a two-way street. We both must risk at least a little if we're going to start earning each other's trust."

"Fine, my name is Adri. It's your turn now—teach me something useful, something that will keep me alive."

He didn't look happy. Actually it was worse than that, it was like he didn't appreciate being told what to do and was having to bite back a response that would have escalated things.

"Very well. Escaping a dream is all about letting go of the alternate version of reality that you or someone else has created. To leave you need to focus on the real world and let what you're seeing in the dream become less real. For me this takes the form of a kind of misty impermanence. It may be different for you."

He paused for a moment before asking his follow-up question. "What state do you live in?"

My insides tightened up. Every piece of information I gave out put him that much closer to finding me. How many Adri's were there in the United States? A thousand? Ten thousand maybe? Of those, how many were my age and blonde? If I told him that I lived in Minnesota that would drop the number down into the hundreds or maybe even a few dozen. He probably didn't have access to any government databases. That would make things harder for him, but still it seemed like too big of a concession on my part.

"No, that's too much. Ask me something else."

I was sure it wasn't my imagination this time. His fists clenched hard enough they turned white and it almost looked like he was shaking. I needed to be more careful how I responded to him from here on out. I didn't want to push him over the edge.

"Fine. Have you run into anyone else in your dreams since your power awakened who was like you or me, someone who seemed in control of their environment? Someone who noticed you, interacted with you in a way that indicated that they knew you were more than just part of the scenery of their dream?"

"Is that important?"

"Answer the question or we're done here."

His voice came out low, lower than mere anger could account for. It had an almost bestial edge to it.

"Yes. There was someone—a woman, I think. I mean she was a woman, but she might have been projecting a different appearance and I just didn't know. She was fast, really, really fast. She wanted to know who I was and when I didn't tell her she started choking me. The weirdest thing was that just before I passed out she sent these odd tendrils towards my face."

"You're going to need to be careful. Supernatural creatures are going to be drawn to you, or maybe you to them, I'm not sure which. It will start out as just dream encounters, but some of them will come hunting you if you give them enough information to track you down."

It took me a couple of tries to get my voice to work. "If that's true then I don't have much of a chance. I don't even know enough to figure out which parts of my dreams are just normal dreams and which parts are something else. Something nasty could just pretend to be part of my dream, blending in until I let something important slip."

"Exactly, that's why I'm trying to convince you to let me come teach you. The safest thing right now is for you to be moving around. If you don't spend more than a day or two in any one part of the country then even creatures that learn more about you than you'd like won't have a chance to act on their knowledge before you've relocated."

I shook my head. "I'm sorry, I want to trust you, I really do, but I'm not going to take that risk. Is there a way to detect other people inside of my dreams?"

He frowned but nodded. "You control your own dreams which means that you can flush people out fairly easily. Change something big about your surroundings and you'll usually notice any intruders. Freezing everyone suddenly like you did earlier works, as does changing your environment. If you go from outside to inside or inside to outside, often times you'll see someone stumble as the ground underneath them literally moves. The same strategy works to a lesser extent inside of someone else's dreams."

"What do you mean?"

"You can't control the whole dream like you can your own, but if your will is strong enough then you can change some aspects of it. If you find yourself in a dream and are unable to make a large global change to it then you know you're in someone else's dream and you must be careful. Leave if you can, or if that isn't a possibility then you need to try to blend in as much as possible."

His shake had pretty much disappeared, but he was looking weaker by the second. He coughed and I got the feeling that it wasn't something that had happened here in the dream, or rather not just here in the dream. He'd coughed because his dream body had been forced to mirror his physical body.

"I don't have very much longer. Being in the dream burns up energy that I can't spare, at least not right now, not with my current injuries. If you're going to tell me how to find you then now is the time to do so, otherwise I'll let you ask one more question as a show of good faith in case we do ever meet up again."

There wasn't any two ways about it. I panicked. I knew so little about this business of sharing people's dreams that I didn't even know what I didn't know, didn't have any idea of what I should be asking. The sheer importance of the next few seconds threw me into a kind of paralysis and I couldn't think of a single question about the dream that I thought might keep me alive if I ran into something as dangerous as he'd indicated I would.

"I want to know about that guy you were spying on. Kaleb. I want to know about him."

The question had just kind of tumbled out of my mouth. It had been driven by nothing more sinister than the feeling I'd had back when I'd first seen Kaleb, the impression that he looked familiar. Not like I'd ever seen him or anything, but he was related to someone who was somehow important to me, someone who had been missing from my life.

I'd thought the question a pretty harmless one, but he lunged to his feet. Pieces of the desk he'd been sitting in went flying across the room. Out of the corner of my eye I saw a couple of my classmates disappear as shrapnel tore through them, but most of my attention was focused on the massive creature that had replaced the Native American between one heartbeat and the next.

"Did he send you? Did Kaleb put you up to this in an attempt to find out what I've learned?"

I fell out of my desk, scrambling backwards on all fours as he stalked towards me.

"I don't know Kaleb. I just asked because he reminds me of someone else!"

The creature's wickedly long claws were fully extended now and he sliced through desks and people with equal abandon as he crossed the last few feet towards me. My back hit the wall and I suddenly realized that I didn't have anywhere else to go. I tried to make the wall disappear—it was my dream and he'd just finished telling me that I should be able to control my surroundings, but it was almost like there was an unseen pressure holding the wall in place.

He took one final step forward and picked me up by the throat again. With the transformation to his beast form the bandages had disappeared, but the glowing slashes across his chest hadn't gone anywhere. In this form they were actually bigger and bleeding more light than they had before.

As the pressure around my neck grew to the point where I couldn't breathe I did the only thing I could think of. I tried to focus on the real world, tried to push the dream away, but it was like there was something holding me there, some unseen wind that pressed me back against the wall.

I pushed harder with my mind and then suddenly the wind stuttered and the Native American started to disappear. That was all I needed to tear myself free of the dream, but I was pretty sure that he hadn't let me go voluntarily. The wounds and the energy he'd expended in an effort to keep me there had simply been too much for him to sustain.

I was pretty sure I wouldn't have been able to escape if his concentration hadn't wavered there at the end.

Chapter 9

I was undeniably jumpy the next morning. I didn't seem to have any of the physical signs of nearly dying for the third time while dreaming. My neck wasn't bruised or anything, but when I climbed out of bed my gray pajama pants slid down off of my hips as soon as my feet touched the floor.

I grabbed my pants, pulling them back up before they hit the floor and then went to retie the drawstring, but it turned out that it hadn't ever come undone. I always tied my bottoms so they were pretty loose, but I was sure that when I'd gone to bed that the pants had been plenty tight enough not to fall down on me like that.

I crept into the bathroom and looked at myself in the full-length mirror on the door. Cindi had been going on about the fact that I'd been losing weight for long enough that I'd finally started to believe her, but I was still shocked by what I saw in the mirror.

Cindi was right, I'd been losing weight for a few weeks now, but the process had accelerated. When I'd looked down at myself during the dream with the Native American I'd seen a body that was still a little on the plump side, but the reality was that I'd lost nearly all of the baby fat that had hounded me for so many years. I was as skinny as any of the other cheerleaders, as skinny as Cindi even. I wanted to say that it was inexplicable, but I knew that wasn't the case.

The Native American had given me the answer, probably without even realizing that he was doing so. Being in other people's dreams was burning up so much energy that the calories taken in during the course of the day weren't keeping up. It was incredible, but no more so than the fact that I was sharing dreams with people I'd never met in real life.

I untied my pants and then retied them again, tightly enough this time that they wouldn't fall off my ever skinnier hips. Having the drawstring that tight bunched the fabric around my waist up, which made me frown. These pants were one of the newest articles of clothing I owned. I'd purchased them a few weeks ago after I started slimming down. If they now fit this badly then I was in trouble. The rest of my clothes were going to be even worse.

My fears were proved out when I started getting dressed half an hour later. My 'skinny' jeans were in the dirty clothes hamper and I had to hold up the next best option, a pair of shorts, with one hand to keep them from sliding down while I hunted through my half of the closet for a belt.

By the time Cindi came out of the shower I was on my third belt and I was starting to lose hope. None of my belts were small enough. So far all of the ones that I'd tried, even on their tightest hole, were too big to keep my pants from falling down.

"Can I borrow a belt, Cindi?"

"Wow, it's almost like I can see you getting skinnier before my eyes. Yeah, here, this one should work."

I gratefully took the proffered strip of black leather and threaded it through the loops on my shorts. The result wasn't pretty. The shorts puckered up around my waist as if yelling to everyone that they'd never been meant to fit around someone as skinny as I currently was, but Cindi's belt served to keep them up where they belonged.

I took a deep breath and tried to tell myself that I didn't care what anyone else thought about me. It was a nice thought, but the truth was I actually did care. I'd always cared, but I cared more than ever lately, maybe not what *everyone* thought, but definitely about what *Jackson* thought.

Breakfast wasn't our usual arrangement. Usually Dad had breakfast with Cindi and me, but Mom tended to be hit-and-miss. Sometimes she stayed up late working on some project or another and then slept in. Other mornings, she was up before dawn so that she could try to capture the sunrise. Occasionally, she held to a more normal schedule.

This morning was apparently one of the unusual days when her art hadn't gotten in the way of socializing with us. Dad, on the other hand, had left for work even earlier than normal. Mom shrugged and mumbled something about a conference call with someone over in France. It was obvious that she didn't really wake up until halfway through her bowl of cereal because that was when she looked at my shorts and shook her head.

"Adri, you can't go out like that. You look like an orphan."

"Yeah, well, losing all of that weight might be good for my heart, but it's really screwing with my wardrobe. Everything else that was clean is even worse than this. I had to borrow the belt from Cindi."

"The top looks pretty terrible too, but it's not quite as bad. Borrow some jeans from Cindi, it's supposed to get cold today, you'll freeze walking back home in those shorts."

Cindi opened her mouth and for a second I thought she was going to argue, but she just shrugged.

"I'll go grab my Tommy's. They are longer because I wear them with my boots. They should be about right for you, Adri."

"I would have been fine, Mom."

"No, Adri, you wouldn't have been. Cindi is fine with lending you some clothes. Besides, it's only for a few days and then I'll take you shopping."

"Dad just finished paying for my cheer uniform, Mom. I doubt there is any money left in the budget for a new set of clothes for me."

"I'll do laundry today and then tonight we'll see what's still salvageable from what you already have. Once I know how bad things are I'll figure something out. Maybe we can go to that new store over on Hillside and trade some of your clothes in for something smaller. Your clothes are all pretty trendy, so they'll probably pay top dollar for them."

I bit back the response that was on the tip of my tongue. I didn't have any clothes that could remotely be classified as trendy. Cindi did, but I'd never felt like I could beg and cajole Mom and Dad into spending that kind of money on me.

We were already running a little late so I rinsed my bowl and headed back to my room. Cindi had been right, the jeans she'd laid out for me fit almost perfectly. They were a lot tighter than I'd ever gone for in my clothes, but the length was good and they didn't need a belt to keep them from falling down.

I grabbed my backpack and my gym bag and then almost ran into Cindi on my way back out into the hall.

"I was just thinking that if it's going to get as cold as Mom said that you probably need some leg and arm warmers. I've got an old pair that you can use."

"Thanks, Cindi. I'm sorry about all of this."

"It's okay, if you hadn't slimmed down a little then you probably wouldn't have made the team. If loaning you some of my clothes is the price to pay in order to be able to cheer with you then it's not a bad deal."

I nodded and headed into the hall, only to pause as Cindi sighed. "I just knew your butt was going to look better in them than mine does."

School was pretty miserable. The popular kids still hated me for causing Janessa so many problems and everyone who wasn't popular still felt like I'd betrayed them by joining the cheerleading team.

I'd made it through school so far by keeping my head down. Now it seemed like every class I went to had at least two or three people whispering about me the entire time.

I didn't catch much of it, but what little I did overhear was pretty vicious. The guys all seemed to think that I was going to turn into a Grade-A slut. The girls all seemed to think I was destined for slutdom too, but they spent almost as much time talking about how losing a few pounds and buying some new clothes wasn't going to change who I really was—a waste of space.

By the time I got to my last class I was just holding out to make it to cheer practice. That was an ironic reversal of the way of the world. I knew that the other girls on the squad would still be as nasty to me as they figured they could get away with, but at least once I made it to practice Cindi would be there.

I was glad Cindi and I had become closer, it was just too bad that it had come at the cost of alienating everyone else in the school. The most graphic illustration of how much had changed happened as I was walking out of my last class and some lowlife, whose name I didn't even know, grabbed my butt.

The two guys with him laughed while I was still too much in shock to react and then the next thing I knew all three of them had surrounded me. I had the feeling that things were going to get ugly and then suddenly one of them was on the ground holding his nose as bright red blood trickled out from between his fingers.

Jackson towered over both of the others and looked like he was ready to rip them apart with his bare hands.

"The next time I see the three of you bothering Adri, I'll put you all in the hospital. If it happens a third time, then I'll put you in the morgue."

Even with the size difference between Jackson and the other boys I still half expected for them to jump him, but there was something in his manner that seemed to welcome the idea of a three-on-one fight. It took only a second or two for the guys who'd been messing with me to decide that they didn't want to tangle with Jackson. The two who hadn't been hit grabbed the one Jackson had knocked down and dragged him away.

"You okay, Adri?"

"Yeah, thank you. I didn't realize that you were going to have to save me outside of games too."

He shrugged. "It's all part of the job description. Let's get you back to your locker and then over to the locker room. I don't think you'll have any more problems today, but I'm going to stick with you anyway so that the rumor mill has a chance to spread the word that messing with you is a bad idea."

I watched Jackson out of the corner of my eye as we walked through the hall. I'd always known that he was built, but seeing him back down three guys had flipped some kind of switch inside of my head. Nothing about his manner had changed, but I was more aware now of the way that he cut a channel through the normal mob of kids in the hall. It was like he dripped testosterone, but not the showy, cocky production that most of the guys our age put on.

He was all calm assurance and I found it even sexier than I'd expected to.

I put my books away, grabbed my workout bag and followed him to the gym. He gave me a nod as I peeled off to go into the girls' locker room. Cindi wasn't in her usual spot so I changed into a pair of Cindi's shorts and a tank top in what I was pretty sure was record time and hurried back out to the gym.

Jackson was already there waiting for me. He'd pulled on some black yoga pants that hit him mid-calf, and a gray t-shirt that he'd ripped the arms out of so that it showed the way the muscles on the outside edge of his back flared out as they traveled from his waist up to his shoulders.

"Are you ready?"

I didn't trust my voice so I just nodded and headed towards the outside door. He paced me, close enough that his arm occasionally brushed against mine. I kept trying to tell myself that I wasn't some twitter-pated freshman, but the truth was that it was all I could do to walk without stumbling. The last half an hour had thrown my attraction to Jackson into overdrive. At this rate it would be a full-blown obsession by tomorrow morning.

Jackson opened the gym door for me, easily throwing the heavy, gray metal door open despite the fact that he was only using one hand. I nearly tripped over Miss Winters, who was standing just outside of the gym rather than waiting over in her usual spot.

"Adri, Jackson, I'm glad I found the two of you. Do you have a second?"

She got a "Sure" out of me and a nod from Jackson.

"I always like to have a backup flyer. That was Cindi up until Janessa left the team. Now Cindi has taken over Janessa's spot and I need a new backup. I'd like for you to be that backup, Adri."

She mistook my wide eyes and slight gasp as disappointment rather than shock and hurried to reassure me. "I'm not saying that you'll have to remain a backup forever. I select based on skill and the other girls have been doing this for a while so you'd have your work cut out for you, but if you really go hard at this it's possible that you could take over one of the other girls' spots."

I shook my head. "I really don't want to bump anyone else, Miss Winters. Honestly, flying scares me pretty badly."

"But you and Jackson were stunting at the beginning of the last game."

"I know, but it wasn't planned or anything. Honestly I got turned around and was headed the wrong direction. Jackson threw me up into a lift because he didn't want me to run over him."

She was quiet for a couple of seconds while she digested my words. "What do you think, Jackson?"

"I think Adri is a natural. If you can convince her to give it a shot she'd make a great backup flyer in case something happens to one of the other girls."

"It really is important, Adri. I'm not going to lie to you, being a flyer is a little risky. I've never had someone seriously injured, but it's not uncommon to lose someone to a sprained ankle at some point during the season. If you're seriously not interested in trying to knock out one of the other girls, then that is even better because it should make for less drama."

"I don't know, Miss Winters. Most of the rest of the flyers are a lot smaller than me."

She shook her head. "You're only an inch or so taller than Sheree and you're just as skinny as any of the other girls. I'd have you work primarily with Jackson though until some of the other guys on the squad start to bulk up a little. Jackson won't have any problem stunting with you. Think it over. It would mean you'd have to come practice on Tuesdays with the rest of the flyers, so it would limit your study time a little bit more, but I really think you'd find it to be a rewarding experience."

My heart started racing. It was like she knew exactly the right force to pit against my fear of stunting. Two weeks ago I would have said that there wasn't anything that could have got me to follow in Cindi's footsteps and allow someone to throw me up a dozen feet into the air, but the possibility of spending more time with Jackson was a powerful draw.

I opened my mouth to tell her that I'd think about it, but the words that came out weren't the ones that I'd meant to say.

"Okay, Miss Winters. I'll do it. I really hope that none of the other girls get injured and I don't want their spots, but I'll do it to help out just in case someone does get hurt."

"That's great, Adri! Even if we don't end up needing you this year we'll definitely need you next year after Missy graduates."

Miss Winters gave us each a smile and then hurried off. I kept thinking that I should follow her, that I should head out to the field where the other girls would be gathering over the next few minutes, but my body seemed almost unconnected from my will. I wondered idly if I was in some kind of shock.

"Come on, Adri. If you stay here much longer you're going to put down roots."

Jackson gently pulled on my arm and I let him lead me further away from the door. We were nearly around the edge of the school when I realized that he hadn't seemed the slightest bit surprised at Miss Winters extending me an invitation to join the flyers.

"Did you have something to do with that?"

"What do you mean?"

His response was a bit too innocent and I felt my suspicion harden into certainty.

"You did, didn't you? You put her up to that."

Jackson shook his head at me. "You are seriously paranoid."

"That's not an answer, that's an evasion."

That earned me a smile and a nod. "Smart too. No, I didn't put her up to it, at least not really. I mentioned to her that you seemed to have good instincts when it came to flying and she took it from there."

He said it like it wasn't any kind of big deal, but he had me wondering. Had he purposefully tried to get me in with the flyers because he'd wanted to spend more time with me? A very loud part of me kept screaming that there was no way that a guy like Jackson could possibly be interested in me, but the evidence was starting to mount.

We walked towards the football field in silence. I didn't know why Jackson had gone quiet, but on my part it was because I was trying very hard to keep the butterflies in my stomach from making a break for it.

Miss Winters announced that I would start training as the backup flyer at the beginning of practice. Everything after that went even worse than I'd expected. At one point, I had to stomp on the urge to look around to see if someone had a voodoo doll dressed like me. I'd read about people staring daggers, but this was the first time that I'd been able to actually feel the hatred coming off of someone.

It was unsettling enough that I missed my cue and screwed up a couple of times in the number five routine. The only thing that got me through it all was the fact that Cindi and Sheree both gave me big smiles and thumbs up every time our eyes met. That and knowing this was my ticket to spend more time with Jackson.

The squad scattered even faster than normal when Miss Winters released us to go home. I tried to tell myself that I was being silly, that the world didn't revolve around me, but the first words out of Cindi's mouth seemed to indicate that my fears weren't completely unfounded.

"Wow, there were a bunch of panties all knotted up today."

Sheree frowned, but it wasn't an angry frown, more along the lines of her not being comfortable with saying something so harsh about the other girls on the squad.

"It wasn't just my imagination then?"

Cindi shook her head at me. "No, you just pulled off the coup of the semester. The older girls are all going to hate you even more because this means that they aren't going to make flyer unless one of us gets hurt."

Cindi took a long pull from her water bottle and then offered it to me. "Not only that, you're going to have seniority, which means that two of us will have to get hurt before they'll get to perform at an actual game."

Apparently we'd moved far enough away from the harsh stuff and close enough to the verifiable truth for Sheree to feel comfortable joining in.

"It really is too bad for the seniors. They aren't like any of us; they can't look forward to another chance at flying next year."

Cindi shrugged. "Realistically, none of the seniors besides Missy are small enough to be flyers anyways."

Now I was the one frowning. "They can't really help their genetics, Cindi. When you get right down to it I'm too big to be a flyer too."

Cindi and Sheree both went into the special kind of reassurance mode that you could only get from other girls. Sheree got her words out first, but Cindi was only half a heartbeat behind her.

"No, you're one of the skinniest girls here."

"Sheree is right, Adri. You're totally small enough to be a flyer now."

It was probably just my imagination, but I almost thought that Cindi put a little extra emphasis on the 'now' bit of that statement. I told myself to calm down and not take everything so personally, but apparently some of what I was feeling made it onto my face. Luckily Cindi wasn't looking at me and Sheree misinterpreted what she was seeing.

"You really will make a great flyer, Adri. I wish there was a way to prove it to you."

Sheree looked around as though she expected to find the proof she was looking for just lying there on the grass. I expected her to realize how silly she was being, but it only took a second before her face brightened up and she let out the kind of yell you usually only heard out of Sheree at actual games.

"Jackson! Could you come help us for a few minutes?"

I turned and had to fight down the urge to blush. Jackson was far enough away that I was astonished that Sheree had known it was him. He'd changed back into the shorts and polo shirt that he'd worn most of the day and had obviously been headed home, but was headed back towards us now.

Sheree was practically bouncing with excitement by the time Jackson made it over to us. "Hi, Jackson. Adri is a little nervous about practice next Tuesday. Would you be willing to do a couple of tricks with her while Cindi and I spot for the two of you?"

"Sure, I can do that."

There was something to Jackson's look that made me want to blush again. I looked over at Cindi to buy myself some time and saw that she didn't look happy about the way things were headed. Her expression shifted so quickly I almost believed that I'd imagined her unhappiness, but it had definitely been there.

"Is that not okay with you, Cindi?"

"Hmm? Oh. No, it's okay, I just have a history test that I need to study for still tonight. I can help out for a few minutes though. It wouldn't be safe for just Sheree to try to spot you."

Sheree excused herself for a minute to call and let her mom know that she was going to be later than expected. Once she was done with her call we got started. Actually, it would probably have been more accurate to say that we *tried* to get started.

I was really bad. Jackson's comment about me having good instincts notwithstanding, I'd expected to be terrible when it came to actual stunts. It turned out that I was worse even than I'd been expecting.

We started out with the same kind of lift that we'd done so unexpectedly at the game the day before. I think everyone figured it was a safe starting point given that I'd already done it once before. We couldn't have been more wrong. Jackson was strong enough to get me up into position almost regardless of how badly I messed things up, but that didn't mean that the stunt looked right, or graceful, or even remotely like I knew what I was doing.

After twenty minutes where I showed a frustrating lack of progress, Sheree suggested that we try something else. We tried an arabesque, but I just couldn't seem to keep my balance during the portion of the lift where Jackson picked me up and put me above his head. I was pretty sure that Jackson was as rock steady as anyone could possibly ask for, but once I got above a certain height I started shaking too badly to get my back leg up into position.

Cindi suggested basket tosses next under the assumption that, at least initially, I wouldn't have to worry about actually *doing* anything, so I could just enjoy the ride as they threw me into the air. I kept closing my eyes, which meant that I came down awkwardly and made it harder for the three of them to catch me.

When Sheree finally told us that she needed to get home, I was surprised to find out that we'd been at it for nearly an hour and a half. I thanked Jackson and Sheree both and then Cindi and I went back into the school for our books before heading home.

It wasn't until we'd been walking for a couple of minutes in complete silence that I remembered that she'd been wanting to get home and study for her history test.

"I'm sorry, Cindi. I didn't realize that we'd been at it for so long."

"It's okay, one bad test probably isn't going to pull my grade down in the class by too much."

I opened my mouth to say something else apologetic, but I knew her well enough to know that she was more pissed off than she wanted to admit. She wasn't going to listen until she'd had a chance to calm down and work through things on her own.

We made it home a few minutes later only to find that Dad and Mom were in a huge fight.

"It's just a couple pairs of jeans and a few tops, John. Honestly, do you want your daughter to run around naked?"

"That's not the point and you know it. Adri had clothes. They may not fit very well now, but you should have talked to me before going out and charging three hundred dollars on the credit card like that."

"What do you want me to do? Should I start selling camera lenses in order to keep our daughters fed and clothed?"

"Yes, if that's what it takes. Maybe if you had to sacrifice a little to keep the wheels from coming off around here you'd appreciate what I go through keeping you in lenses and photography supplies."

Cindi and I hadn't meant to sneak into the house, we'd come in through the front door just like always, but Mom and Dad had been yelling so loud that they hadn't heard us arrive. Mom's voice was getting really pitchy just like it always did when she was nearly to the point of tears.

"That's not fair, John, and you know it—to me or Adri either one. Why should Adri have to settle for the cheapest clothes we can find while Cindi gets designer labels? As for my equipment, you haven't had to lay out a single red cent in years. I pay for my supplies and whatever else I want out of my own earnings."

"Fifteen thousand dollars."

My dad's voice was low enough that I almost couldn't make out what he'd said, but my mom obviously heard him and it apparently was a long-standing point of contention between them.

"Not that again."

"Yes, that again. We spent fifteen thousand dollars on your hobby six years ago. You said that it would be a fun thing you could do on the side to bring in money while the girls were at school. The truth is that every miserable penny you've earned has gone right back into buying yet more gear and it's so far beyond a simple hobby that the girls and I hardly see you anymore. It's become an obsession."

"You're a fine one to speak of obsessions. How many hours did you work last week? Seventy? Eighty? I turned to my photography because *you* were never around. The girls have each other and their friends at school. You have your coworkers and your work, my photography is all I have"

I opened my mouth to tell them that we were here but Cindi grabbed my arm and shook her head. Dad responded to Mom's latest allegation before I could tell Cindi that I thought it was a really bad idea for us to be listening to them fight.

"I took this job specifically for you. I took a pay cut because you were singing this exact same song back then."

"And how long exactly did that last? You're working just as many hours now as you were six years ago."

"I started working more hours because you were never around, and putting Cindi through cheer camps and keeping her in those damn designer jeans was eating into what little savings we had left. If I can close this project out at work then I'll finally have something to show for the last few years. I'll be able to move back up into the kind of position I had at my last job."

"There will always be another project, John."

"Just like there will always be another print that needs developed?"

I was saved from hearing Mom's response by the fact that Cindi burst into tears. She ran through the house and slammed our bedroom door with a crash that was too loud even for Mom and Dad to miss.

Chapter 10

The next hour or two was kind of a blur. Mom yelled something about Dad being an insensitive jerk and stormed down to her cave. Dad came into the living room for just long enough to give me a hug and then he followed Mom down into the basement. He shut the door on the stairs, so I couldn't hear much of what was said after that. Even when they were shouting at each other I couldn't make out more than a word here or there.

I didn't want to eat, but between the calories I'd burned off in the dream the night before and the calories that got consumed at practice, I figured that skipping dinner wasn't an option. I made myself a club sandwich and then pulled out my English homework. Normally I was a pretty big procrastinator, but between normal cheer practices and the extra Tuesday practices that I'd just agreed to, I figured I'd better keep my nose to the grindstone homework-wise or I'd be in pretty big trouble.

The yelling downstairs went on for nearly another hour without much in the way of pauses. I heard Cindi come out of our room to use the bathroom at some point, but she went back into our room without saying hi, so I decided to continue giving her space.

Dad finally came back up about the time the sun went down. He looked tired, but then he always looked tired lately. This was something more than that, he looked like someone who'd been fighting a battle for a very long time. Someone who'd just realized that maybe the battle wasn't worth fighting after all.

"I'm sorry that you girls had to hear that, Adri."

"It's okay, Dad. I'm sorry you and Mom are struggling."

Dad gave me a sad smile. "It's not your fault, sweetie."

"Isn't it?"

He grimaced. "This fight wasn't about the clothes. Honestly I wish I could dress all of us in the height of fashion, but with the economy going the way it is right now things are just too tight."

"I understand, Dad."

"I'm not sure you do, not really, but I appreciate you being so willing to forgive. I'm sorry that I haven't put my foot down before now and made your mother stop buying Cindi such outrageously expensive clothes without doing the same for you."

"What are you going to do now?"

The look of exhaustion was back on his face. "I'm going to go talk to your sister and try to convince her that I still love her despite what she heard when the two of you got home."

"That's probably a good idea, Cindi could use some reassurance right now, but that wasn't what I was talking about."

I made an awkward gesture that I hoped took in the fact that I wanted to know more, wanted to know what the future held.

"I don't want to drag you into the middle of the fight your mother and I are having, Adri."

"Are the two of you going to get divorced?"

Dad rubbed his eyes, but I was pretty sure it was more just to buy himself time than anything else.

"You know, when you were little anytime you asked me a question I didn't want to answer I just distracted you with a toy. Sometimes I miss those days."

"That's a yes, then."

Tears started pooling in my eyes, but my dad grabbed my hand before I could run out of the room.

"I don't know, Adri. I'm sorry, I wish I could give you an unqualified no, but I can't any more. If you'd asked me even a couple of months ago I would have said no without hesitating, but I'm just not sure now."

"What happened? Is there someone else?"

I was old enough to understand that divorces happened, that it didn't have to necessarily be my fault or Cindi's fault, but I knew that they'd loved each other when we'd been little if nothing else. That, seemed to demand that someone be at fault.

"No, sweetie, there's nobody else. You heard the summarized version earlier. Your mother feels like I've been an absentee husband and father while I feel like she's been an absentee mother and wife. The truth is that we're both right. And we're both wrong. It's just one of those things."

I knew my dad better than anyone else except for maybe my mother. I could tell when he wasn't telling me the full story and this was one of those times.

"What else? That's not the only reason."

Dad nodded. "You're going to think less of me for saying this, Adri, but I'm tired of working and having nothing to show for it. I've been in this profession for nearly two decades and at various times I was making pretty good money, but even after all of that your mother and I don't have enough in savings to cover a few hundred dollars' worth of clothes for you. Our retirement is in just as bad a situation. Honestly, at this rate I'll be working until the day I drop dead of a heart attack."

"Don't say that!" I managed to keep my outburst down to little more than a whisper, but it took nearly every ounce of self-control that I had. I managed it only because I knew that it would destroy Cindi if she overheard what Dad was saying right now.

"I'm sorry, Adri, but it's the truth. I tried to tell myself otherwise for the longest time, but over the last few months things have gotten even worse. We've gone from having only a little saved up to starting to rack up credit card debt. The balances are small still, but they get a little bit bigger every month. Your mother has nearly a hundred thousand dollars in photography equipment down there."

I didn't even try to hide my surprise. Dad tucked a stray strand of hair behind my ear as he nodded.

"She's been quiet about it, but every time I go down there to talk to her she's got another lens or a new camera. She might wish otherwise, but I can read our tax returns and last year alone she made nearly forty thousand dollars. The truth is that I've been keeping a close eye on her equipment as a way of proving to myself that she's reinvesting all of her earnings. As bad as her current actions are, if she started socking away tens of thousands of dollars into a separate bank account somewhere that I didn't know about, that would be worse."

"Because it would mean that she was getting ready to leave you."

"Yes. I hate to admit to having those kinds of doubts, but there it is."

My stomach hurt and I suddenly wished that I hadn't eaten. If I'd skipped dinner like I'd been thinking about doing then there wouldn't be anything in me to come back up.

"I'm sorry, Daddy. I didn't mean for Mom to buy all of those clothes for me. I try not to ask for very much."

The tears that had been threatening to escape earlier started down my face now as my dad pulled me into a gentle hug.

"You haven't done anything wrong, Adri. I love you and Cindi both. I don't begrudge you the money we spent taking care of you. You've been a real trooper and hardly ever asked for anything, and even some of the extravagant spends on Cindi aren't her fault. I should have reined your mother in years ago, but I just couldn't bring myself to deny her any more than I could refuse you when you said that you wanted to join the cheerleading squad. This is as much my fault as anyone else's."

"What are you going to do?"

As much as I didn't want to hear the answer that I suspected he was going to give me, I had to know. It would be better to know what was coming than to have it hit me completely by surprise.

"Your mom and I are going away for a week. We don't have the money for anything fancy, but we need some time away from everything else to try to reconnect. Your mom has all of the hiking gear we'd need and she's agreed to pay down the credit card debt and buy a tent out of her photography money, so we're going camping. We'll go up to St. Croix and try to keep the distractions to a minimum. I'll bring my cell phone but no way to recharge it and your mom will bring her camera but no way to recharge it either."

"So work will be able to call you if there is a real emergency, but they won't be able to steal you away very much and Mom has a limited number of pictures she can take before she's out of juice too."

"Yes. We'll bring your mom's cell phone and a solar charger for it so that you can get ahold of us if something happens, but other than that, it will just be the two of us with nothing to do but talk to each other."

"What about your big project at work?"

"They'll just have to get by without me for a week. Your mom suggested this trip I think partly because she thought I wouldn't take the time off. My boss isn't going to be happy about losing me on such short notice like this, but you girls and your mom need to come first. I didn't understand that as well as I should have early on in my marriage and this is one of the consequences of that."

Chapter 11

Cindi didn't say anything when I finally went into our room to go to sleep. I was a little worried that she'd overheard Dad and me, but there wasn't anything I could do. If she hadn't overheard us, then anything I did to try and make things better would just result in her finding out what he'd said and being hurt as a result.

Once I was ready for bed, I told Cindi good night and then fell asleep almost as soon as my head hit the pillow. The dream about the Native American had still bothered me a little when I'd been awake, but once I fell asleep some of the raw terror I'd felt when he'd tried to kill me again came back. It was odd the way that the dreams seemed less important, less immediate, once I was awake.

It was possible that it was some kind of mental defense mechanism from having come so close to death. The more I thought about it the more sense that made to me. My mind was probably shying away from the sheer distress that the dreams had been causing me, but once I was back in them it was bringing it all back so I'd have the best chance possible of surviving long enough to wake back up.

I was just outside of the school this time and there wasn't anyone around. I'd been walking, but I stopped and pretended to tie my shoe while I scanned for the telltale shimmer of someone trying to hide themselves.

A slow turn in place once my shoe was tied satisfied me that there wasn't anyone watching me. I reflexively dusted my hands off and then realized that in the dream there wasn't any dust. I'd put my hands on the ground at one point to steady myself, but the ground hadn't been made up of individual grains of dust and dirt, it had been one single hard surface just textured such that it looked like real dirt from a distance.

I bent back down to look at the ground in closer detail and watched in astonishment as the ground transformed before my eyes. I ran one finger along it and this time my finger dug a track in the soft dirt and came away just as dirty as I would have expected it to.

The grass was just as unrealistic as the dirt had been a second ago, but as I focused on it and remembered what it was supposed to be like, it changed too. Individual blades of grass formed where before there had been only a springy mass of green.

I tickled the sharp, soft edge of a single piece of grass with my thumb and then looked back at the dirt and found to my dismay that it had returned to its former state. A few minutes of experimentation taught me that I could, with great difficulty, simultaneously hold both the grass and the dirt at a state that was close to what they were in real life, but when I did so everything else around me became obviously fake. The school took on a two-dimensional feel and some of the trees in the skyline behind the school became misty and disappeared at random times.

I let the grass and dirt go back to their normal dream state and watched as everything else around me became a little sharper, a little more realistic. It was like my brain only had so much processing power when it came to populating my dreamscape.

All of that manipulating of my surroundings made me wonder what I could do when it came to manipulating my own appearance. I made myself taller, changed my hair color and even changed my shape from the slightly plump version of me that I'd started out as to anorexic skinny and then over to obese before shifting back to the pleasingly skinny version of me that had been staring at me from the mirror this morning.

Changing how I looked was actually harder than changing my surroundings, and the further I got from how I'd started out the dream the harder it was to hold the change. It was interesting that my subconscious still seemed to think that I was as chubby as I'd been a few months ago. There was probably some kind of big insight there, but I didn't want to dwell on my psychological issues right now. A better use of my time would be to try to continue to learn whatever I could about manipulating the dream. I didn't expect to make any huge breakthroughs, but even small bits of knowledge might be what kept me alive the next time I ran into the wax lady.

I thought about trying to find the Native American again. Presumably if I was subconsciously pulling him into my dreams somehow then I should be able to do the same thing consciously, but so far neither of our encounters had been pleasant. The first time he'd purposefully let me go, but this last time, when he'd lost control of himself, he'd been trying to hold me there inside of the dream. I was pretty sure that he would have killed me if his wounds hadn't robbed him of the strength required to hold me there.

I didn't want to run into the Native American right now, but that didn't mean I couldn't still try and acquire the skill of finding a particular person. I might need it at some later point. It only took me a second to settle on Sheree as the one that I wanted to find.

I was torn on whether or not to keep my real face and body while I went looking for her. So far all of my encounters other than the most recent one with the Native American had been inside of someone else's dreams. I was pretty sure that I'd actually been in the wax lady's dreams when I ran into her, but there wasn't any guarantee that someone else couldn't find me while I was with Sheree. In the end, I shifted into as good of a match for Missy's tiny body and scowling, but beautiful, face as I could manage.

I had no real idea how to find Sheree, but everything else in the dream world seemed to be based on visualizing what I wanted and willing it into existence. I took a deep breath and then started thinking about Sheree. The details were a struggle but I forced myself to create a clear picture in my mind of her smile, the way that her wavy brown hair perfectly framed her face, and the tiny frame that made her a perfect flyer.

It felt like my mind was stretching, like it was being pushed right up to the edge of what I could handle and then slightly over that thin, pulsing line. It hurt, not necessarily in a bad way, but in a way that told me that if I pushed even harder that it could turn into the bad pain of a tear rather than the good pain of a stretch held slightly too long.

I got the last bit of detail inside of my mind right and then *pushed* in the odd way that I'd done when I made the dirt and the grass conform to my will. I opened my eyes and found Sheree standing in front of me, perfect in every detail.

We stood there for a couple of seconds, neither moving, and then I recovered enough from the effort of bringing her to me that I managed a smile.

"Hi, Sheree."

"Hello, Adri."

I started to ask her what she'd been dreaming about before, but the words died in my throat. I looked back down at myself to confirm that I was still wearing Missy's body and found that I was. There wasn't any way for the real Sheree to have known that I was Adri instead of Missy. This wasn't Sheree, it was a construct that I'd created inside of my own dream just like I'd changed my shape and size. She was calling me by name because that was what my subconscious was expecting her to do.

I idly thought about seeing how good of a conversation this Sheree would be able to maintain, but ultimately that was just a very convoluted, very odd way to talk to myself. I sent her away without really knowing what I'd done until after she was gone.

I stopped for a minute to try and figure out how I'd made her disappear. My mind felt different now that she was gone, it was more...relaxed. I visualized a bench where there'd never before been a bench and then tested it to make sure it was up to my weight.

As I sat down on it I realized what was different. I wasn't having to think about it, but some part of my mind was busy maintaining that bench. The closest parallel I could come up with was that a corner was knotted up from the strain of keeping my dream from switching back to whatever my subconscious actually wanted it to be.

I stood back up and relaxed my mind, smiling as the bench vanished. Now that I knew what I was looking for it wasn't difficult at all to find the tiny bit of my mind that was maintaining the illusion that I was Missy rather than Adri.

I could feel exhaustion starting to pull ever so slightly at me, but I had one more idea that I wanted to try before I let myself lapse into a more normal rest. I closed my eyes again and thought about Sheree again, but this time I focused more on how she made me feel.

Sheree was the kindest, most non-judgmental person I knew and being around her was almost like being wrapped in a soft, fuzzy blanket of acceptance. I felt a smile tug at the corner of my lips as a sense of happiness rushed through me. The happier I felt the stronger the sense of her presence became.

There was a kind of tightness in my skin, like maybe I was being pulled through a keyhole, and then the exhaustion that had been hovering at the edges of my being moved a little closer, dragging at the happiness that had been buoying me up.

HUNTED

I opened my eyes and my jaw dropped when I found that my surroundings had changed. I wasn't outside of the school any more, I was inside someone else's bedroom.

"Mom, please don't make me get up. It's a Saturday. Can I please just sleep in for once?"

Sheree's voice sounded more tired than I'd ever heard out of her before now. The perky excitement that was normally part and parcel of interacting with her was gone, but it was still Sheree, she was just buried underneath her green comforter.

I was pretty sure that I was in her dream this time. Things felt different, for one thing, and there were some things that didn't look right. Sheree's hands were enormous for one thing, which seemed to indicate that she was much more self-conscious than I ever would have guessed about that particular attribute. Just to be sure I tried to change the color of the walls in the room. I imagined the blues and greens switching over to yellow and then once I had that image fixed in my mind I pushed in an effort to enforce my will on our surroundings. There was a flicker of something on the wall closest to me, but it disappeared so quickly that Sheree didn't even notice the change.

I definitely wasn't in my dream now. The level of effort I'd just put into that simple change would have more than sufficed if we'd still been in a construct that I'd made. Another wave of exhaustion crashed through me and I momentarily had to lean against the chair and desk behind me. I was going to have to be careful not to try and change anything

"Are you tired, Sheree?"

She looked up at me and nodded. "Yes, I'm exhausted. I was helping poor Adri try to learn stunts for what seemed like forever last...well, I'm not sure when it was. I was going to say last night, but that can't be the case if today is Saturday..."

I didn't want Sheree to think that through too much. I figured I was much better off with her in her normal dream state than if she were experiencing some kind of lucid dream. I'd just found out how hard it was to change things around when in someone else's dream. It seemed like a really bad idea to let her or anyone else dictate what my environment did.

I shuddered slightly at the thought of just how unpredictable it could be to experience someone else's dream. You would never know which physical laws were going to be working at any given time.

Sheree misinterpreted my shudder and frowned at me. "I don't understand why you hate Adri so much. It's not like she made Janessa take those drugs. The whole thing was unfortunate, but it's hardly Adri's fault that things ended up going *that* badly for Janessa."

"I don't care about Janessa, I just don't like Adri."

I got another frown, but it looked like this was just par for the course when it came to Sheree's interactions with Missy. So far, she didn't seem to think anything was out of the ordinary.

"You're not going to lose your spot as a flyer, Missy. I know—we can practice right now if you want."

I opened my mouth to tell her no, but something made me stop. I had only vague memories of the dreams where I'd learned the routines that had gotten me on the squad. It seemed like I'd watched for the longest time and then Cindi or Sheree had invited me to join them. It had worked for that, maybe it could work when it came to learning to fly as well.

"Okay, let's practice. You'll have to hurry though, I don't have long. It's a good thing that we're already at the school."

We weren't actually at the school when I said it, but I'd been acting on a hunch. My saying that we were at school nudged Sheree's subconscious into putting us there. We were standing on the football field with no breeze and a clear blue sky above us.

"Hmm, we're going to need more than just us if we are going to do this, Missy."

"Ah, look, there's Jackson and Cindi."

I pointed behind her as I said it and once again that caused her subconscious to do exactly what I wanted her to do. Jackson and Cindi appeared as she turned around to look for them, and Sheree didn't seem to think it was odd that they were wearing the exact same clothes as they'd been wearing when we'd practiced earlier that day, and she didn't seem to notice the fact that they were rendered like some kind of low-resolution computer painting. Apparently her mind wasn't up to holding much if any more in the way of detail than mine was.

"Oh, this is perfect. Hi, guys, would you be willing to help Missy?"

We all got the preliminaries out of the way and then we got down to business. I'd hoped that it would be easier to practice in the dream, but I hadn't expected it to be as easy as it turned out to be. In the real world I'd spent the entire time scared that I was going to get seriously hurt. In the dream, I just figured that any sprains or breaks wouldn't still be a problem when I woke up, so I relaxed and let Jackson and the others throw me to their hearts' content.

Everything from basket tosses on down went smoothly. I didn't start out perfect obviously, but Sheree just kept telling me what I was doing wrong and I kept making slight adjustments to my technique until she started telling me I had it.

The thing that was most surprising of all was that I actually started enjoying all of the different stunts. The feeling of soaring through the air, the centrifugal forces as I did a backflip, it was all much more fun than I'd expected it to be.

I thanked Sheree profusely after what felt like a couple more hours of practice, which caused her to look at me oddly. Apparently gratitude wasn't one of Missy's strengths. As I let Sheree's dream dissolve away from me I realized that I could really get to like this whole dream traveling gig. I could practice with Sheree or one of the other girls pretty much whenever I wanted to without it getting in the way of studies or any of my other waking activities.

I even liked interacting with Sheree better in the dream world than in the real world. Don't get me wrong, Sheree was super nice in both places and I felt a little bad at having fooled her by making her think I was Missy, but there was something addictive about being able to interact with people completely on your terms.

Chapter 12

It turned out that there actually were some consequences to dream traveling. By that, I mean negative consequences. I already knew that dream traveling used up calories, but that came down decidedly on the benefit side of things.

I was the most tired I could remember being in months by the time morning finally rolled around. After finishing my impromptu practice session with Sheree I'd slept the sleep of the dead. I didn't remember any more dreams, normal or otherwise, almost as though I'd dreamed myself out and hadn't been capable of dreaming after that.

I hit the snooze button two more times than normal before finally stumbling down out of my bed. Mom and Dad were both gone already, apparently both trying to get ahead with their respective projects before they left on their mini vacation. I hadn't expected that, but it wasn't entirely a surprise. What did shock me was the fact that Cindi was gone too by the time I stumbled out of the shower.

She hadn't said anything during the minute or two when we saw each other before I went into the bathroom, so I hadn't realized I was going to be walking to school by myself. It was surprising just how different it felt to leave the house without Cindi by my side. We'd been walking to school together each morning since middle school and I honestly couldn't remember a day where I hadn't talked to her before sitting down in my homeroom class.

I spent the first hour or so of school worried that Cindi had overheard Dad and me talking. There wasn't anything I could do to make things better if she had been listening to us, but that didn't stop me from wondering how bad things were going to be when she finally exploded. Just trying to keep up with the lectures when all I wanted to do was lay my head down on my desk and sleep took nearly all of my mental resources.

I finally caught up with Cindi at lunch, but even then it was just because I happened to see her head outside with her salad just as I was headed into the cafeteria. I grabbed a big serving of greasy yellow French fries and a slice of pizza and then headed outside to see if I could find her.

She was sitting outside, back against the school, staring off into the distance as she ate her salad. It was maybe the only time I'd ever seen her eat by herself in the last year.

"Can I join you?"

She looked up at me and nodded. "Sure. Those jeans look good on you by the way."

I was wearing the clothes that Mom had bought me. I'd actually forgotten that I'd put them on this morning, but I suspected that she'd commented on them less out of an effort to be polite and more as a way of covertly bringing up what had happened last night.

"Thanks. I almost didn't wear them, but I didn't want to borrow any of your stuff without asking and without your belt none of my other pants would have stayed up."

Cindi's nod was oddly noncommittal. "You should be careful, Adri. You have to watch what you're eating if you want to stay this skinny. Just because you're stressed out and unhappy doesn't mean you can just eat whatever. I know it's a temptation, it's hard for me too."

I looked down at my pizza and fries and nodded. She was right, at least she would have been right if I'd been normal. I debated telling her about my dreams, but now didn't seem like the right time. Things had been better between us lately, but if I was going to tell her something that crazy then I wanted to be certain that she would believe me. As things stood right now she was just as likely to think that I was making it all up as some kind of play for attention.

"I'll be careful, Cindi. Thanks for the warning. I think I'll be okay for today though.

Yesterday took a lot out of me. It wasn't even just the exertion from trying to stunt, I was all tensed up and nervous the entire time too, which also burned up calories."

I wasn't sure I wanted to dive right into Mom and Dad's fight, so I cast about for something else to talk about.

"Did you take your test yet?"

"Yeah, I had it second hour."

"How did you do?"

Even as I asked, I realized that the answer wasn't going to be good, not given how little time she'd had to study for it and how terrible last night had been.

"I'm pretty sure that I failed it. I didn't even know what he was talking about with about half of the questions."

"I'm so sorry, Cindi. This is my fault. I never should have agreed to practicing last night."

She shrugged. "One test probably won't drag down my grade too much. I can probably still get a 'B' out of the class. Maybe Mr. Cruthers will even let me do some extra credit work."

She hadn't disagreed with me, which meant that she did think her bad grade was my fault. A tiny part of me wanted to tell her that she was a big girl, that she could have told the rest of us when our impromptu practice ran long, but I stomped on the impulse and tried again.

"I'm sorry about the way things went down when we got home last night. I tried to leave you alone because that was what I thought you wanted. I'm sorry if that was the wrong way to have handled it."

"It's fine. Look, I've got a test next week that I should probably get started studying for. I'll see you at practice."

I went through the rest of my classes in a haze of misery. I'd joined the cheerleading squad mostly because of Cindi. The idea had been that both of us being on the squad would bring us closer together. The reality was that things were tenser now than they'd been for weeks.

I was so deep in thought that Jackson had been walking next to me for several seconds before I realized it was him.

"You okay, Adri?"

"Yeah, sorry. I...well, it was just a rough night after the four of us got done yesterday."

He gave me a surprisingly understanding smile. "I'm sorry to hear that. If there's something I can do to help make things better just let me know."

"Thanks, I don't think that there is, but I appreciate the thought."

We were nearly to my last classroom and all of a sudden I realized that he hadn't just happened to run into me, he'd purposefully come and found me.

"Not that I'm complaining or anything, but why are you following me around?"

Jackson shrugged. "It's probably nothing, but I made a promise to those three lowlifes yesterday. I figured that if they were going to try anything they'd probably do it in about the same place, which means either before or after your last class."

A rush of warmth and happiness moved from the tips of my toes up through the top of my head. Jackson was acting like it was no big deal, but no guy, other than my dad, had ever made that kind of effort on my behalf.

"Thanks, Jackson. I appreciate it. I appreciate it a lot actually."

"Don't worry about it. I'll be here a few seconds after school gets out and we can go to the locker rooms together."

I practically floated over to my assigned seat. I'd actually been considering quitting the team in an effort to make things better between Cindi and me, but there was no way I was going to do that right now. I finally had an iron-clad reason to spend time with Jackson; I wasn't just going to throw that away, not without a lot more in the way of proof that quitting would make things better with Cindi, and not until I'd had a chance to get to know him better.

I went slower than usual when it came to gathering up my books, and when I stood up from my desk and turned back to the door

Jackson was waiting for me just as promised. We walked back to my locker and then over to his more or less in silence, but it was the companionable kind of silence that you usually only find between people who've known each other for a really long time.

Half of the team had arranged their schedules so that they had their PE class last. It was actually kind of smart because it meant that they just changed into their practice clothes once and then didn't have to worry about getting sweaty and going back to their other classes.

It was hard to be sure around all of the other girls who were changing back into their street clothes, but it seemed like there weren't as many cheerleaders in the locker room as normal. I slipped on some of Cindi's old clothes that she'd gifted me when I joined the team and then put all of the rest of my things in my duffle bag.

It was actually a good thing that I didn't have PE this semester. Cindi's clothes more or less fit now that I was skinnier, but some of the stuff she'd given me was from a year or two ago when she was a little shorter than she was even now. I was pretty sure that the shorts and tank top I was wearing now weren't quite in keeping with the school regulations. Miss Winters wouldn't mind, but Coach Bellor would.

Jackson was waiting for me outside the girls' locker room and the smile he gave me when he saw what I was wearing made my face heat up. I honestly didn't know how to handle guys looking at me like that. It had never been an issue before now, but I decided I liked it. I wasn't about to go start dressing like a skank, but anything that helped Jackson notice me wasn't all bad.

Miss Winters was out on the sidelines of the football field in her normal place, but she was obviously unhappy about something.

"Ah, Adri, Jackson, good, you're here. I was starting to wonder if I was going to have a team left by the time that school got out."

I looked around and realized that while she was exaggerating slightly, she wasn't that far off. Half of the team still looked like it was missing.

"What happened?"

My question drew another frown out of her. "PE is what happened. Coach Bellor started a game of girls-against-guys dodgeball and then left to go take a call. Apparently there was more than the usual amount of trash talk and a bunch of girls got hurt."

"How hurt? Will they be okay?"

"Yeah, nothing serious, at least it doesn't look like any of the injuries are really bad, but we're down five girls. Two of them got slight concussions from running into each other, and the other three have sprained ankles."

I had to force myself to close my mouth. What Miss Winters was describing was that amazing. Stuff like that just didn't happen in real life. Movies and TV sure, but not real life.

"That's a third of the team."

"Yeah, but that's not the end of it. Jesse and Jenny both asked to be excused from practice. Normally I would have just told them no, but given how many girls we've already lost I decided to let them go, which means that we've got exactly ten girls left."

Miss Winters took a deep breath, visibly calming herself down before continuing. "Given all of the missing girls, and the fact that some of the girls who are going to be here are a little worse for wear from the dodgeball game, I've decided that we're going to do a flyer practice today. We have just enough people that we can have the three regular flyers and you all practice at the same time."

My stomach started doing flip flops. Practicing with Sheree in the dream world had actually been kind of fun, but I didn't know how similar that would be to the real world. Miss Winters patted me on the arm.

"Don't worry. You're the tallest flyer, so I'll have Jackson with you all of the time. Some of the others will rotate so that everyone gets a chance to work with different spotters and the like, but Jackson won't be rotating."

My nod was a little shaky, but she didn't seem to notice. I watched as she hurried over to talk to some of the other girls. I'd been trying to keep my nerves from being on display for the entire world to see, but Jackson obviously knew how badly our first practice together had gone. He touched my shoulder and pulled me around slightly so that I was looking at his face.

"This is going to be okay. Nothing bad happened to you yesterday and nothing bad is going to happen today. You can do this. It's no different than the stunt we pulled at the game. You just need to relax and trust me. You're still overthinking everything."

I nodded and closed my eyes for a second. "I do trust you; it's just there is so much that could go wrong despite your best efforts."

Jackson smiled. "Nothing will go wrong. You're safer with me spotting you than with anyone else in this school."

Our conversation was cut short as the last few girls trickled out onto the field and Miss Winters called for us to group up. I tried to listen as she explained what we were going to be doing, but my mind kept skittering away from the fact that I was about to simultaneously risk my life and humiliate myself in front of half the cheer squad.

No matter how hard I tried to focus on Miss Winters' words, my attention wandered. While she was explaining about the injuries that had sidelined the other girls, I noticed the fact that a slight breeze had started up sometime between lunch and now. As she started assigning spotters to flyers, my gaze drifted over to the football team, who looked like they were going to be practicing on the field at the same time as us today.

Miss Winters threw her hand into the center of the circle and as I followed suit and yelled the obligatory "Go Wolves," I realized that I didn't know what I was supposed to do next. Jackson put a surreptitious hand on my back and guided me over to the far end of the line of girls.

"We're over here, we're starting with basket tosses."

I wondered if I was in shock as Tessa and Daphne interlocked their arms and crouched down slightly. I felt Jackson's hands on my waist and heard him softly count to three and then I was standing on the basket with one hand on each girl's shoulder. Four seconds later I was airborne.

It wasn't a great launch, but that was my fault more than theirs. The dozens of times that I'd practiced this stunt with Sheree last night hadn't been enough to completely hardwire in a new set of reflexes, so I didn't push off with my hands hard enough, but Tessa and Daphne were much stronger than Cindi and Sheree and they launched me impossibly high into the sky.

The extra hang time should have terrified me even more, but instead it gave me time to get past the initial rush of fear. There was a brief instant at the very top of my jump when I was completely weightless and the world slowed down enough for me to appreciate just how vivid the colors were here in the real world.

Things really were a little different in the dream world and it went beyond just the colors and the way that objects tended to get soft and blurry when you weren't directly looking at them. That initial thrust of acceleration as the girls launched me skywards hadn't been as strong with Sheree and I hadn't gotten the timeless instant at the top of the jump with her.

Maybe it was because she'd been doing it for so long that some of those things were old hat for her, or maybe it was just that she experienced a basket toss in a different way, but doing the basket toss for real had a surge of excitement to it that was exactly what I needed. I couldn't have done it without the drills Sheree had put me through, but it wasn't the drills that finally made me okay with putting my life in other people's hands, it was the sheer thrill.

I nearly messed up the landing. If Jackson hadn't reached up and grabbed my shoulders at the last second the girls probably couldn't have caught me safely, but he did and they did. As soon as my feet hit the ground I spun back towards them with a smile on my face.

"Let's do it again. I can do better than that."

The next basket toss went off almost perfectly. I assisted with the launch and even kicked my legs out a little at the top before coming down for a much more controlled landing. My grin just got bigger and bigger as the practice went on.

Miss Winters ran us through all of the stunts that I'd screwed up so terribly with Cindi and

Sheree the day before. I didn't get them all perfect, but I did really well and I got better and better with each stunt. I lost Tessa and Daphne a couple of stunts in, but Jackson stayed with me and somehow I knew that he really wouldn't let anything happen to me.

By the end Miss Winters was having us synchronize our jumps, which was harder than I expected because different bases threw the different girls at different speeds, but it actually went pretty well all things considered.

I ended the practice hot, sweaty, and feeling drunk from the endorphins. Miss Winters congratulated us all on a good practice session and then dismissed us. I was leaning against Jackson, still trying to catch my breath when Miss Winters came over to us.

"That was really, really well done, Adri. I was hoping that you'd display at least a little of the natural talent that Cindi has so much of. I never expected you to be this good so fast. I'm not sure I've ever seen anyone pick up stunting this quickly before."

"Thanks, Miss Winters. I'm not sure what happened, it just all clicked for me. It helped to have such good bases, especially Jackson."

She nodded and gave me a brilliant smile. "You've given me a lot to think about today, Adri."

I watched her walk away for a few seconds and then turned back to Jackson. "Thanks again,

Jackson. I couldn't have done any of that without you."

"I'm glad that you've started to trust me, Adri. I really won't let anything happen to you out here on the field."

There was a teasing look in his eyes, but the words had the feeling of being carefully measured out. Jackson gave me one last nod. "I'd offer to walk you home, but my mother is expecting me."

"That's okay, I should probably spend some time alone with Cindi anyways and the walk home is about as good a chance as I'm probably going to get."

I knew I should probably go back to the locker room and change into my street clothes, but I just couldn't seem to bring myself to turn away from Jackson. I told myself that I had all of my clothes and books with me between my backpack and my duffle bag and that I could always just walk home in my workout clothes.

Under normal circumstances it wasn't something I would have been very keen on, but apparently it was enough of an option for me to just sit there and watch Jackson until he turned onto the street and disappeared behind one of the houses.

Jackson no longer being where I could see him broke some kind of spell and I realized that given how unhappy Cindi was with me that there was a chance that she'd just choose to leave without me.

I walked over to my bags and picked them up, but when I turned back towards the school I realized that I wasn't by myself any more. Tristan flashed me the winning, all-American smile that always made Cindi's heart flutter and then held out a hand as though offering to help me with my bags.

"Hi, Adri. I've been trying to catch you by yourself for a couple of days now, but you're like a ghost. I don't even know where your locker is and you weren't at lunch today."

"You could have asked Cindi. Since I started cheering she knows my schedule better than I do."

Tristan shrugged. "It's okay, luckily Coach let us go about the same time as you got done, so we can talk right now."

I debated for a couple of seconds and then put my backpack in his outstretched hand. "Okay, we can talk, but let's talk while we're walking. I need to find Cindi and you'll want to say hi to her anyway."

Tristan grabbed my arm, completely stopping my forward motion and pulling me back around to where I didn't have any choice but to look him in the eye.

"You didn't come to the party after the last game, but you said maybe another time. A few of the guys and I are planning on going up to a cabin in St. Cloud the week your parents are going to be out of town. Come with me."

It wasn't the most romantic gesture ever. Actually it wasn't even the slightest bit romantic, but it took me a second to process what he'd said because the way he was holding onto my arm was making me nervous. Tristan wasn't as tall as Jackson, but he had slightly broader shoulders and he was built like someone who spent a lot of time in the weight room.

Jackson was all lean muscles, almost like a swimmer, while Tristan was bulky, more like a running back than I'd always thought a quarterback was supposed to look like. I told myself that nothing was going to happen out here in broad daylight despite the weird vibe I was getting from him, and then shook my head at him.

"I'm flattered, Tristan."

Actually I wasn't really flattered, more like creeped out due to the fact that he had to have at least some inkling of the fact that Cindi liked him or he wouldn't be trying so hard to get me off by myself to talk. Still, I was pretty sure that he was used to girls all but swooning when he asked them out and I figured that things would go better if I didn't let on that his pitch had been the epitome of underwhelming.

"That sounds fun and all, but I don't think it would be a good idea."

"How come?"

"I don't think it's really my place to say."

He looked at me for a few seconds almost as though he was expecting for me to cave just based off of his smoldering good looks.

"Is it because of Cindi?"

"You know that she's interested in you, don't you?"

He nodded. "Yeah, but it's not like I asked for that. Cindi is a nice girl, and she's super attractive, but she isn't the one I'm interested in. You are."

I didn't know what his issue was for sure. I suspected that he was getting bored of girls throwing themselves at him and just wanted a challenge.

I didn't actually care what was making him act like a jerk, but I needed to come up with a way of warning him off without ruining the possibility of him and Cindi getting together later on. Assuming that she was still interested in him once she got to know him better.

"I really am flattered, Tristan, but I'm not going to do that to Cindi. Even if you were my type, which you aren't, I still wouldn't do anything to hurt her like that."

Tristan waited to see if I was going to say anything else for several seconds and then shrugged. "I have a feeling you're going to change your mind at some point, but I won't push the issue right now. One way or another you're going to end up spending that weekend with me. Tell Cindi that I said hi."

HUNTED

I opened my mouth to ask him what he meant, but he just shot me a snarky grin as he looked over my right shoulder and then turned and walked off. I turned to see what he'd been looking at and my heart sank as Cindi hurried towards me.

Chapter 13

I had only a second to wish that Cindi had been a few minutes slower changing and then she reached me and I had to start answering questions.

"What did he say? Tell me everything!"

Fat chance of that. Cindi was already mad at me. If I told her that her crush had asked me out then she'd stop talking to me altogether. It wasn't fair. I hadn't done anything to try to capture his attention, but she wouldn't place the blame on him, she'd lay it squarely at my feet.

"It was mostly just small talk. He's got some kind of trip up to St. Cloud planned when Mom and Dad are away on their vacation."

"Did he invite us? Did he mention me?"

"He didn't invite us."

Technically he hadn't invited us, he'd invited me, so it wasn't quite a lie.

"You came up in passing, I tried to bring you up more than that, but he really seemed pretty focused on himself."

Again, not quite a lie, he'd definitely cared more about himself than anything or anyone else. And I had brought up Cindi, he just hadn't wanted to talk about her.

"You can't just leave me hanging like that, Adri. What did he say?"

"He said you were nice and super attractive."

Something that hadn't quite added up during our conversation suddenly crystallized for me.

"Cindi, how did Tristan know that Mom and Dad are going to be gone? I haven't said anything to anyone, did he hear it from you?"

Cindi gestured for me to pick up the backpack that Tristan had set down on the ground before making his abrupt exit.

"Let's get started for home. I'll tell you on the way."

She'd already started walking so I didn't have any choice but to grab my stuff and follow if I wanted to carry on a conversation with her.

"I want to throw a party while Mom and Dad are gone. Not a huge one or anything, I just want to invite a few friends. I had Patty Conners mention it to Tristan so that he could make sure not to plan anything else. I was thinking that you could invite Jackson."

"Are you crazy?"

The words came out harsher than I meant for them to, especially after how pissed off she'd been at me lately. It wasn't like I could take them back now though and they pretty much summed up how I felt.

"I've seen how you look at him, Adri. It's obvious that you like him. Maybe not to everyone, but you're my sister. I've never seen you act like that around any other guy. I think you should invite him and see where things go. It's not like we get many opportunities to have the house to ourselves."

"That wasn't the part I was talking about. You can't really be thinking that it's a good idea to throw a party while Mom and Dad are away."

"So you *do* like him. I thought as much."

"Okay, yes, I'm very interested in Jackson, but that doesn't change the fact that these things never work out like they are supposed to. More people than you invite are going to end up coming to the party and then you'll completely lose control of it and they will trash our house."

"Just because you saw it happen that way on a sitcom doesn't mean that it's gospel, Adri."

She had me there. I hadn't actually been to any parties since I'd been eight and those had been heavily supervised. I knew I was right though, knew that the risks were huge, but she preempted me.

"Missy threw a party last month and everything was fine. The key is to make sure you invite three or four of the biggest guys on the football team and have them throw out anyone who shows up that you don't want to be there."

"What if they don't do their job? Or end up being the ones who get out of control."

"That's easy. You pick guys who are dating your friends and make sure that they know they'll be going through a major dry spell if they screw things up."

My face heated up immediately. It was like this whole conversation was one blindside after another.

"I can't believe you just said that! Please tell me that you haven't…well, you know."

Cindi had the grace to look a little embarrassed. "No, I haven't, but you and I are about the only girls on the squad who haven't. Just because I haven't doesn't mean that I don't know what's going on though or how to use it to my advantage."

"Wait a second, were you at Missy's party?"

"Of course. You're a pretty heavy sleeper, especially lately. I waited until Mom and Dad fell asleep and then I snuck out through our window. Patty picked me up half a block from our house and then dropped me off again a couple of hours before dawn."

I was still reeling or I probably would have handled things better. Instead I let the first thing that came to mind slip out of my mouth without filtering it.

"I'm not going to go along with this."

"Yes, you are, Adri. The only way for you to stop it would be for you to tell Mom and Dad, and you're not going to do that."

"Yes, I am!"

Cindi shook her head at me. "Think that through, Adri. If you were to tell them then they'd probably cancel their vacation so that they could stay home and make sure that the house didn't get trashed. You'd be ruining their chance at working things out. Do you really want to do that, Adri? You know they aren't going to just go and then punish me when they get back. Mom is never going to be okay with a bunch of kids she doesn't know being here at the house without any supervision, not when there isn't anything to keep them out of all of her photography equipment."

I opened my mouth to tell her that she was wrong, but nothing came out. She wasn't wrong and we both knew it. She could have just left things there and I probably wouldn't have said anything to our parents about her party, but she didn't stop there. She had to drive one last nail into the coffin.

"Besides, Adri, you owe me. I've been nothing but nice to you lately. I'm the reason you tried out for the cheer squad, I'm the reason that Jackson is starting to notice you. Everything good that is going on in your life right now is because of me. You're even wearing my clothes."

"I didn't ask for this, I didn't even want any of this."

"You keep saying that, but it's not the truth and we both know it. I don't know how you're doing it, where you're finding the time, or who is teaching you, but this is obviously something that you've been working towards for weeks, maybe even months. People don't just suddenly learn our routine like that, not without serious effort, and you're picking up stunting way too fast."

I wanted to respond, but I didn't know what to say. There was no way that she was going to believe that I was learning everything from sharing dreams with members of the squad. Cindi nodded, as though in satisfaction that I wasn't going to dispute her version of events.

"Most of all though, you owe me because you wasted my time yesterday with a practice that you didn't even need when I had other, more important, things that I should have been doing."

"I did need that practice. I'm sorry that it went long, but you should have said something when you realized that it was time for you to go."

"Whatever. One way or another you're lying to me. You're not going to tell Mom and Dad and that's pretty much all there is to it."

I didn't eat very well at dinner. Cindi seemed to take that as a proof that I had a guilty conscience, that or maybe that I was taking her advice from earlier about not eating like a pig so that I didn't balloon back up to my old size.

The truth was that I actually *did* need to eat. I'd burned through a lot of my reserves during my midnight practice with Sheree and I wasn't sure that I'd managed to replace them yet today, which could be a problem if I ended up in another shared dream tonight.

Mom and Dad were actually both at dinner with Cindi and me, which was a rare treat, but I couldn't enjoy it while worrying about what Cindi was planning. Apparently Mom and Dad were really trying to make a go of things—there wasn't any other explanation for them both having torn themselves away from their respective projects in time to have a normal, sit-down dinner like everyone else had.

My apathy even cast a pall over their efforts there, because instead of talking to each other they spent most of the meal trying to get me to tell them what was wrong. I excused myself from the table after twenty minutes of picking at my food and retreated to my bedroom.

I tried to work on homework, tried to read a book, nothing worked. I finally just went to bed about an hour earlier than normal. I didn't particularly want to sleep, but I didn't want to talk to Cindi right now. This wasn't something that we wouldn't work past eventually, at least I didn't think it was, but it wasn't something that I could just forgive right now.

Once again I fell asleep instantly, but this time I didn't end up inside of my own dream to start out with. I was in someone else's dream, and it had happened without any kind of conscious effort on my part, which meant that I was in danger. I looked down at myself and found that I was once again a chubbier version of myself.

I didn't waste precious seconds this time around wondering what that said about my subconscious. Instead I visualized my body becoming even more rounded and then pushed that illusion into the pseudo-reality of the dream. I changed my hair and skin color and then reached up to confirm that my face had also shifted around as I'd changed the rest of my body.

I debated for the briefest of instants and then I changed my eye color to brown and stretched my face so that it looked like something you'd see in one of those curvy mirrors at the circus.

The whole process had taken less than a second. I'd done it out of a reflexive paranoia at what I'd find here, but it felt like the right thing to have done.

I could feel the tightness off in a corner of my mind that told me that my psyche was sustaining the illusions without any kind of massive effort on my part. I knew there would be a constant, slow drain of strength and energy out of my real body as a result of the seeming that I'd created, but tonight I felt strong and well-rested, so it wasn't something that I needed to worry about in the short term. Hopefully I'd be gone before it became a concern.

I looked around and finally realized how I'd known that I wasn't in one of my own dreams. Everything was much more vivid than I could manage with my own efforts. I was standing in a field of gorgeous sunflowers under a blue sky that had only the faintest white wisps of clouds as a gentle breeze caused the flowers to bob up and down.

The flowers, at least the ones in easy reach of where I was standing, were all individual plants rather than the textured, colored mass that would have been the default surrounding in one of my dreams. Even more impressive, the soft, delicate petals on the plants were likewise individual and varied.

There had been a little different of a feel to Sheree's dreams than to mine, but this was incredible. These dreams were almost compelling enough to mistake for the real world. I tried to change the color of a single leaf, fixing the image I wanted in my mind and pushing, but the faintest of flickers was my only reward for the effort and strength I'd just expended.

Any lingering question I might have had about this possibly being my own dream was settled. I sat down in the middle of the sunflowers and started trying to flee this particular dream. There had been the tiniest of inclinations to explore my new surroundings, to see if the dreamer whose hospitality I was imposing on might be a potential friend rather than an enemy, but I knew that would be stupid. I needed to build up my endurance, needed to master those few things I already knew before I went looking for allies in the dream.

I took a couple of slow, deep breaths and then tried to block out this dream as I simultaneously focused on the real world. I expected it to be a little bit of a challenge, but I'd done this four times now—twice on purpose—so I expected it to be doable.

I hadn't counted on the way that the breeze continued to caress my cheeks or the deep, earthy smell that it carried. Even the feel of the ground underneath me and the flowers brushing against my back served to enforce the immediacy and strength of this reality.

It was harder than I expected to remember all of the little details about the real world. The exact feel of my sheets against my bare arms and the sound of Cindi's breathing were just out of my reach and with them the easy escape from this dream that I'd been expecting to accomplish.

I sat there for several minutes, but each attempt failed and each failure drained some of my limited supply of strength. I was just about to start my fourth attempt when I heard someone walking through the field of flowers.

I tried to stand just enough to see without being seen, but he happened to be looking directly at me and stopped moving as soon as he saw me.

"Interesting."

He didn't seem angry, and he hadn't tried to kill me or anything yet. It was actually a much better start to things than I'd been expecting. I cautiously stood up, both to get a better look at him as well as to let him see that I wasn't at all threatening.

I tried a hesitant smile as I looked him over. He looked like he was ninety and had a white beard that had to be nearly as old as he was. His skin was wrinkled and had the liver spots that I would have expected in someone that old, but there was one detail that didn't match with the rest of his appearance.

He wasn't moving like an old man. He had an elaborately carved walking stick in his right hand, but he wasn't at all stooped over and the simple brown robe he was wearing seemed to be hiding shoulders that were surprisingly broad for someone who otherwise looked like they should be nearly to their deathbed.

"What's interesting?"

"You don't belong here in my dream."

"You know this is a dream?"

"Indeed I do. It's one that I dream on a regular basis, one I've dreamed for more years than you've been alive."

"You never dream of other people being here with you?"

"Occasionally, but never someone like you."

His gesture took in my appearance. I looked down and felt myself blush. I'd been so busy trying to make sure that I wasn't recognizable that I hadn't really stopped to think about how the total package might look. My face was distorted enough he probably hadn't even been sure I was human to start out with.

"I'm sorry, this isn't how I normally look, but it's important that I keep who I really am a secret. I've been told that it's not safe for me here in the dream world, that there are a lot of supernatural...beings that would harm me if they could."

He frowned, but it wasn't an angry frown as much as it was sad.

"Secrecy is almost always a tool of those with evil intentions, and it requires someone very far gone indeed to see danger behind every tree and bush. I will give you the benefit of the doubt though. Why did you seek me out?"

I shrugged. "I didn't, not really. Maybe you brought me here somehow. I'm not completely in control of where I end up when I go to sleep. Sometimes I just go straight to my own dreams, sometimes I end up in the dreams of other people."

"No, I'm afraid it's nothing I've done. In all of my years I've never encountered a...dream walker before now."

"Still, you have some kind of power though, don't you? You have to be unique in some way."

He gave me an appraising look. "Each person is unique. You'll excuse me if I choose not to share more than that given your own reluctance to be forthright with me."

His words were delivered with such calm that it didn't sound like any kind of stinging rebuke, but I felt myself recoiling away from him regardless.

"I'm sorry, child. That was unnecessarily harsh. Tell me what you can about your situation and ask me what you will. I can't promise to tell you all, but I will tell you whatever I can if it seems that it will help you."

"I'm not sure what to tell you, or even what to ask."

He just nodded patiently, so I asked something that felt relatively harmless.

"How is your dream so detailed? I've been in other people's dreams and they aren't nearly this vivid."

"Ah, I hadn't realized that my dreams were in any way different from anyone else's. I don't know for sure, but I suspect that it has something to do with my age, and possibly some of the mental disciplines that I have practiced over the years."

I didn't know what else to ask him, but before the silence could get too awkward he cleared his throat.

"How long have you been traveling into other people's dreams?"

"A few weeks, maybe more, but definitely not more than a month or two. I started out sharing dreams with some of the kids from my school. It was pretty harmless really, and I didn't even realize what was happening until it became obvious that some of the things I knew weren't things that anyone had told me."

"But at some point you started running into people you didn't know, dangerous people."

I nodded. "There was this Native American guy who shifts into some kind of monster, and then there was this wax lady. The Native American told me how to leave someone else's dream, but both times I ran into him he practically killed me."

"And this...wax woman?"

"She tried to strangle me and right there at the end it was like she was sending these tendrils of smoke into my head."

"Were you able to see her face? Would you recognize her if you saw her again?"

"No, she was all deformed and melted. All I really know is that she was female and skinny, and I guess I don't even know that for sure because I found out that people can change how they look. I would recognize the Native American though because he wasn't hiding his real face from me."

"And you can tell when someone is not showing their true form?"

"Yes, there's a kind of shimmer around them when they do that."

"Like now?"

As he asked me the question he transformed, becoming taller even as he became less substantial. The process of the change took less than a second and when it was done he'd been replaced by a glowing figure that seemed constructed by nothing more than light. As I watched, his glow intensified to the point where I almost couldn't look at him, but if I put my hand between him and me just right to cut out most of the light I was able to see the faintest hint of the shimmer I'd seen when the Native American had made himself invisible.

"Yes, I can see that isn't your true form. Do you mind toning it back down?"

Between one heartbeat and the next he shrank back down and solidified into the form he'd been wearing when I'd arrived in the dream. It happened so fast that it was almost instantaneous, but there was a split second there where it had almost looked like he'd been someone I knew. It was one of those things that was over so quickly that afterwards you were pretty sure that it was just your imagination, but the feeling that I'd recognized something about his intermediate shape had been so strong that I had a hard time shaking it.

I double-checked to make sure that the old man in front of me was really his actual identity. There wasn't any shimmer or other indication that he was forcing his dream to take on anything other than his normal appearance.

He looked strangely satisfied as he resumed his normal shape. "Although I generally know that I'm dreaming when I come here, I've never been able to control things to that extent. Talking to you like this is making me more aware of just how much I can change."

The sunflowers were wilting before my eyes, but he didn't seem to notice that or the way that the sky was clouding over.

"I think that you're right to be wary of these other two that you encountered while dreaming. I can't teach you about the dream itself, but I would be willing to teach you the mental exercises that I believe have allowed me to create a dreamscape which is more complete than others you have seen."

The sun was almost completely occluded by the clouds now and the sky had darkened ominously. I almost thought I could hear laughter, but it was so faint as to be almost indistinguishable.

The old man looked around at our surroundings and frowned at the way the landscape was changing. A second later, the flowers were back and the sky was a cloudless blue, but the flowers had lost some of the detail and individuality that had impressed me so much when I'd first arrived.

"I appreciate your offer. How do I start?"

"Oh, no. I'm afraid I can't teach you here in this place. It will take time, even just getting started is the work of more than a single night. Not only that, there is no guarantee that we'll meet again like this. It would be best if we were to meet up in the real world. There I'll be able to teach you the beginning exercises."

I shook my head. I knew I needed to stall for time, but I was out of ideas on how to do so. "I'm sorry. I really appreciate your willingness to teach me, but the only thing that's keeping me safe right now is the fact that none of the...people I run into in the dream know how to find me in real life. Maybe if we meet again in the future I'll get to the point where it would be okay for us to meet, but right now that's just not a possibility."

There was a flicker of something in his expression that was gone too quickly for me to identify it.

"Are you really so sure that you're safe, even with your real identity a secret?"

Before I could answer he struck, not physically, but with his superior control over the dream we were in. The ground opened up, causing me to stumble, and then closed back over my ankles, trapping me in place.

I was still reeling from the attack when I felt pressure starting to build. It was like a giant vice was somehow pressing against every single inch of my body at the same time. The part of my mind that was maintaining the illusion that altered my appearance felt like acid had been poured on it.

My body shrank and then expanded slightly back out as I put more of my strength into countering his attempt at unmasking me.

"You're like a child. You have no idea what you're up against, no idea what's at stake if you fail."

The pressure from the vice doubled and my body collapsed in on itself. It wasn't an exact match for my real body, it was still the chubbier version of me that my subconscious still conjured here in the dream, but he'd stripped away that layer of my defense.

I tried to fight back, tried to reestablish the false body that I'd been wearing just a few seconds previously, but my mind was pure molten agony. Another wave of psychic pressure started to build and I did the only thing I could think of to hide my identity. I threw myself as far forward as my entrapped feet and ankles would allow, obscuring my face with the fake black hair that he hadn't managed to shift back to its normal color yet.

"I don't think so."

Even as he spoke something rough wrapped itself around my waist. I was forced backwards against my will until finally I came to rest with my back tight against the rough bark of a tree that hadn't been there just a second before.

The knotty branch that had wrapped itself around my waist was joined by two more, one around my thighs and the other around my chest just above where my ribs started. My arms were free and I clawed desperately at the topmost branch in an effort to free myself, but all I succeeded in doing was ripping my nails free of my fingers.

The old man walked over to me and ran his fingers over my clothes, shaking his head at the way that they hung from my body now. They'd shrunk down somewhat as my body had diminished in size, but not completely, and I knew I looked like a little girl playing dress-up in her mother's clothes.

"We really must do something about these."

The pressure built so suddenly that I never even had a chance to fight back. One second I was wearing clothes and then in the next, the outer layer of my clothes had disappeared. I reacted out of instinct, covering the underwear he'd just revealed, and only then realized my mistake.

I'd dressed myself in my cheerleading uniform.

I tried to recover from my mistake, tried to change into a featureless black jumpsuit, but he was obviously prepared for that because my clothing darkened only slightly before snapping back to the blue-on-white cheerleading shell and skirt that I'd owned for less than a month.

I looked down at myself as he forced the branches to rearrange themselves to better display the school name and mascot. I'd managed to blur them slightly, but I was pretty sure that I hadn't managed to hide enough of the detail.

He came even closer, touching my uniform and then looking up at me and smiling. "I thought as much. Your accent is a dead giveaway, you know."

My hands were free so I did the only other thing I could think of. I punched him in the throat. It wasn't a great punch, but he'd leaned down to look at the lettering across my chest so my hand didn't have to travel very far, and I put everything I had into the blow.

He grabbed his throat as he collapsed to the ground. I envisioned the tree disappearing and my legs coming free of the ground, but when I tried to push my version of reality into the dream I met with resistance so strong it might as well have been real iron.

Even choking and gagging like he was right now, his will was just too strong for me to affect his reality. In that instant I realized that I'd run out of options. I was going to die here and nobody would know why my heart had just stopped beating partway through the night.

As the old man pulled himself back up to his hands and knees, still gasping for air, a host of regrets washed through me with shocking force. The startling thing wasn't that I had more regrets than I'd anticipated, it was how different some of them were compared to what I'd been expecting.

I was sorry that I hadn't worked harder to bury the hatchet with Cindi years ago. I wished that I'd realized just how bad things were between my parents and tried to do something there instead of being so self-involved all of the time.

Those were the more or less predictable regrets, but I also regretted the fact that I'd never applied myself to anything with my full heart and soul. School, cheerleading, having a social life, I'd never gone all-out in an effort to excel at any of it. I'd just wasted a lot of time when I could have been doing something worthwhile.

Most of all though, I was sorry that I'd never acted on the persistent urge to fill the absence that I'd spent so many months denying. It wasn't a lack inside of me so much as it felt like a missing potential. I was a key without a lock, a bow without a violin. I was perfectly acceptable as I was, but I could be so much more with the right person.

I didn't know whether or not Jackson was that guy, but I should have tried harder to find out. I was going to die never having even kissed him.

The thought of Cindi waking up tomorrow morning to find me dead, my body already cold, wracked me with grief. I could see her in my mind's eye, tears streaming down her face, darkening my sheets wherever they landed, and the fact that it hadn't actually happened didn't matter. That was real, that was what was *going* to happen.

I looked around at my surroundings one last time and realized just how dreary and artificial they looked. My conscious mind didn't know what to do with that knowledge but some deeper level of my subconscious reached for Cindi and my parents.

Strength gushed out of me like blood from a mortal wound.

And then I sat up in my bed. I was shaking from exhaustion and my sheets were soaked in sweat, but I was alive. I even managed to make it to the bathroom before throwing up.

Chapter 14

I stumbled back to bed, more because I didn't know what else to do with myself than for any other reason, and fell asleep despite the terror I was still feeling. I wouldn't have said it was possible to sleep when you were that scared, but I literally had no reserves of energy left.

I felt a little better when I woke up, but I was starting to look gaunt. I'd gone beyond skinny and if this kept up I was going to look like a famine victim pretty soon. The fear was still there. It was muted compared to what I'd felt during the dream the night before, but it had been too strong for it to be completely washed away by the arrival of daylight.

Cindi seemed almost back to her old self. She smiled at me as I was going into the bathroom. I say almost because there was a definite edge of smugness to her manner. It was kind of annoying that she was so happy about having maneuvered me into not saying anything about the party she had planned, but I had much bigger problems to worry about.

I pulled my clothes off and stepped into the shower, letting the water wash away the sweat that was the only physical sign of my near brush with death the night before while my mind worried at the invisible results.

I'd never come so close to dying before this, and it hadn't just been death in the dream that had been threatening. The old man had very nearly unmasked me, which would have put my whole family at risk too.

As it was, if he'd really recognized the uniform like he'd seemed to, then all of the other girls on the squad were in danger already, but I had a feeling that he wouldn't do anything drastic until he'd narrowed the possible targets down to just one or two. Surely even supernatural creatures couldn't get away with killing or kidnapping more than a dozen girls at once.

I debated quitting the team, but that didn't particularly seem like a good idea. The key to staying safe right now was to blend in as much as humanly possible. Quitting the team would make me an anomaly, which would make anyone who knew that the new dream walker in town was a cheerleader, examine me more closely. No normal cheerleader would go to all of the time and effort of getting on the team and then walk away from that accomplishment without a really compelling reason to do so, and I didn't have an obvious reason for doing something crazy like that.

What I really wanted was to tell someone else what was going on, but that also felt unacceptably risky. Mom and Dad would be convinced that I needed counseling, and I'd already established that I couldn't tell Cindi, at least not right now, not while she was acting like Machiavelli.

Actually, I could probably convince anyone I wanted as to the existence of my powers. All it would take would be to spend a couple of nights sharing their dreams and then telling them exactly what they'd dreamed about. The only problem with that was that it would either freak people out because I'd been invading their privacy, or they'd immediately start trying to figure out how to profit from what I could do.

If I didn't play my cards just right then the best-case scenario was that I'd end up in a government lab somewhere, locked up while they ran every test under the sun on me and then figured out a few hundred different ways to weaponize me. The worst-case scenario probably involved me disappearing without warning and then spending the rest of my life locked up inside someone's basement.

Just because I was now pretty sure that there were actual supernatural beings out there didn't mean that every monster was of the creepy-crawly variety. There were plenty of sickos out there of the purely human variety and I didn't even want to begin contemplating the kinds of things that someone who was really demented might try to use my power for.

Telling other people about what I could do was undeniably dangerous, but I was still tempted to do it anyway. In the end, the only thing that stopped me from choosing that route was the fact that I couldn't take it back once I started telling people.

Right now I just wanted to have as normal a life as possible, which kind of precluded running away as a solution to my problems. The chances of having anything remotely like a normal teenage existence were rapidly approaching zero, but there was still *some* chance and I wanted to cling to that possibility for as long as I could. Maybe it was the wrong thing to be doing, maybe I was already past the point where the smart thing would be to go ahead and get whatever help I could from the adult in my life, but I knew I was going to wait a little longer in the hopes that the old man hadn't seen enough last night to act. If he didn't come after me in the next few weeks then maybe I'd be able to get enough of a handle on my abilities to avoid continuing to attract supernatural threats.

It was a long shot, but by the time the hot water started to run out I knew that it was the route I was going to try for.

As I walked back into our room, I happened to look at the calendar that Cindi had hung on the wall. Today had a big blue border drawn around it, which meant that we had a football game today. I looked closer and realized that it was an away game.

I looked at our clock and then muttered a swear word under my breath as I realized just how far behind schedule I was. I pulled on the rest of my clothes—a mixture of the stuff that Mom had bought for me a couple of days ago, Cindi's old clothes, some of which were even long enough that the school administration might not send me home for being indecent, and some of my old stuff that probably wouldn't fall off of me before the day ended.

I double-checked the calendar to confirm that we were headed to an away game, and then packed my duffle bag up with my away game shell and skirt. Dad was already gone, and Mom was rattling around the kitchen still looking like she was half asleep as I blew through it on my way out the door.

"Hold on there, young lady, you need to eat *something*."

There was some cold pizza in the fridge, the greasy, fatty kind that Cindi would never dream of eating, which was perfect because unlike her, right now at least, I didn't need to worry about getting too big to fit into my cheerleading uniform. I grabbed three slices out of the white cardboard box and promised Mom that I'd eat them on my way to school.

School went by in a blur. People were still whispering nasty rumors about me just loud enough to make sure that I'd overhear them, but it bothered me less than it had before. It was still mean and completely unjustified, but now I was also able to see just how petty it was too.

A lot of what had happened in the dream with the old man was already starting to fade into a distant, untouchable mist—which was simultaneously frustrating and welcome—but I could still remember how it had felt to see my death barreling towards me with enough advance warning for me to realize just how badly I'd messed up my priorities. There was a lot about that experience that my mind seemed still unready to deal with, but that wasn't one of those things and I tore into my classwork with a zeal that astonished my teachers and surprised even me.

I'd never actually realized that I was capable of focusing on one thing for more than four or five minutes, but while the old man had probably lied about a lot of things, I was pretty sure that he was right about mental discipline leading to more power and strength in the dream. I didn't know what mental exercises he'd done to gain such an incredible level of mastery, but I figured that I could at least start by getting to the point where I could complete an assignment in one sitting rather than it taking an entire evening.

I was working on my U.S. Government assignment when my fingers started hurting. At first I thought it was just a side effect from doing so much writing, but when my left hand started hurting in almost the exact same fashion I realized that there was more going on than just that.

I didn't have an explanation though, so I just gritted my teeth and kept going. It wasn't until after lunch, which consisted of another slice of pizza and some French fries again, that I realized what was causing the pain that was threatening to stop me from being able to continue with my homework.

The pain I was feeling wasn't the result of anything I'd done at school, it was a shadowy reflection of what had happened in the dream. I'd mutilated my hands clawing at the branches that had been holding me up against the tree. At the time, I'd been too freaked out to worry about the damage I was doing to myself or how badly it hurt, but now I was experiencing some of the pain that I'd been feeling in the dream.

My fingers weren't bruised and bleeding and my nails looked fine, so it had to all just be inside of my head, but it felt like I'd just run them over a cheese grater. It represented one more unpleasant side effect from my dream walking that I was going to have to deal with. I filed it all away, along with the fact that it had taken hours after the actual 'injury' for the pain to start up in the real world.

Jackson walked me to my last class again, which was super nice, but I was too worried about everything else going on in my life to get as googly-eyed at him as I normally did. I was actually so caught up inside of my own head that when the bell rang to dismiss us I left without waiting for Jackson.

I was a third of the way back to my locker when I felt someone brush up against me. It wasn't quite a groping, but it was right on the border, something that could possibly be explained away as an accident, but a very unlikely one.

I turned around and saw the guy Jackson had punched smirking at me. His expression dared me to react, dared me to say something so that he could claim that nothing had actually happened.

I'd been through so much crap in the last few days that I didn't even think. I slammed my foot down on his instep as hard as I could and then smiled as he collapsed to the ground with tears streaming down his face.

"I hope it's broken, you piece of trash. The next time you try that kind of sleazy crap on me you'll really be sorry."

I turned and walked away without looking back, but a few seconds later I felt someone following a couple of steps back from me. I turned, ready to give the perv a piece of my mind, but it wasn't him, it was Jackson.

"It looks like you don't actually need my help after all."

"We'll see. If he tries it again you can go ahead and put him in the hospital for all that I care."

Jackson nodded and then pursed his lips. "I'm starting to think that I misjudged you, Adri. I never would have guessed you had it in you to do something like that."

"I don't, not usually, but things have been so crappy lately that I think in some way I was just looking for an excuse, looking for someone to take my frustrations out on."

My newfound zeal meant that I was carrying more books than normal. We'd arrived at my locker and Jackson held his hands out to take my books so that I'd have a hand free to spin the tumbler on the combination lock.

"What's going on? You made the team, you're a backup flyer, and you're gorgeous. Most girls would practically kill to be in your shoes."

He'd leaned in close as he'd said it, his voice dropping to something that was only barely more than a whisper. I knew it was just an effort to keep our conversation from being overheard by every other junior who happened to share this section of the hall, but it was still strangely intimate and the way that his breath caressed the side of my neck was incredibly sensual.

A tiny tremble ran through me, but I was pretty sure that I managed to keep all of that off of my face.

"The entire school hates me, half because I joined the team and the other half because I got Janessa kicked off of the team. Most of the people in both groups are convinced that I'm now some kind of massive slut, and my sister now hates my guts for about a dozen different reasons. Oh yeah, my parents are constantly at each other's throats lately, and I'm pretty sure that it will take some kind of minor miracle to keep them together long enough for me to graduate. Life is just peachy."

Jackson sighed. "I'm sorry, Adri. I guess that nothing good happens without something bad happening to balance things out a little. I wish that there was something I could do to help make everything better. Is there anything else?"

Yes. I wanted to say it, wanted to confide in him, but I shook my head.

"Isn't that enough?"

"I guess it is. I don't suppose that my hitting people will do anything to convince them to like you?"

His expression was so deadpan that I couldn't help myself. I broke out into the kind of laughter that invariably turns heads as people try to figure out what you think is so funny.

"No, I don't think it would, but thank you for the offer. I'll definitely keep it in mind."

Jackson nodded and gave me a warm smile that still somehow had some of the smoldering heat that he'd used on me a couple of times before.

"Well, then I guess we'd better get moving. The bus is leaving in twenty minutes and if we don't hurry we're going to get left."

We made the bus with a couple of minutes to spare and then had an uneventful ride to the game. Miss Winters was apparently still a little jittery about having the guys on the team and therefore on the same bus as us, so she put the girls in the back of the bus, Jackson and the other guys in the front of the bus and then sat between the two groups.

By the time I arrived, Sheree was already curled up in one of the seats and sleeping soundly. Cindi beat me to the bus too and was sitting in the very back of the bus with Missy and a couple of the other seniors.

It was possible if I went back there that Cindi might talk to me. She'd been relatively pleasant earlier in the day, but I had a suspicion that she was still at least a little mad at me and I didn't particularly want to make the trip to the back of the bus and then be humiliated by Missy and the others if Cindi didn't stand up for me.

With Cindi and Sheree out as possible travel companions, I knew I was pretty much out of luck. None of the other girls were going to talk to me, so I just plugged my headphones into my phone, exchanged one last smile with Jackson and then turned on some music and zoned out.

Cheering at the game went better than my first game. I managed not to run into anyone and I hit all of my marks. Jackson gave me a look a couple of times that seemed to ask if I wanted to stunt with him, but I was more than happy to leave that kind of stuff to the three flyers. Flying during practice was one thing, doing it during a game would probably just cause me to tense up again. Besides, I didn't want Missy or Sheree to feel like I was gunning for their spots.

The most annoying thing that happened during the game was the way that Tristan looked me up and down every time our defense was on the field. There wasn't anything I could do other than ignore him and hope that Cindi didn't notice, but I knew it was only a matter of time before one of the other girls noticed and said something to her.

We won the game by two touchdowns, which was quite the feather in Tristan's cap since the first-string quarterback was still out with an injury. I still knew pretty much nothing about football, but I suspected that we were going to have a really good team next year with the way that he was playing. It was a perfect example of the fact that being good at football doesn't mean you're a decent human being.

This school was big enough to have a locker room for the visiting team, but only one. Miss Winters had told us that the football coach had agreed to let us use it first, so once the game ended I just headed in to change. The rest of the girls pretty much all made an instant beeline towards our football team.

Predictably Cindi was practically hanging off of Tristan's arm, but I didn't want any part of that. Besides, I figured it would be better to get changed back into street clothes by myself before the rest of them all came into change. The less interaction I had with the other girls the better as far as I was concerned.

I was most of the way changed before they struck. I was in the middle of pulling my white tank top over my head when I heard giggling and an odd hissing sound. A split second later I felt a trickle of liquid running down my back and I realized that the hissing had come from one of those cheap squirt guns you buy at a dollar store. I pulled my tank top down and turned to see what was going on, but they'd already turned and run out of the locker room. I caught a flash of blue, but didn't see enough to identify them.

I reflected that it seemed like a pretty lame prank and ran my hand across my back so that my top would soak up the water. It wasn't until I saw the black on my hand that I realized that I hadn't been sprayed with water. A quick trip over to one of the mirrors revealed what looked like black ink staining the bottom of my hair and the back of my shirt.

I wanted to cry and scream all at the same time, but I just grabbed some paper towels and used them to blot the worst of it off of my top so that it wouldn't run onto my jeans. My tank top had actually protected the top of my head, but the bottom inch and a half of my hair had turned a splotchy, streaky black.

I used some more paper towels in an effort to try to strip off the worst of the ink, starting at the top with a clean paper towel and working down so that I didn't spread the ink further up. It probably would have been quicker to just strip back down and wash my hair, but I wanted to make sure that I had plenty of evidence to show Miss Winters and I was pretty sure that it was going to take hairspray or some kind of specialized cleaner to get the ink out anyways.

I cleaned my hands off, grabbed my stuff, and then headed back outside. A mostly-full garbage can had the squirt gun lying on the top of it along with the plastic gloves that they'd used to keep the ink from staining their hands.

Pretty much the entire squad except for Cindi and Sheree were lined up outside, just kind of standing around inconspicuously, but I knew that they were there just so they could see me come out covered in ink. I was suddenly very glad that I hadn't started crying or yelling. I didn't want to give any of them the satisfaction.

Miss Winters showed up before anyone said anything and her eyes went super wide.

"Adri, what happened?"

"Someone from our squad sprayed me with ink while I was getting changed. I didn't see them well enough to be able to tell who they were, but they were wearing blue uniforms."

I was pretty sure that the school paid Miss Winters a little bit to coach us, but mostly she paid the bills by working as a cosmetologist during the day. What had been done to me wasn't just wrong, it probably insulted her professional sensibilities. She looked at me for a couple more seconds with her mouth open than then closed it with an audible click.

"Let's get you taken care of, Adri. The rest of you girls stay right here. I don't want you in there with us, and any girl who leaves to go home with her parents or someone else is off the squad, no questions asked. Once I've helped Adri I'm going to come back out here and we're all going to have a rather pointed discussion."

I followed her back into the locker room. "I don't think that there's much we can do, Miss Winters. The ink isn't going to come out with just soap and water. It will just have to wait until I make it home."

She looked positively miserable. "How long has this been in your hair, Adri?"

"I don't know, maybe ten minutes."

"Sweetie, it's not ink. It's hair dye, I can tell by the smell."

I closed my eyes and took a deep breath as I tried to stop myself from completely losing it.

"It's been too long, hasn't it?"

"More than likely. If you had darker hair maybe not, but your hair is so light that it will have had some effect by now."

Apparently my distress was more evident than I meant for it to be because she rushed to reassure me.

"Don't worry though, I've fixed worse than this. We can bleach it back out so that you're a blonde again, or we can change it to pretty much whatever color you would like."

I shook my head. A few of the girls at school had used Miss Winters to color their hair and I knew that she did a good job, but I also knew that there wasn't any way that she could recreate the sheer depth of the high and lowlights in my hair. She'd probably get a good match for my base hair color, but even then it wouldn't be quite right.

I'd never realized just how vain I was. I'd told myself for years that I didn't care what other people thought, that what was on the inside was more important than what was on the outside, but that wasn't quite true. My character was the most important thing, but I did care how I looked and for years my hair had been the one physical attribute that I'd been proud of.

Other girls bleached their hair in an effort to make it look like mine did naturally, but no matter how hard they tried it was never as rich as mine. If I bleached it then I'd be making myself look just like all of them. I'd look like just another artificial blonde cheerleader who wasn't happy with the color that nature had given her. They would be winning.

"Can you just cut off the ends instead? Turn it into a bob, or if there isn't enough unstained hair, maybe you can do a pixie cut."

She was backing away from me now with her hands raised. "Let's not do anything hasty, Adri. Cutting your hair isn't something you should do on the spur of the moment like this. Let's just get the dye rinsed out enough that you won't get it all over your other clothes and the bus. We can figure out where to go from there tomorrow or Sunday after you've had a chance to think things over."

She was right and I knew it. It was stupid to just hack my hair off like this, but a wave of stubbornness washed through me. I didn't dig my heels in very often, but when I did nobody had ever managed to budge me.

"I'm not going back out there like the ugly stepsister because that will mean that whoever did this to me has won. I want to go out there like they didn't manage to get to me. If you won't do it then I'll cut the ends off myself. I think I've got some nail clippers in my bag."

I set my bag down and started rummaging through it. Miss Winters took a deep breath and then put her hand on my arm.

"If you're that determined then I'll cut it for you, just please, please, please make sure you're positive that this is what you want to do."

"I'm sure."

"Okay, I came directly from work and I was bringing my scissors home so I could cut my niece's hair. I'll go send someone for them."

She left the locker room and I thought I could hear snatches of conversation as she ordered one of the girls to go get her bag.

Whoever she sent must have run because she was back in less than five minutes. Miss Winters sat me down on one of the hard wooden benches and pulled out her scissors.

"This is your last chance to change your mind, Adri."

"It's okay, just go ahead, please."

I'd heard that she was good, but I was surprised at how quickly she worked. The black ends fell to the floor in rapid succession despite the obvious care she was taking to make sure she didn't let any of it fall on my jeans.

She then wiped her scissors clean on a paper towel, and started in on the undamaged hair. The whole process took less than twenty minutes after which she let out a deep breath.

"Okay, it's done. If you come by my house tomorrow I'll finish cleaning it up for you and I'll show you how to style it, but that's as much as I want to do tonight and the guys are no doubt starting to get antsy."

I nodded. I'd actually forgotten that the football team still needed to change. I just wanted to sit there, but I forced myself to go stand in front of the mirror. My hair had been just barely past my shoulders and almost completely straight. I'd been trying to grow it out for almost a year now. Before then I'd kept it a little shorter so that Cindi and I had almost the same hairstyle.

It was short now, shorter somehow than I'd expected it to be even though Miss Winters had done exactly what I'd asked her to do. I looked at the golden strands that now framed my face and told myself once again that I wasn't going to cry. It was short, but it was still my color.

"Thank you, Miss Winters. It's perfect."

I was sure that she heard at least a little bit of the lie in my voice, but she'd probably heard the same tremor in the voice of hundreds of girls over the years who'd gone in and asked for an extreme change and then second-guessed the decision after it was too late to do anything about it.

"I'll give you a few minutes to change into something that isn't ruined."

I couldn't get my voice to work so I just nodded and then watched as she walked out of the room. There wasn't a good way to get my tank top off without getting more dye on my hair or other clothes, so I just stripped back down and slid it down far enough that I could step out of it.

Five minutes later I was dressed again. Jeans still, but I was back into my shell and my sports bra as everything else was ruined. I looked at my tank top and bra for a couple of seconds and then just threw them into the garbage on my way out.

The football team and the guys from the cheer squad were all lined up waiting to use the locker room. I mustered what I hoped was a genuine-looking smile.

"It's all yours, gentlemen."

Tristan looked me up and down again as he walked past, and Jackson gave me an indecipherable look, but nobody else seemed to really even notice that I'd just lost half of my hair. Miss Winters was standing with the rest of the girls just around the corner of the school.

"Adri, why don't you go for a walk? You don't need to hear what I'm about to say to the rest of the team. Sheree, you can go with her if you'd like."

I shook my head. "I'm fine. Someone can just call my cell when you're ready to go."

I turned around and went back the other direction. The team was between me and the football field, so just going to the bleachers was out. I didn't particularly feel like going back to the bus either, so I just kept walking along the edge of the school until I found a bench.

I felt like I was in shock, which was stupid, but I hadn't realized that the other girls hated me this much. If things kept escalating then eventually I'd have to just quit the team and hope that doing so didn't make me stand out too much when the Native American, the wax lady or the old man came calling.

I kind of lost track of time, but I felt something changing in me as I sat there. I wasn't just in shock now. I was starting to get mad. The other girls on the team had no right to be so mean to me. They were trying to get me to quit the team, but I didn't want to quit.

I didn't love cheering, not really, but I loved spending time with Jackson and I still had some hope that being on the team would help me patch things up with Cindi. Besides, I really wanted to see how good I could get at stunting.

"Adri, are you okay?"

I looked up to find that Tristan of all people was approaching me.

"I'm fine, and I haven't changed my mind about dating you. Please go away."

He shook his head at me. "You don't have to be so hardcore about everything. Look, I heard what happened and wanted to say that I'm sorry. If you want I can find out who did this. Plenty of guys on the team are dating girls on your squad. If I ask around one of them will find out who did it. Girls talk."

I was surprised. I hadn't thought that Tristan was that insightful, or that he'd even care. Of course he was probably just trying to get in my pants, but even so I hadn't been expecting it.

"I don't know. I guess go ahead and find out, but don't tell me who did it unless I ask. I'm not sure it would be good for me to know."

"Okay, it's your call."

I heard footsteps and turned to find Jackson approaching. He gave me a slow smile. "You look gorgeous."

My cheeks tried to heat up, but I clung to my anger.

"Thank you, but right now I want to be mad and you reassuring me doesn't help with that."

Tristan stood a bit closer to me as though staking out his territory. "Why don't you get lost, Jackson?"

"Because she'd rather be with me than with you."

Any points that Tristan might have earned by offering to find out who had sprayed dye on me disappeared as he stepped away from me and into Jackson's space. It was obvious that he was gearing up for a fight, but it wasn't something he was doing for me, it was one hundred percent for his own ego.

"If you seriously start a fight with Jackson then I'll never talk to you again, Tristan."

"You've already said that you won't date me, so that's not exactly the most effective threat anyone has ever come up with. Besides, I've wanted to beat the tar out of Jackson for months."

"You can try. It's actually better this way because it means I've got a witness who can make sure everyone understands that you started this."

Jackson's words came out strangely unconcerned. I'd seen a couple of fights start over the years, and usually the two guys involved had to work themselves up to fighting. Jackson wasn't getting worked up, but I was positive that he was ready to fight.

"You really think you can narc me out after I beat you down and there won't be any consequences?"

Jackson shook his head. "No, it's more like I hate dealing with the authorities after I hospitalize someone. It's always better when I can point out that it was self-defense."

It was like he'd poured gas on a forest fire. Even I knew that Tristan couldn't back down after a statement like that. I did the only thing I could think of to stop the fight. I stood up and walked away.

"This isn't about the two of you, this is supposed to be about me right now. If you want to fight then fight, but I'm not going to sit here and watch. You're not going to impress me or have a witness to tell the cops who started what."

I didn't look back, but a second later two sets of footsteps started following me. They caught up to me all too quickly, Jackson walking on my right side, Tristan walking on my left.

Out of the corner of my eyes I saw Tristan open his mouth, but I already knew it was going to be some lame attempt to justify what he'd been doing.

"Don't even start with me, Tristan. You screwed up, deal with it like a man and accept it. Maybe then you'll start to grow on me a little."

Whatever he might have said in response was preempted by a muffled scream. I took off at a run without even thinking about the fact that it might be dangerous to get involved in whatever was going on. There were a couple of outbuildings a short distance away from the main school building and I was currently running around the side of what looked like a metalworking shop.

I'd expected to find one or more guys assaulting some poor girl. I didn't expect to find one girl, a slender Hispanic, being punched and kicked by four other girls. Normally I would have just grabbed my phone and called 911, but the anger that I'd been nursing over what had been done to me flared into an incandescent point of brilliance. The parallels to this girl's situation and my situation were too close for me to just watch and wait for the police to get there.

The building was nearly twenty yards long, but I covered the distance in a couple of seconds before they'd even realized they weren't alone any more. I grabbed the arm of one of the girls and shoved her into the side of the building to stop her from landing another kick.

"Get off of her!"

All four girls turned on me with a speed that took my breath away.

"Get lost, wolf girl. If you leave now and keep what you saw to yourself we won't track you down and beat your head in."

It took me a second to realize that she was talking about our mascot. I was still wearing my cheerleading shell, so it didn't take a genius to know which team I belonged to. I was slowly backing away, trying not to do anything to cause them to actually attack me, but they were following me, keeping the distance between us from growing.

With a start I realized that all four girls were in red and white cheerleading uniforms. It took me a minute to remember that we'd played against the Waterford Red Devils.

"Sorry, devil girl, but I can't just stand here and watch you kill her. If you have a problem with her, then come at her one by one after she's healed back up instead of just ganging up on her."

The girl they'd been beating on had pulled herself up to a sitting position, but she still didn't seem very with it. I wanted to yell at her to make a run for it, but I knew that would just focus the attention of the cheerleaders back on her.

I was starting to think of the girl who was doing all of the talking as the head cheerleader. She was so furious she was practically spitting.

"You don't know anything about what's going on here. She looks like a normal girl, but she isn't. She's some kind of supernatural freak. Two of the football players we knew turned up dead after a party last week. She was the one they were last seen talking to. She ripped their throats out."

A supernatural freak. Parallels indeed. I took a deep breath and shook my head. "Listen to yourself. You really think someone our size overpowered and killed two burly football players? Even if she was capable of that why would she then let the four of you kick the stuffing out of her? It doesn't make any sense."

I'd continued to carefully retreat the entire time we'd been talking. We were nearly a dozen yards away from where they'd been attacking the girl. If she was unhurt enough to run it should be more than enough room for her to escape, but she was just sitting there in a daze.

"You're out of time."

Even as she said it the head cheerleader sprang at me. I was still pissed, but four-to-one odds had gone a long ways towards calming me down enough to realize that I couldn't let any of them get their hands on me. I tried to turn and run but there was something unexpected in my way.

Jackson steadied me with one hand as I bounced off of him and then straight-armed the head cheerleader with an open hand to her sternum. It wasn't a blow, more like he'd just let her run into his arm, but it knocked her on her butt.

Somehow in all of the craziness I'd completely forgotten about Jackson and Tristan. They'd followed me, but stayed back far enough that apparently the cheerleaders from the other school hadn't thought they'd interfere.

"Are you okay, Adri?"

"Yeah, thanks. They'd knocked that other girl down and they were kicking her."

One of the other devil girls spoke up for the first time. "You guys aren't going to hit girls."

I stepped to the side a little so that I could see Tristan and Jackson without turning my back to the other girls. Tristan actually didn't look very happy at the idea of fighting with girls, but Jackson was doing a lot better job keeping his poker face in place.

"Oh, I don't know. I probably won't actually need to hit you. Besides, girls who will gang up against one girl like that are nothing more than bullies. I don't like bullies."

Jackson's comment apparently made Tristan feel like he needed to man up and defend me too.

"We're not going to let you hurt Adri or that other girl anymore."

Fighting another girl when you outnumbered her four to one was one thing. Throwing yourself at two guys the size of Jackson and Tristan was something else entirely.

"The next guy she kills is on your conscience."

All four cheerleaders started moving away from the building so that they could go around us without getting too close to the guys. Jackson just pivoted in place so he could keep an eye on them, but Tristan took a step forward as if to go help the girl they'd been beating on.

I grabbed his arm before he could get very far.

"She looks pretty traumatized. Let me go talk to her first, you guys stay back there and make sure that the devil girls don't bring a bunch of guys of their own."

It wasn't until I said it that I realized just how skittish the other girl looked. If she'd been a small animal she'd have been right on the verge of running up a tree or otherwise fleeing for safety.

A breeze had picked up. It was mostly running parallel to the building, but as I took my first couple of steps towards her a stronger than normal gust came in at a slightly different angle. The wind made the thin, white material of the peasant top she was wearing flutter and it came up far enough that I was able to see some of the bruises that they'd left on her stomach and side.

I gritted my teeth and reminded myself that it was more important to make sure she was okay than it was to chase down the other four girls and beat their heads in. There would be plenty of time for the police to deal with the four devil girls.

"My name is Adri. How can I help? Are you okay?"

I reached a tentative hand towards her in an effort not to startle her, but something still set her off. She recoiled so fast that I almost didn't see her move. One moment I was only inches away from her and then she was a couple of feet away with her arms and legs underneath her as though ready for fight or flight.

"I'm just trying to help. I won't hurt you, I promise. Do you need an ambulance?"

It seemed a stupid question given how quickly she'd just moved, but people could move on broken legs and not even feel the pain if they had enough adrenaline in their systems. I could see her visibly trying to regain control of herself. She was breathing erratically, sucking in huge drafts of air in between each gust of wind, but finally after one last deep, calming breath she seemed to come back to herself enough at least to respond to me.

"No, no ambulance. I'll be fine. They were just getting started, I'm mostly just bruised up."

She accepted the hand I offered her and pulled herself to her feet.

"I'm glad you're okay. Do you know those girls, I mean like names and stuff? You're going to have to file a police report and names would help."

It was like a switch flipped inside of her. She went from normal to aggressive so quickly that I didn't realize what had happened until her hands clamped down on my arms with a grip stronger than I'd ever felt out of any girl before.

We were about the same size but she'd crouched down slightly such that she was looking up at me with her lips pulled back slightly, less of a smile and more of a snarl like what you'd see out of a feral dog. That would have been plenty unnerving all by itself, but her eyes were molten yellow pools of rage.

I told myself that it was just a trick of the overhead lights scattered around the parking lot. That was the only logical explanation, but I'd been dealing with a whole host of things lately that weren't rational, that didn't follow any of the rules I'd grown up believing were absolute. Even more than that was the fact that I'd never seen eyes like that anywhere before, not under any kind of light.

"You don't tell me what I have to do."

The words came out as a barely audible hiss that I almost couldn't make out over Tristan's question.

"Adri, are you okay?"

She'd used my body to mostly screen her from the guys, but Tristan must have caught my involuntary wince of pain when she'd clamped down on my arms.

"Keep them back."

The order was accompanied with an increase in the pressure she was exerting on my arms, but I managed to keep from gasping at the pain.

"I'm fine! Stay back there, she's just scared." I dropped my voice to a whisper. "You're right, you don't have to do anything. I just thought that you'd want to make sure that they didn't come after you again later."

"I'll be gone before morning arrives. It was a mistake to stay here for so long, a mistake to try and build a normal life for myself."

She released my arms and seemed to shed the fury that had been so close to consuming her.

"We all want normal lives, no harm in that."

She gave me an odd look. "Not all of us deserve normal lives."

"That doesn't stop us from wanting them."

Her nod was a short, choppy motion. "Thank you for your help."

"You're welcome. Do you want help getting somewhere? Do you need to call anyone?"

"I don't know anyone who could help me."

With that cryptic remark she turned to go, but she stumbled and only the fact that I was there to grab onto saved her from a nasty fall.

"You're hurt, let me help."

She shook her head and left without another word, walking with only a slight limp.

Chapter 15

It was silly, but as soon as the Hispanic girl disappeared from sight my thoughts went back to what had just happened with the other girls from my squad. Once that happened, I knew I had a very limited time in which to lose Jackson and Tristan unless I was willing to let them see me lose my composure.

They of course didn't want to go. Honestly I would have liked for Jackson to stay, but I couldn't think of a way to send just Tristan away. Tristan was a self-centered jerk—he'd backed me up against the cheerleaders, which counted for something, but not enough for me to let him see me cry.

Jackson had pointed out that it probably wasn't safe for me to hang around unprotected after having pissed off the devil girls, so we came to a compromise. We continued on around the school so that I could sit on the bleachers at the football field and he and Tristan would give me some privacy while staying where they could keep an eye on me in case the cheerleaders from the other team showed back up.

Once I was by myself, I did cry, but only a little. I was still pissed at the other girls enough to take the edge off of the worst of my sadness, but there was no getting around the fact that I was sad. Hair seemed like such a stupid thing to cry over, especially considering the fact that I wasn't sure that I'd survive to graduate, but in a very real sense, Missy and the rest of the squad had won. I'd had to cut my hair and they were going to get off with nothing more than a slap on the wrist.

I didn't want my eyes to get all red and puffy so I forced myself to stop crying after only a minute or so, but it didn't change how I felt, didn't change the fact that the world seemed to be closing in on me.

Sheree found me a couple of minutes after I got control over myself again. "Adri, I just had the oddest conversation with someone."

"What do you mean?"

She handed me a phone which I realized after a second was mine.

"This girl walked up to me and asked if I knew an Adri. I told her yes and she gave me this phone. It's yours, isn't it?"

I unlocked it and confirmed that it was displaying my background and that the contacts were mine.

"Yeah, I guess it is."

"How did she get ahold of it?"

I'd been busy asking myself that same question.

"A dark-haired girl, Hispanic-looking and who maybe looked like she'd been in a fight recently? She would have been wearing a peasant top?"

"Yeah, that was her, do you know her?"

I shook my head. "Not really. I...ran into her earlier on the other side of the school. She must have stolen my phone when she stumbled and grabbed ahold of me for balance."

"That's really odd, why would someone steal a phone and then give it back?"

"I really wish I knew. It was kind of an odd conversation. Is everyone ready to go?"

Sheree looked uncomfortable, like maybe she didn't like talking bad about the other girls on the squad, even though she knew that they deserved it.

"No, Miss Winters only just barely let them go in and change. The football team was in there first, but it was the fact that she was yelling at everyone that kept them from changing earlier. The guys have been done for a little while."

I nodded. That made sense seeing as how Tristan and Jackson had been back in street clothes when they'd found me.

"She's really mad. Nobody admitted to having done it, but she said that you saw two girls and that they were wearing our uniform.

She said that the fact they were all there waiting for you to come out of the locker room means that they are all complicit, everyone but Cindi and I, so between them they all need to come up with four hundred dollars to replace your clothes that they ruined or she'll kick *all* of them off of the squad and hold a new set of tryouts."

My eyes went wide in shock. "Wow, I didn't expect that."

Sheree nodded. "Yeah, she's pretty unhappy. She sounded like she was trying to come up with something else to punish them with too when the guys came out of the locker room and she told Cindi and me that we could go in and change."

In the grand scheme of things making the girls pay thirty or forty dollars each to replace my clothes wasn't that big of a punishment, but it was actually far and away more than I was going to need, which meant that if I wanted to I could buy something really nice just to rub their noses in the fact that they'd had to pay for it.

As far as revenge went, it was a pretty good option and I was pretty sure that Miss Winters had known that when she'd stipulated the amount. Visions of designer purses and jeans flashed through my head for a second until I remembered that the jeans I was currently wearing had been the cause of things boiling over between my parents. No article of clothing was worth that.

I pushed away thoughts of the money and focused on Sheree again.

"I'm really sorry that the girls have been so mean to you, Adri. I hope you don't feel like I've been mean too. I'm sorry if I haven't been as friendly as I should have, I've just been really, really tired for the last few days."

I shook my head at her. "Sheree, you're a darling. You have nothing to be sorry about. Nobody else on the team has been as nice to me as you have."

Even as I said it I realized it was truer than I'd realized. Sheree hadn't just been nicer than the other girls on the team, she'd been nicer than Cindi too. Cindi was my own sister and she'd been released to go into the locker room at the same time as Sheree. Why wasn't *she* out here telling me how sorry she was that I'd been pranked in such a mean way?

In fact, the more I thought about it, the more I wondered if she'd actually known what they were going to do to me. She'd been in the back of the bus with Missy and the others. Had they really not said anything to her?

It was a nasty thought, but Cindi had been pretty nasty to me lately. It was a concern for another time though. I reached out and gently squeezed Sheree's arm.

"I really do appreciate how nice and thoughtful you've been to me."

Sheree blushed, but it was just a little darkening of her cheekbones. "You would have done the same for me."

My phone picked that second to start ringing. I held it up to Sheree and asked, "Do you mind?"

"Oh, no, go ahead."

It wasn't a number I recognized, but I got so few calls that it went against my nature to let a call ring through to voicemail.

"Hello."

"Are you by yourself?"

I recognized the voice—it was the girl who'd stolen my phone, the one who'd never actually told me her name.

"No."

"Then get alone and hurry. I don't have much time."

I frowned, but I covered my phone with one hand and pointed out into the field.

"I'm sorry, Sheree, I really need to take this. Do you mind if I just walk over there? I'd love to sit with you on the ride back home, if that's okay with you."

"That would be nice, thanks, Adri."

I waved goodbye to Sheree and then started across the tired green grass towards the center of the field at a fast walk.

"Okay, I'm by myself."

"How by yourself? Where is the closest person?"

"I'm in the middle of the football field and my friend is back behind the bleachers already and headed the other direction."

"That will have to do." She sounded tired, like maybe the beating from earlier had taken more out of her than she'd let show at the time. "You're in a lot of danger. Someone close to you, probably one of the two guys you were just with is extremely dangerous."

"What do you mean?"

I could almost hear her debating what to tell me through the silence on the other end of the phone.

"It's not safe for me to tell you more than that. You need to stay away from the dangerous one no matter the cost. I tried to get close enough to figure out which one was the threat, but there are too many humans around. You're just going to have to trust me on this. You're better off staying away from both of them than risking that you'll pick the wrong one and get hurt down the road at some point."

"You said that like you aren't human."

There was more silence on the other end of the line, more debating as to how much to tell me.

"If I said I wasn't, would that make you more or less likely to believe me?"

My voice caught for a second. I swallowed a couple of times and then managed a response.

"I'm not sure."

"Yeah, that's what I thought."

"What if I told you that I wasn't entirely…normal myself?"

She sighed. "Are you faster and stronger than a normal person?"

"No."

"I am, but I wouldn't go up against him by myself, so I guess I'd say it doesn't make any difference."

I was starting to shake. Everything I'd ever learned growing up, every physical law I'd ever had explained to me told me that this girl was crazy. Intellectually I knew that she might be nothing more than some loony escape from the insane asylum, but something told me that wasn't the case. She had some of the answers I needed. Maybe not about how to survive in the dream, but about what I was going to have to do to survive in a world where things I didn't even know existed were going to try to kill me. I was so close, and out of all of the people I'd met so far she seemed the most trustworthy, but even before I asked my next question I knew that she wasn't going to tell me what I needed to know.

"That's not what I meant. Would you tell me more about what kind of trouble I'm in if I told you I was different than other people somehow?"

"No, I'm sorry, but I'm already taking too much of a risk as it is. There are people who would kill me for what I've told you already. Just because we're both different than other people doesn't mean that my kind doesn't want our true natures to remain a secret. Good luck. I suspect you're going to need it."

She hung up on me. I called her number again, but it went straight to voicemail. I was pretty sure that she'd turned her phone off already. I knew I was going to try to call her again over the next few days, but I would have bet money that she would toss the phone as soon as she had another one.

After everything else that had happened over the last few hours this was almost too much, but I didn't scream or throw things. Instead I just turned back towards the school and got a profound shock when I saw that Jackson was standing next to the bleachers.

The girl had said that I'd probably be safe out in the center of the field with nobody closer than the bleachers, but the key word seemed to be *probably*. Just how good was this *thing's* hearing? I was pretty sure that Jackson wasn't the threat, but there wasn't any way to be sure. I took a deep breath and put the best smile I could on my face as I walked back to them.

Jackson was the first to speak. "Is everything okay?"

I nodded. "Just a call from my mom checking up on me. Given all the...drama at home right now I figured I'd better get far enough away that nobody would hear me."

"Understandable. Miss Winters is ready to load the bus up. Tristan and the rest of the football team left twenty minutes ago."

Right after they'd left me alone.

"Okay, then I guess we'd better get back to the bus."

I got an even bigger shock when I made it to the bus. Someone had dropped off a bouquet of brilliant yellow sunflowers for every single female on the team, including Miss Winters. The old man from my dream had indeed recognized my uniform.

Every single one of us was in danger now.

Chapter 16

It was a good thing that I had Sheree with me for the ride home. It took everything I had to get in the bus without freaking out, but I knew that my life depended on maintaining an appearance of calm. There was no reason for the old man to send the entire team sunflowers unless he was going to watch us and see who became the most unsettled as a result.

I tried to covertly look for him as I sat down in a seat next to Sheree, but just because I couldn't see him didn't mean that he wasn't there. It was possible he was just using binoculars or something similar to watch from a long ways away, but I knew that wasn't the only option. The mere fact that I'd ended up inside of his dream was pretty conclusive evidence that he wasn't normal, that he had some kind of supernatural power. For all I knew he could make himself invisible and he'd watched me from a distance of inches at some point during the night.

It was the kind of thought that made me want to start screaming and crying, but I held myself together because I didn't have any other choice, not if I wanted to survive what was coming.

Sheree was a godsend. We didn't talk about anything earthshattering, but Sheree wasn't just nice, she was also a surprisingly good storyteller. I got her started telling me about some animated show that she loved and got sucked into the story almost in spite of myself.

Originally she hadn't wanted to tell me about what happened in it because she said it would ruin the story when I watched it myself. I told her not to worry about that, that I didn't expect to ever watch it myself, but by the time we'd made it halfway back home I'd started to reconsider my stance there. The series sounded silly on the face of things, but she painted the characters as such lively, sometimes silly, individuals that I started to think that maybe I should watch a few episodes just to see if it was as good as she made it sound.

Sheree started yawning when we were still forty minutes from home. She apologized profusely, but I could tell that she was exhausted. It took some convincing, but she finally agreed to close her eyes and take a nap.

I was starting to think that Sheree's lack of energy lately might have something to do with our stunting practice session. I didn't remember her being this tired all of the time before I'd stopped in for help that one night. I knew I was tired a lot after I spent an extended amount of time in someone else's dream or manipulating my own dream, but it didn't linger for me like it was doing for her. It was possible though that my ability to dream walk somehow cushioned me from the worst of the fallout.

Hopefully Sheree would be okay in another few days, but it was one more thing to worry about. I resolved to leave Sheree's dreams alone for the next few weeks at least. Maybe once I'd confirmed that she bounced back without any long-term problems then I might practice with her again one night, but not for now.

Once Sheree fell asleep I was alone with my thoughts. I was doing the best I could to keep from breaking down, but it was a losing battle. Just when I felt like I couldn't take it any more, I looked up and saw Jackson watching me. His smile was a little hesitant, but it was enough to remind me that for all that my new powers had brought a lot of bad into my life, they had brought good with them too.

I got a text from my dad about fifteen minutes before we got back to the school.

Sorry, Adri, I'm stuck at work still. Will you guys be okay walking home or do you need me to try to get away?

A text from my dad, even one telling me that he wasn't going to pick us up, brought a smile to my face.

We'll be fine. Don't work too late.

Once we arrived at the school, I woke Sheree back up and then the two of us made our way to the front of the bus. Miss Winters stopped me just outside of the bus and handed me a wad of cash.

"One of the benefits to what I do is that I always have a lot of cash from tips. Here's some money to pay for the clothes that were just ruined. Don't worry, it's not coming from me, the girls on the team are all chipping in to cover this."

I wondered if she was going to say anything about the fact that the 'chipping in' hadn't been voluntary, at least not if they wanted to stay on the team, but after several seconds of silence I just nodded.

"Thank you, Miss Winters. I really appreciate it."

Sheree gave me a tired smile and then frowned. I followed her gaze and felt my stomach sink a little. Cindi was already a block away. Sheree and I had been pretty close to the front of the bus, while Cindi had sat in the very back with Missy and the others. I knew that she hadn't made it off of the bus before me, but she'd apparently come straight off of the bus and started towards our house without waiting for me. I said a hasty goodbye to Sheree and then started after Cindi. I was walking fast, but I didn't manage to catch up with her.

Something was obviously still bothering her because she was in her pajamas and pretending to be asleep by the time I made it into our bedroom.

HUNTED

Luckily I had a dreamless night, which meant I woke up on Saturday morning full of energy and ready to go accomplish anything. Dad and I had a quiet breakfast together. I wondered if we'd see Mom or Cindi before we got done, but neither of them ventured out of their respective bedrooms. I thought about telling Dad what had happened the night before, but I didn't want to tell him about the money yet, and if I told him about the rest of the events without telling him that I had a way of replacing my clothes then I'd just stress him out.

Instead, he read through the news on his tablet while I planned which stores I would be hitting. We cleaned up our dishes and then I told him I wanted to go to the mall. He nodded and an hour later I was walking into the mall.

Shopping wasn't usually something that I enjoyed, but then again, I didn't usually have any money to spend. This time I not only had money, but I needed to spend it or I'd run out of clothes before the end of the week. It made for a more enjoyable time except for the fact that I constantly had to stop myself from spending too much. There was a dizzying array of gorgeous clothes to pick from, but I knew just how much I normally paid for my clothes and after walking through the fifth store where jeans were more than one hundred dollars each I realized that shopping still wasn't any fun when you had money but were trying to stick to a budget.

After nearly an hour and a half of wandering through the mall I finally remembered the store that my mom had told me about back when she'd first decided that I needed new clothes. I double-checked the address on my phone and then decided to walk there.

It was like heaven. The prices were only a little higher than I was used to paying, but the clothes were incredibly cute. I replaced my jeans and tank top, picked up some new shorts, and another top that would work for the winter, and still had enough to go back over to the mall to pick up a bra and stay inside of my budget.

I started back for home a little after two as my stomach reminded me that going without food wasn't really an option these days. Mom and Cindi were gone when I got home, which was convenient considering that I wanted to talk to Dad alone, but it kind of bugged me that they'd slept in late and then left Dad all by himself.

The door to Dad's office was open, so I went in and sat down next to him. "Do you have a minute, Dad?"

"For you? Always."

"So...some girls squirted me with hair dye at the game last night."

His eyes went wide and I saw him looking at my hair, trying to decide whether or not it was different than he remembered. I continued before he could get a word out.

"Everything ended up okay...sort of. My clothes were pretty much ruined and they got the bottom inch or so of my hair, but I just had Miss Winters cut the black part off."

"I'm so sorry, Adri. Are you sure you're okay? Is that why you went to the mall today?"

I nodded. "Yeah. Miss Winters was actually a lot cooler about everything than I expected her to be. I didn't see who did it, but they were definitely cheerleaders from our team and most of the team was waiting outside of the locker room to see how bad they got me. When I told Miss Winters what had happened she yelled at the rest of the team for something like half an hour. When nobody would tell her who did it she told the rest of the team that they were buying me new clothes, and if they didn't chip in that they were off the team."

"Ah, that was rather shrewd of her. If any of the girls' parents complain she can just point out that their daughters can get out of contributing just by telling her who actually did the prank. It also has the benefit of possibly creating some friction between the real culprits and the rest of the team."

"Yeah, she's actually a lot smarter than I gave her credit for."

"Good, I'm glad that she's taking such a stern position with this. Did you manage to find clothes that you liked at the mall?"

"No, but I went to this used clothes store that Mom told me about and shopped there. I got some cute clothes that I'm pretty happy with."

There was a twinkle in his eye as he looked down at the bags in my left hand. "Did you want to show me what you found?"

"No, it's okay. I can show Cindi later. Mostly I just came to tell you that I bought everything I needed to and I have about two hundred dollars left. I want you and Mom to have it. Mom racked up extra credit card debt to get those other clothes for me and this should cover at least some of what she spent."

As I spoke, I pulled out what was left of the cash that Miss Winters gave me and tried to place it in his hand but he pulled back out of my reach.

"That's a really amazing gesture, Adri, but I don't expect you to do that."

"But I want to help out. Things are tight and I can help so I should."

He shook his head at me as he closed my fingers back around the money, making a fist.

"I don't mind taking care of you girls and your mother. I think that's my responsibility as a man. I know it's not fashionable these days for guys to say that kind of thing, it means we're the kind of chest-beating Neanderthals that used to club our women over the head before dragging them back to our cave, but that's how I feel. I have a good education and there's no reason that I can't take care of the family from a financial standpoint."

"But the economy is so bad right now, Dad."

"You're right, it is bad, but I still have a job and while this isn't always the case, usually I've found that when a man has to depend on his wife or kids to help support the family it's because he's either chosen not to earn as much as he could, or because he's refusing to sit someone in the family down—possibly himself—and tell them that they are trying to maintain too extravagant of a lifestyle."

I dropped the money on his desk. "You just finished saying that isn't true in all cases, Dad. Let me help."

"It's true in our case though, sweetie. I'm guilty of both of those things. I've had some time to think about things since we talked about all of this last. This bit about your mother and the money she's spent on her photography equipment is just a smokescreen in some ways. If I hadn't changed jobs a few years back, we'd be making forty or fifty percent more than we are right now."

"But you did that for us. You did that so that you'd be working fewer hours so that you could spend more time with us."

"Yes, and I think that is a valid life choice, but having made that choice I should have sat Cindi and your mother down and told them unequivocally that certain expenditures were going to go by the wayside. I didn't do that, and now we...I...am reaping the consequences. Money is constantly tight despite the fact that I'm back to working long hours."

"Are you guys going to get a divorce?"

I couldn't stop my voice from quavering a little bit, but I did manage to keep my eyes from filling up with tears.

"I still don't know, honey. Hopefully our little vacation this week goes even better than I'm hoping and we'll come back with a good foundation to start working through some of these issues."

Dad looked out the window for a second as though searching for the right words to say.

"I really do love your mother and I care about her deeply, just like I care about you and Cindi. I see a lot of things in her that I still admire. I love that she throws herself into projects with such reckless abandon. I love that she doesn't let the details get in the way of trying to go after what she wants. I think those are really good things in the right amounts, I just feel like she's lost the rudder that would allow her to use them as strengths rather than weaknesses. Maybe we've both lost our rudders."

"Where did things go wrong, Dad?"

"I'm not sure, Adri. I've looked back over our lives trying to figure that out. I think I took that stroll down memory lane partially out of a desire to fix things, but I think it's also been because I want to know so that I can warn you and Cindi before you're both my age and suffering from some of the same regrets."

Dad cleared his throat, probably trying to hide the fact that his voice was becoming thick with emotion, and continued.

"I think it was a lot of small things. When we got married, I was so sure that we were headed towards a happy, full life. I could see all of the ways that we complemented each other, all of the strengths we had individually and the way that they worked well together. I've thought back again and again and I just can't see any one individual event or even two or three events. It was like a hundred small branches in a path and while we didn't choose the wrong fork every time, we chose the wrong path most of the time."

"So you just kind of drifted apart?"

"I guess, but it was more like we just became two different people, people who cared about different things, people who didn't have anything in common except for the two of you."

The tears that I'd been fighting started to pour down my cheeks, which then caused Dad to stand and pulled me into a hug.

"No matter what happens I'm still going to love you, Adri. Your mom will too. Even if the worst comes to pass we'll still make sure that our feelings about each other don't get in the way of taking care of the two of you."

"Thanks, Dad. I really hope that it doesn't come to that."

"Me too, sweetie. Me too."

Chapter 17

I called Miss Winters after Dad and I talked and set up a time for her to touch up my hair. It turned out that she was only a fifteen-minute walk away from us. It was crazy to think about just how many people were packed into such a small area around us. We didn't live in the center of the city or anything, but I still saw hundreds of homes on my walk to Miss Winters' house and I only knew a handful of our neighbors.

Miss Winters greeted me with a smile and then seated me in her kitchen and started working on my hair.

"I'm really sorry that things have gotten so bad on the squad for you, Adri. I really do wish I could just wave a magic wand and make all of you girls the best of friends."

"It's okay. I never expected to fit in on the team anyways. To be honest I never would have even considered trying out, let alone joining, if not for Cindi practically begging me to."

"Well, I for one am glad that you joined up. It would have been a real shame for you to never have developed your talents, you're a natural. You're already as good a flyer as anyone else on the team."

I felt myself blushing. "That's very kind of you to say."

"It's no more than the truth, Adri. Speaking of which, I've had a little more time to think about that extra punishment that I mentioned. I'm still a little up in the air about it, but I don't think that replacing your clothes inconvenienced whoever sprayed you down very much. I had hoped that doing that would have made someone else on the team step forward, but that hasn't happened either."

I nodded. She was more or less going back over the same ground as Dad and I had covered earlier.

"Anyway, I feel like I have to do something else to drive home the point that while I can't make you all be friends, I at least want you all to treat each other decently. I think that Missy is the key. Even if she wasn't involved she should have known what was going on, and as the captain of the team she should be better than that. I'm thinking of putting you in her place as one of the three starting flyers."

I shook my head. "I don't think that's a good idea, Miss Winters. That's just going to make the other girls hate me even more. Besides, I may be picking things up quickly, but I still don't have any experience doing stunts in games."

"Everyone starts as a novice somewhere, Adri. I understand your reluctance, but it wasn't that long ago that I was in your shoes. I remember being on the team, I remember some of the pressures and I remember just how catty the girls can be. I just hope that if it comes to it that you'll agree to help me out. I have to punish whoever did this or I'll continue to run into the same kinds of problems next year and the year after that."

"I'll help you however I can, Miss Winters, you know that."

"I appreciate that, Adri. Your hair is done. What do you think?"

She'd done an amazing job. She hadn't just cut it, she'd styled it and I looked like some kind of movie star or something. I told her as much, which made her smile, and then she showed me how to style it and I headed home.

I expected for Mom and Cindi to be back by the time I got home from my hair appointment, but they stayed out late. Not just a little bit late, late enough that Dad and I both ended up going to bed before either of them came home. Dad texted Mom about the time that we started preparing dinner, but she just texted back saying that we shouldn't wait for them.

I couldn't blame Dad at the way he frowned when he received the text. They were supposed to leave on their camping trip tomorrow and Mom was leaving him to do all of the packing by himself. It wasn't a very promising start to the vacation that he was hoping would save their marriage.

Chapter 18

The sound of Mom and Dad packing pulled me out of bed almost two hours before I'd originally planned on getting up. Cindi didn't even stir when I left our room. Apparently she and Mom had been out *really* late.

Things weren't pretty when I got out to the living room. The pile of camping gear that Dad had spent the evening putting together had mostly disappeared into two large blue backpacks, but Mom was sitting bleary-eyed at the table while Dad finished up the last of the packing.

"Honestly, John, there isn't any reason to be such a jerk about things. It wouldn't have hurt you to let me sleep for a couple more hours before we left."

Dad didn't look up from his packing. "We can discuss it on the road."

"No, I want to discuss it now. I'm tired of you trying to dictate to me."

"Fine, you want to discuss it, let's discuss it. I'm tired of trying to keep the girls from seeing just how much of a child you've become over the last couple of years. I thought maybe we should spare Adri another fight, but if you want to force a confrontation I'll be more than happy to give you one."

Mom opened her mouth, probably to snap back at him, but Dad didn't give her a chance.

"We're leaving right now because that is when we agreed to leave. I didn't dictate that, we jointly agreed that we wanted to get an early start so that we could finish the first leg of our trip and get the tent set up before dark. I woke you up because I'm tired of your incessant tendency to disregard things like this and then expect me and the girls to pick up the pieces."

"That's not fair!"

"You're right, it's not fair. It's not fair for you to spend money we don't have and then expect me to come up with it rather than chipping in yourself. It's not fair that you haven't cooked a dinner in months, instead expecting the girls or I to do all of the cooking while you selfishly pursue your hobby to our detriment."

"That's not what I meant, and you know it. You're so high-and-mighty, always treating me like a child. Well, I'm tired of *that*. Do you realize how many guys expressed an interest in me at my last gallery showing, a showing that you didn't even bother attending?"

My dad's knuckles went white on the backpack's frame, but Mom apparently didn't see the warning signs—that or she just didn't care, just wanted to goad him into the most excessive retort she could manage.

"I would point out that I didn't go to your show because you scheduled it the same night as Adri's first cheerleading game, but I somehow suspect that you wouldn't actually care about that. Please tell me, Nichole, how many guys propositioned you?"

I could tell that Mom was surprised. She'd expected Dad to lose it. I'd never really seen him mad, but something there hinted at the fact that he must have had a temper at some point.

"Do you not even care?"

"The number is immaterial, Nikki. You're a beautiful woman, that isn't the first time that you've had guys express interest in you. The real question is how you responded to them. If you returned their interest then it doesn't really matter whether it was one or a hundred."

"I haven't called any of them back."

Dad stood up, and for the first time I realized just how much bigger he was than Mom. "You gave them your number?"

"Some of them were buyers or gallery owners."

He nodded, but it was like he was nodding at something else, like he'd made a decision of some kind.

"So our marriage is even further gone than I thought. Fine. Your gear is all packed. I'll be out in the car and I'm leaving in fifteen minutes, which is forty-five minutes after the time we agreed to last week. Frankly right now I don't particularly care whether you're in the car when I leave, but if you're not, then when I get back I'll file for divorce. And I'll make sure I take half of your photography gear as part of the settlement."

Dad stood, his backpack in one hand, and walked out the door before Mom could say anything else. I just stood there in shock, unable to process everything that had just happened. Mom looked at me and her lips shrank down into a thin line. She obviously wasn't happy to have had an audience for this particular fight, but after a couple of seconds she stood up from the table and carried her bowl over to the sink.

"I want you and Cindi to behave and get along while we are gone. We'll be back on Saturday."

∽つ ✷ Cつ

I sat around in shock for most of the rest of the morning. Cindi didn't get up until after noon, and then proceeded to spend the rest of the day on the landline talking to her friends about her party plans. I hadn't exactly forgotten about the upcoming bash, but I'd managed to put it out of my mind.

Sometimes I was good at ignoring things I couldn't change—not usually, but sometimes. I was glad that this had been one of the things that I'd been able to leave alone rather than picking at it incessantly.

I'd had a fuzzy idea that the party was going to happen on Friday night after the next game, but it turned out that we had Wednesday off from school because of some kind of teacher prep day, so Cindi had scheduled the party for Tuesday night.

For the most part Cindi ignored me as she went about locking down all of the final details. I felt like it should have bothered me more than it did, but the truth was that I was feeling less guilty and more mad about everything that had happened recently.

She had been the one who had pushed for me to join the team. I hadn't set out to upstage her, and I resented the fact that she hadn't even acted sad when the other girls had pranked me and ruined my hair. She still hadn't said anything to me about it. Instead she'd gone on some kind of super-secret combination shopping trip and night on the town with Mom. It was obviously supposed to be a secret, but she hadn't done a very good job hiding the bags they'd brought back with them. I saw them over in one corner of our closet when I came back from the shower to get dressed.

I wanted to scream when I saw them. I probably would have gotten into an epic fight with Cindi right then and there if she'd been in the room when I first saw the evidence. It was the single most selfish thing she could have done. She'd heard Mom and Dad yelling at each other over the fact that we were out of money. Given that, letting Mom take her shopping was pretty much just coming right out and saying that she thought having cute clothes was more important than their marriage.

Dad obviously hadn't noticed anything before they'd left, but I kept thinking about how Mom was going into their trip in bad faith. He was trying to save their marriage and she'd just finished doubling down by spending hundreds of dollars more that we didn't have to spend.

There was always a chance that I was wrong, that Mom had purchased Cindi's clothes with her photography money, but in some ways that was just as bad. The idea that Mom would spend that much on Cindi, who already had more nice clothes than she could possibly wear, and not spend a dime on me, was like a knife to the heart. I'd always known that Mom liked Cindi the most, but she'd never been this obvious about things.

I managed to get control of myself by the time I saw Cindi again, and by all appearances she never even realized that I knew what she'd been up to with Mom. She just continued to talk to her friends with a kind of smug self-assurance that made me want to punch her in the face.

It was dinner time before Cindi actually deigned to talk to me.

"Have you invited Jackson to the party yet, Adri?"

"No."

My terse answer didn't discourage her in the slightest.

"You should. This party is happening despite how badly you wish it wasn't. You can either cower inside of our room while it's going on, or you can try to make the best of it by making sure that there is at least one person there who will talk to you."

Half a dozen different nasty things were on the tip of my tongue, ready to be said, but I swallowed them down for the simple fact that she was right. I either needed to leave the house entirely and risk my stuff all getting trashed, or I needed Jackson there. The alternative, sitting in my room by myself for hours, was too terrible to contemplate.

"I'll invite him."

"You'd better, Adri. Don't think that I haven't seen the way you've been making doe eyes at Tristan."

"I'm not interested in Tristan and I've told him that. I told him he should ask you out."

"And yet the star quarterback, who just led the team to two wins, has decided not to go after any of the girls who actually want to date him and instead is spending every minute he can with you. Yeah, right."

HUNTED

I was beyond pissed at Cindi. I was nearly to the point of saying all of the things I'd been thinking in the back of my mind, things that I knew she would never forgive.

"You know what, Cindi, I don't care. You can believe what you want, but I've done nothing but try and have your back where Tristan is concerned. If you don't believe me then maybe I should stop trying and just date him like he wants me to."

I slammed the door to our bedroom and then climbed into bed. None of this was fair. I had some kind of supernatural creepy-crawly guy after me, I shouldn't have to deal with all of the normal, stupid teen drama too. I was used to dealing with this kind of crap at school, but this was the first time I'd had it follow me home like this.

Cindi was my sister, she wasn't supposed to be my worst enemy too.

Chapter 19

Monday passed in a blur. I didn't remember having any unusual dreams, but I was as tired as if I'd spent the whole night dream walking. I was pretty sure that it was just the normal result of not sleeping well due to all of my worries. As poorly as I'd eaten on Sunday, I was pretty sure I would have been skin and bones if I'd actually dream walked Sunday night.

The cheerleaders were nasty to me, but they had all matched up their schedules with each other and I hadn't, so I didn't have any classes with them. That meant that the harassment was primarily either in the halls or by non-cheerleaders in my classes. My having put that one guy on the ground after he'd tried to grope me meant that nobody was willing to escalate things too far, which was nice. I couldn't have taken it if things had gone beyond nasty rumors and whispered insults.

The teachers seemed to have clued in, at least a little, towards the end of the day, but there was only so much they could do since they were outnumbered by the students and couldn't be everywhere at once. I told myself that this didn't really matter, that it was a temporary problem, but it still took a toll on me. By the time Jackson met up with me to go to my last class, I had a headache and just wanted to curl up in a corner somewhere and rock myself to sleep.

"You okay?"

"Yeah."

"And by 'yeah' you mean not really?"

I shrugged, but Jackson didn't seem like he was going to let me get away with avoiding the question.

"Yeah, not really, but there isn't much that can be done about it, so I'll just have to deal with the fact that everyone in the school now hates me."

"Not everyone."

"You're right, you seem strangely immune to the mind-control powers exhibited by Missy and the rest of the girls."

As feeble as my joke was, it still earned me a smile, which lifted my spirits more than I would have said was possible. Just being around Jackson washed away some of the exhaustion of dealing with everyone else all day.

"I was actually thinking of Tristan, but you're right, I don't hate you."

"Jealous, Jackson?"

"Hardly. It's just been a long time since I told someone to get lost and they didn't obey. Tristan doesn't make sense on a lot of levels and I don't like things I can't explain."

"Well, I wish he had left. My sister is convinced that I'm tricking him into liking me, but the truth is that I wish he'd chase her. I think they deserve each other."

We were nearly to the gym when I remembered the dreaded party. I bit my lip. I'd never actually asked a guy out to anything, let alone to an unsupervised party, but the only thing I could think of that was more terrifying than spending Tuesday night alone was the prospect of the old man or the Native American finding me in real life.

"Cindi is throwing a small party tomorrow night while my parents are away. Will you come so I have someone there who doesn't hate me?"

I pushed the words all out in a rush so that I wouldn't lose my nerve and chicken out partway through inviting him. That would have been bad enough all by itself, but I also put my hand on his arm as I said it.

He practically turned to stone at my touch.

"I would really like to come, but I'm not sure whether or not I'll be able to make it. My…mom has some stuff planned for us that night and it might be late before I can sneak away."

It was like being punched in the stomach. I knew a polite refusal when I heard one, I just didn't understand *why* he was turning me down.

The only logical explanation was that I'd somehow misread the signals I thought I'd been getting from him.

"Okay, well, I'm sure it will go for hours, so if you end up able to come a bit later you should drop by."

"That sounds good, I'll do that."

I plastered a fake smile across my face and ducked into the girls' locker room before he could say anything else. My mind retreated into a kind of white noise as I changed into my workout clothes. I could still respond when someone talked directly to me, I still hit my marks during practice, but all of the other stuff happening around me faded out into unimportance.

I think that Cindi and I walked home together, but I couldn't have said for sure. Once practice was over I simply picked up my stuff and started towards the road. As I went to bed that night I idly wondered whether or not I'd snap out of my current state.

Part of me felt like I should be worried, that this was dangerous, but mostly I was just relieved that I didn't have to worry any more. Maybe I'd always had this capacity to tune everything else out and just never exercised it fully. Maybe that was why I'd never been as concerned as Cindi about fitting in.

Even the prospect of dying when the old man eventually found me didn't really seem to matter now.

Chapter 20

I made it all the way to Tuesday afternoon before something managed to crack the artificial bubble of calm that I'd layered around myself. I'd somehow gotten up on time, gotten ready and made it to school out of nothing more than habit. Somewhere along the way I'd apparently eaten breakfast and lunch too because I didn't have that hollow, ravenous feeling that was my near-constant companion lately.

Despite all of those hours of class, I couldn't remember a single bad thing that anyone had said to or about me, and I liked that. Part of me resented Miss Winters when she pulled me aside just before practice and thereby tore my sanctuary away from me.

"Adri, are you okay?"

"Yes, Miss Winters, why?"

I could tell that she didn't believe me, but she wasn't quite sure how much to say.

"Adri, you've continued to lose weight. I'm glad that you have a desire to take care of yourself and that you've slimmed down from where you used to be, but you're approaching the lower end of what could possibly be considered healthy. I don't care how badly you want to cheer or fly, or what guy you think will like you if you're just a little skinnier than you are now, it's not worth it."

It took a second for her words to sink in.

"Oh, you think I have some kind of eating disorder. I don't. I hate being hungry, so I rarely miss a meal. At lunch I usually have pizza and French fries because I've been trying to make sure that my calorie intake keeps up with my expenditures."

"Calories in don't count if they don't stay down, Adri."

I was suddenly tired. Actually that was odd, had I not been tired before? I was usually tired these days.

"I'm not throwing it all back up. I'm not throwing any of it back up. I'm not even trying to lose weight. I'm just exercising with the squad a lot more than I ever used to."

"How much exercising are you doing outside of practice then, Adri? I've seen a lot of different ways that girls abuse their bodies in my time. Compulsively exercising to the point where your body can't keep up with the punishment you're doing to it isn't much better than starving yourself."

"I don't really exercise outside of practice."

"Is it stress then? Something isn't adding up between what you're telling me and what I'm seeing. The kind of calories you're *saying* you eat each day don't just disappear, they have to go somewhere."

Saying yes, that it was stress that was causing me to slim down despite how much I was eating was a tempting option. It seemed like an easy out, but even as I opened my mouth to tell her that was the cause I realized I couldn't say that, not if I wanted to stay on the team.

Miss Winters was a good person, one who cared about us girls as individuals, not just as cogs in a machine that she hoped would win her trophies at the regional cheer competitions. If I told her that stress was causing me to lose weight beyond the point where she thought I could still be healthy, then she'd kick me off the team. She'd let me down as gently as she could while still encouraging me to get some kind of professional help, but she wouldn't have any other choice.

"It's not stress. I've been more stressed than this before and I didn't lose weight like this. I promise that I'm not doing anything bad. If you don't believe me you can ask Cindi. She's constantly telling me that I can't eat the way I am and still hope to stay skinny on a long-term basis."

"You're sure that cheerleading isn't causing you too much stress?"

I wanted to say yes so badly. When you stacked all of the cheerleading fallout up against the fact that someone with powers I couldn't even guess at was trying to kill me, it was pretty small change. Even so, eliminating even that small amount of drama from my life would go a long way towards clearing my head enough to think about possible ways to deal with the Native American and all of the other people who might be trying to hunt me down.

I knew that quitting the team would paint giant crosshairs on my back though, so instead I lied.

"I really am fine, Miss Winters."

She gave me a long look. "Okay, I'm willing to trust you at least a little, but I want you to go see a doctor next week and get a physical. Ask him to write up his findings and then I want you to bring them to me. If you don't, or if the findings indicate that you're getting into any kind of dangerous territory, then you're off the team."

"Yes, Miss Winters."

I turned to go, but she reached out and touched my arm. "Adri, I really am just worried about you. I want to believe you, but your physical transformation over the last month or two is nothing less than astonishing."

"It's okay, I probably wouldn't believe me either. I know it's crazy, but I really haven't been doing any of the stuff you're worried about."

Something in my eyes must have convinced her because she took a deep breath and nodded. "I need you on the team, Adri. It's past time to break Missy's clique and I can't do it without you."

Practice went by in a kind of slow agony where time couldn't seem to manage much more than a faltering limp. True to her promise when I'd first agreed to become a flyer, Miss Winters kept Jackson with me the entire time. It was torture.

I could tell that Jackson was trying to pretend like nothing had changed, but I knew it was just an act. I tried to lose myself in the stunts, but even that didn't work. The second or two when I was in the air was pure joy, but I always had to come back down and I always came back down to Jackson's arms.

His touch seemed to burn. I knew it was my imagination, knew that nothing had changed other than me being hyperaware of him, but having him touch me now was painful. It was silly, we hadn't ever kissed or even held hands, but I'd started thinking of him as *mine*. Only he wasn't, not even close.

Making it home didn't provide any relief from my misery either. Missy and a few of the other girls walked home with us—home with Cindi, really—so that they could help get things ready for the party. Nobody even pretended to include me in the conversation as we walked the few blocks to our house. It was too much for me; once we arrived I just went to my room and shut the door.

I came out after a couple of hours so that I could grab something to eat and was astonished at the transformation that had taken place. I vaguely remembered Cindi doing some prep work the night before, but that had involved little more than moving everything that was valuable or breakable into Mom and Dad's bedroom so that she could lock it up once the party got started.

Things hadn't looked all that different then, but now there were black lights, strobes and all kinds of crazy stuff scattered all over the house. They'd even put black paper over all of the windows, probably in an effort to keep the strobe lights from alerting the neighbors to the fact that there was a party going on.

It was actually a pretty smart thing to do. We weren't particularly close to our neighbors, but that didn't mean that they wouldn't tell my parents about any parties that took place while Mom and Dad were gone.

Missy apparently didn't have to go home before the party, because she'd already changed into a black tube top and shorts so tiny that she wasn't particularly hiding much. The rest of the girls were still just wearing the clothes that they'd worn to practice, but Missy's clothes were a definite preview of what was still to come.

I grabbed some cold cuts, put them between two slices of bread and then retreated back into my bedroom. It was amazing how much homework you could get done when you no longer had anyone to talk to or anything else to do.

It had taken a while for my bubble of indifference to fully dissipate after Miss Winters had pulled me aside, but as the last of it started to disappear a slow, burning rage began filling me up. There was nothing about this situation that was fair. It was bad enough that I had to deal with all of the squad's crap when I was at school. Having it—having them—follow me home was a million times worse.

My first instinct was to bow out, to spend the night in my room and just make the best of a bad situation, but I was realizing that I needed to take a stand or they'd just continue to push. I needed to go out there and pretend like I was having a good time. I needed to go out there and flirt with whatever guys showed up. I couldn't change how the cheerleading team felt about me, but possibly I could start showing some of the rest of the student body that I wasn't as bad as they all seemed to think.

I was still wearing my workout clothes, so I started there. I changed into a different tank top and some clean shorts, not because I was trying to compete with Missy when it came to who could be the most slutty—my shorts weren't anywhere as revealing as hers—but because I didn't want to come across as a prude.

Some small part of me thought it was a sad state of affairs when wearing jeans made you a prude, but it seemed like that was how things worked now, at least when it came to the kind of party I was suspecting this was going to end up being.

I snuck back out to the bathroom and checked my hair before putting on some mascara and eyeliner. Honestly that was about all of the makeup that I owned and I wasn't going to borrow any of Cindi's, not as pissy as she was being lately, but even if I'd had more options I still probably would have just stuck to the basics. I'd never felt like putting makeup on was going to make enough of a difference for the average guy to get past my chubbiness, so I'd never bothered learning how to apply lots of makeup like Cindi usually did.

Five minutes later my teeth were brushed and I'd decided that I looked as good as possible. All that was left was to go out and deal with the bevy of skanks that I'd heard leave an hour or two ago and then start trickling back in over the last little while.

It was obvious that the party hadn't really gotten started yet, there were only a dozen or so people there, but as I stepped out of the bathroom someone turned on the music and it was like some kind of signal had been given.

Lights started going out and being replaced by strobes or black lights as couples started dancing or making out depending on how long they'd been dating. Part of my mind kept up a running commentary about the stupidity of what I was seeing, but I shoved aside thoughts about the strobe lights causing us all to get headaches and started towards a couple of football players who were standing off in a corner of the living room holding red cups and talking.

The music was thankfully quiet enough that it was possible to carry on a conversation with someone as long as you stood really close to them. That surprised me for a second until I realized that Cindi and the others were probably keeping the music to a dull roar in an effort to help make sure that none of the neighbors realized we had a party going on here.

"Hi, I'm Adri."

The bigger one nodded. "Right, the new cheerleader. You're Cindi's sister, aren't you?"

"Yeah, what are your names?"

"I'm Vince and this is Reginald."

Reginald, the smaller, African American guy, gave me a look that was almost as smoldering as Tristan usually hit me with.

"The pleasure is all ours. I've seen you cheering at the games, you're slamming out there, girl."

It took me a second to process his compliment. The look threw me for a bit of a loop. I still wasn't used to guys who were that confident directing those kinds of looks at me. What was it with the football team—did they all take classes on how to sweep girls off of their feet with nothing more than heavy eye contact?

Vince apparently didn't want to just give up without a fight. "You are awesome out there. You're a year older than Cindi though, right?"

"Yeah, I'm a junior."

"Why didn't you try out last year or the year before? You're good enough and hot enough you would have totally made it onto the team."

"They wouldn't have wanted me back then. I...well, I lost a bunch of weight recently."

Vince's smile hadn't been quite as impressive as Reginald's but it lost most of its brilliance as he realized what I'd just said. *Once a porker, always a porker.* Maybe that wasn't exactly what he was thinking, but I was pretty sure it was close.

Things had already gotten awkward, but before they could get more awkward someone put their arm around my waist. I could only think of one person who would display such easy familiarity and I turned to smile at Jackson in relief that he'd been able to come after all. Only it wasn't Jackson.

Tristan started to return my smile, but stopped when I frowned at him.

"I liked it better when you were happy to see me."

I stepped away from him, moving his arm away from my body, but he followed—not too aggressively, but enough so that I knew he was going to be harder than normal to discourage.

"I wasn't excited to see *you*, I thought you were someone else."

"Jackson, right? What is it about that freak show that draws you in so much?"

"He's not a freak show, but for starters he doesn't throw himself at me like a drunken idiot."

Tristan smiled, but it was just a happy smile rather than something designed to turn me into a little puddle at his feet. "Just because he doesn't know how to have fun doesn't make him better boyfriend material than me."

He'd completely missed the point, but until then I hadn't realized that he'd been drinking. As he got closer to me again I could smell it on his breath and I winced a little. I had zero experience dealing with drunk people, but I had a suspicion that Tristan was going to be even more difficult drunk than he was sober.

"Tristan, please give me a little space."

"I could do that, but I have an even better idea. Let's go find somewhere private and talk about us."

He'd pretty much backed me into a corner. I looked over at Vince and Reginald, hoping that they'd come help me, but it was like I didn't even exist now. They were busy talking to each other and very carefully not looking over at Tristan and me.

"There is no us, Tristan."

"I know you keep saying that, but we could be incredible together. You don't know how to deal with all of the crap that comes with being in the popular crowd, but I do."

His face was only a couple of inches away from me, but I shook my head, carefully so as not to make him think I was trying for a kiss or something.

"I don't want to be part of the popular crowd; I just want to be left alone."

He leaned in even closer so that he could whisper in my ear. "That's too bad, because you're already part of the popular crowd despite how hard they are trying to keep you out. You're a cheerleader and you're hot, that automatically puts you in. You're lucky though because I want you for my girlfriend. You're not bitchy like the rest of the girls on the squad. I've had enough of that to last me a lifetime."

It was more insight than I expected out of Tristan, and I mentally moved him up a couple of ranks. He was probably still a jerk, but the mere fact that he'd decided not to let Missy and her friends be mean to him was a plus. There didn't seem to be many guys who could walk away from a hot girl regardless of how badly they were being treated.

The sheer shock of finding out that he was more than just a pretty face and a strong arm set me back enough that I didn't have an immediate response. I never got to find out what I ultimately would have said because a flicker of movement pulled my head around so that I could see past Tristan.

I was just in time to see Cindi walk up and pull Tristan back away from me. I opened my mouth to thank her, but she slapped the side of my face before I could get the words out. My ears were ringing badly enough that I missed the first part of what she said.

"…stupid whore! Is there anything you won't try to take from me? You're a fat cow and I'll hate you forever."

Cindi stormed off towards our bedroom and Tristan grabbed my arm, stopping me from following her.

"Let me go! This is your fault."

Tristan shook his head and pulled me in close again despite the fact that I was pushing on his chest with all of my might.

"I told you I could find out who pranked you. Don't you want to know who it was?"

"I'm only going to tell you this once. Let me go right now so I can go try to explain stuff to Cindi."

"What if Cindi was involved in ruining your hair?"

The question hit me with nearly as much force as Cindi's slap from a few seconds earlier. I looked at Tristan, trying to determine whether or not he was telling the truth, but I couldn't seem to get past the fact that he no longer looked drunk.

The girl who'd stolen my phone had told me he was dangerous, but somehow I'd thought I'd be safe as long as I wasn't alone around him. Looking at him now I wasn't so sure of that.

"Was she?"

"She didn't spray the dye on you if that's what you're asking, but she knew about it and didn't even try to stop them."

"Who sprayed me?"

"Missy and Wendy, but everyone else on the squad other than Sheree knew. They figured that she wouldn't be able to keep her mouth shut if they told her."

"Why are you telling me this?"

He looked at me for several seconds before responding. "I don't like bullies, but I really don't like people who pretend to be your friend and then stab you in the back."

My mind was spinning too fast to make sense of everything that I'd just heard, but I suddenly wasn't so sure that I wanted to go and try to smooth things over with Cindi.

"Do you still want me to let you go? Are you still going to go tell Cindi that you're sorry?"

"Yes to the first question, and I don't know about the second part."

Tristan released my wrists and then stepped back slightly so that I could get around him.

"What are you going to go do now?"

"I'm not sure, I guess I'll just try to keep this party from boiling over into something that gets me into trouble."

Tristan nodded. "That makes sense. How can I help?"

"I'm going to go sit in the kitchen to make sure that nobody goes down into the basement and messes with my mom's photography gear. Whatever you can do to help out in the living room would be awesome"

"That's smart, otherwise someone will probably sneak down there to...well, you know, for some privacy."

"Yeah, I know. If you can just try to keep people from breaking things or getting too loud that would be awesome. Also make sure nobody crashes."

"Sure, I can have a couple of the guys help me take care of that. Would you rather I just shut the party down instead?"

"Actually, yeah, that would be even better, except if I did that I'm not sure that Cindi would ever forgive me."

Tristan shrugged. "Okay, I can respect that. I think you're giving her way too much credit, but I can respect that. You realize that you're going to owe me one after this, right?"

I nodded. I knew he was going to want something in return, but I still didn't even know if he was safe to be around, let alone if he was the kind of guy that I'd be willing to date.

The appearance of the sunflowers at the last away game had distracted me from the crazy girl's warning, but I hadn't forgotten about it. My number one problem was still figuring out a way to throw the old man off of my scent, but I still had to keep in mind the fact that Tristan was more dangerous than he seemed.

Maybe the girl I'd saved really was crazy, but I couldn't take that chance. I needed to find a way out of all of this, but I had to do it without Tristan, the old man, or anyone else realizing that I was on to all of them.

Chapter 21

To say that I spent the next few hours in a state of misery would have been a profound understatement. Tristan was as good as his word, keeping at least one fight from starting and generally stopping things from getting out of hand.

A little after 3 a.m. he told me the party had been going long enough. I wasn't sure he was right until he took my hand and pulled me to the doorway between the kitchen and the living room. I'd never seen so many people passed out in one place before. It was hard to tell how many of them had had too much to drink and how many of them had just fallen asleep because it was so late, but Tristan was a pro at getting people to their feet and sorted out. He sent the drunk girls home with other members of the cheer squad who were less drunk and then he and a few of the other guys from the team started hauling their teammates outside.

By the time 4 a.m. finally arrived, the house was empty except for Cindi and me. I looked around at the mess in the living room and the disaster in the family room and decided to just go sleep in my parents' room.

It was a good plan except for the fact that Cindi had locked their door and I didn't have any idea where she'd put the key. I stood outside of the door to our bedroom for a couple of minutes before deciding that regardless of how big of a fight it provoked with Cindi, I wasn't going to be sleeping anywhere other than my own bed.

"Open the door, Cindi."

"Go to hell!"

I wanted to yell at her. The anger that had been slowly simmering before the party was at a roiling boil now and it took all of my willpower to take a calming breath instead of coming unglued on her.

"Open the door or I'll call Tristan up and have him come put his foot through the door."

It was a bluff. I didn't have his phone number, but it did the trick. Two seconds later Cindi had the door open and was in my face.

"How dare you even threaten to get him back over here. I can't believe that I felt sorry for you. I thought it would be fun to have a sister I could do things I liked with instead of one who just sat around like some kind of depressed lump all of the time."

I started to respond, but she'd already moved into my personal space and I realized that this could escalate beyond just words.

"I had this childish dream of us being best friends, but instead you've done everything you could to ruin my life ever since I got you on the team. It's just like Mom said."

My rage hadn't disappeared, but between one second and the next it went from hot and frothy to a frozen anger that I could feel corroding everything it touched.

"What do you mean just like Mom said?"

"You're just like Dad. You make everything about yourself, you push people around, you take and take from them to get yourself ahead and then when they finally start to stand up for themselves, you pull the old 'woe is me' card."

"Mom told you that?"

"She told me that and a lot more. Dad knew that we were home when they were fighting, he knew that I was listening when he called me a spoiled brat. That's what he does, he hurts people in order to get what he wants. That's the truth, Adri. That's the truth that Dad doesn't want you to know."

I reached up and slapped her, hard. I didn't even think about what I was doing, but I hit her with enough force that she stumbled into the wall behind her.

"Let's talk about the truth, Cindi. The truth is that you *are* a spoiled brat even though Dad never actually said that. How much have he and Mom spent on your clothes just over the last year? Two thousand dollars? Three? How much did they spend the year before that or the one before that?"

She tried to get a word in edgewise but I just yelled louder. "That's Dad's money, Cindi. He slaves away year after year trying to put something away for retirement, but you just keep sucking him dry. Mom doesn't help, she just keeps buying more and more crap that doesn't do anything to actually make her a better photographer. The truth is that you're a spoiled brat because Mom's a spoiled brat. She doesn't even bother to cook dinner anymore and half of the time you and I have to do all of the cleaning too."

"She's good and you know it, Adri. She's going to be rich and famous and then you and Dad are going to be sorry that you doubted her."

"I don't care whether she becomes rich and famous or not. I know that's hard for you to believe, but that's the *truth*. Tonight I finally realized something that I should have realized years ago. I stopped trying in school, stopped trying socially because of you and her. I stopped working for any kind of worthwhile goal because I let your example convince me that the only way to get ahead in life is to use people like the two of you have used Dad. I was wrong, that's not actually the case, but it doesn't change the fact that I'd rather be a dirt-poor failure than succeed by knocking the people who love me, the people who I should love back, into the dirt and walking across their backs to get what I want without ever thinking about the cost to them."

Cindi ran down the hall without looking back. I heard the front door slam and thought about going after her, but in the end I just waited a few minutes to see whether or not she'd come back before locking both the front and the back doors and going to bed.

She knew where the spare key was hidden. I was done sacrificing to keep her happy.

Chapter 22

The next few days were surreal. The house was still a mess because I refused to clean up after Cindi and she hadn't come back after leaving the night of the party. Our room and the kitchen were both fine and I did clean up the bathroom, but Cindi was the one who had planned the party and she was the one who was going to be in the most trouble if the house was a disaster when Mom and Dad got home.

Some clothes disappeared out of Cindi's side of the closet sometime between when I left for school on Thursday and when I got back home, so she must have ditched school to come back for just long enough to get some of her things.

Tristan had pleasantly surprised me by continuing to be helpful without pushing for some kind of payback for his assistance the night of the party. He slipped a note into my locker telling me that Cindi was staying with

Missy. I'd been starting to get worried about her by that point, so it was nice to know, even if it did feel like she was escaping the consequences of her actions yet again.

Things with Jackson were still strained at practice on Thursday night. He still pretended like everything was okay, but he spent most of practice with Wendy and didn't walk me to my last class. I'd nursed some kind of childish hope that I'd been wrong, that he hadn't really been freaked out by my inviting him to Cindi's party, but it was obvious that I hadn't misread that particular set of signs. Seeing him nearly every day at cheerleading practice hurt a lot more than I expected it to.

It wasn't even the whole almost-boyfriend part of things either, it was the simple fact that I didn't have anyone to talk to about all of the craziness that was going on with Cindi. I probably would have even started opening up a little to Tristan if he'd been around more, but apparently his coach was extra worried about the game on Friday because by the time we made it out onto the field they were already practicing and they kept going until after Miss Winters released us to go home.

The rest of the cheerleaders were as bad as I'd expected them to be. I heard an almost constant stream of whispered insults whenever I was around any of the other girls on Thursday, but apparently they were still wincing from having to pay for my new clothes because nobody did any more than just talk.

It was pretty clear that the battle lines had been drawn and it was Missy, Cindi and everyone else against me. Sheree was the only one of the girls who didn't actively hate me, which meant that the rest of the cheerleaders were starting to exclude her too. She was too good of a person to just turn on me because everyone else was being mean to her now, but I could see that it was taking a toll on her. Sheree was so nice that usually everyone couldn't help but respond in kind, this was probably the first time she'd ever had real enemies.

It took all of my strength just to make it through Thursday so that I could go home and curl up in my bed. As I drifted off to sleep I realized that the only positive thing that had happened all week was the fact that I hadn't been dream walking.

It seemed like not having dream walked for the last few nights had recharged my metaphysical batteries, because as soon as I fell asleep I found myself in another dream that was too vivid to be a normal one.

I turned in place, taking in my surroundings. I was in a reddish-brown wasteland of a desert that was different than my home in almost every way, but as I blinked it became even more different. There wasn't much in the way of vegetation, a few cacti and some scrubby brush, but every living thing seemed to be giving off a faint white light that was only visible due to the fact that the sliver of a moon above gave off almost no light.

I tried to manipulate the dream, tried to create a tree just in front of me, but the result was ghostly and short-lived. Now that I was positive I was in someone else's dream, I looked around for somewhere to hide, but before I could start running towards the dry streambed that I'd identified, a huge black wolf came bounding up out of it.

I knew I should be scared. The wolf was way bigger than any dog I'd ever seen before. It looked like it could easily tear me in half with a single bite, and yet there was something other than just wild savagery in its eyes.

A cool breeze kicked up between one second and the next, but even more incredible was the fact that the wolf was gone now, replaced by a guy who was about the same size as Jackson. He was looking away from me at first, as though worried about someone following him.

I started to take a step backwards in an effort to get somewhere I could hide, but he turned before I could get very far. My breath caught as I saw his face for the first time. He was gorgeous with wavy dark hair and piercing blue eyes, but it was more than that.

In a way that I couldn't explain, this guy was the piece that had been missing from my life. It was like having a dislocated shoulder put back into place. This whole time I'd been feeling an almost irresistible draw towards Jackson and it had all been because physically Jackson looked like this guy.

It was like I'd been wowed by a child's watercolors for months only to now see a Monet. I couldn't go back to just being happy at the prospect of being with Jackson. I was pretty sure that I'd never be satisfied now unless I was with this guy.

The resemblance to Kaleb was clear, but where Kaleb was somehow unfinished, somehow lacking some critical ingredient, the guy looking back at me now was a kind of perfection that went beyond just the physical. I'd never before realized that you could see someone's character in their countenance, but with him I could.

He was dangerous. The mere fact that I was sharing his dream would have told me that even if I hadn't just seen him transform from a wolf, but I somehow knew he wouldn't hurt me, not casually, not without a reason, and not if there was any other option.

"You're Kaleb's son, aren't you?"

The words slipped out without conscious effort on my part, but they didn't seem to alarm him.

"Yes, although I'd give a lot to have it be otherwise. Who are you?"

"My name is Adri."

It was a reckless risk, but it never even crossed my mind to refuse him my name. I wasn't sure that I was capable of refusing him anything.

"Why do I feel like I know you, Adri? Why do I look at you and wonder when you cut your hair? It should be longer than that."

My heart was in my throat. For a second I thought I wouldn't be able to manage anything more than a shrug.

"I'm not sure, but I think I know what you mean. I feel like I know you from somewhere, like I should be incredibly happy to see you, like you're a long-lost friend of some kind or another."

He didn't look satisfied with that answer, but it was the only one I could offer to him. We stood in silence for several seconds before he shook himself and then looked back up at me.

"Curious. You'd think that I'd become immune to the surprise of having the world drop impossible things into my lap, but so far that hasn't been the case. Why have you brought me here, Adri? You're not one of us, are you?"

"One of you?"

"The moonborn, a shape shifter."

"No, I'm not. How did you know?"

His smile was sad. "You didn't respond to my transformation with a flare of power from your own beast. That's a pretty good sign that you're free from my curse."

"Is it really a curse?"

"Most of the time. You don't know what it's like to have something alien inside of you, something that has its own ideas of right and wrong, its own ideas of how things should be handled."

It wasn't something that I'd ever considered. The movies made werewolves and the like seem so glamorous. Maybe not as cool as vampires, but still something awesome.

"It's got to be pretty awesome though to be stronger and faster than normal humans though, right?"

He seemed to consider my question for several seconds.

"I suppose. There are a lot of times in my life where my beast's speed and strength were the only things that kept me alive, but then again, I wouldn't have been in those situations if I hadn't been a shape shifter in the first place."

"I guess that makes sense. The truth is that I didn't actually bring you anywhere. This is your dream; I'm just sharing it with you."

He looked around at our surroundings. "This isn't like any other dream I've ever had before. It's more real, more vivid than it should be."

I looked over at him in confusion. "This is more vivid than *I* can usually manage. That's odd, but it has to be your dream because I can't change our surroundings."

A frown of concentration briefly spoiled his expression, and then a large rose bush grew up out of the ground like we were watching some kind of time-lapse photography.

"I guess you're right, this is my dream, but you being here has somehow made it more than I can manage on my own."

A second later he made a black, wrought-iron bench shimmer into view. He sat down on it like he'd been carrying the weight of the world on his shoulders, like he'd been dying to put his load down and rest, but hadn't been able to do so in longer than he could remember.

"Well, Adri, I guess the proper question isn't why you brought me here, but rather why you've brought yourself here."

"Does there have to be a reason?"

"Not necessarily, but I'm starting to believe that gifts like the one you've displayed tonight operate out of need more often than not. It's possible that we met here on this particular night out of nothing more than chance, but I doubt it. I suspect that you have a need greater than any you've ever before known, and that some part of you thinks that I can help you."

My throat had gone dry. It took a couple of attempts to get a response out.

"Even if that is the case, why should that matter? Why would you bother helping me?"

His smile was odd. It was mocking, but he wasn't mocking me. It was more like he was mocking some memory or misadventure from his past.

"Trust. It always comes down to trust, doesn't it?"

"I guess so. I can't survive in the world that my ability has thrown me into. I'm not fast or strong or deadly. The only thing keeping me alive is the fact that I'm safely anonymous here where I do all of my interacting with other supernatural beings."

"I guess I spoke more truly than I realized. Your problem is deciding who to trust. You're in physical danger already, aren't you?"

"How did you know?"

He suddenly looked tired, almost as though my asking him that simple question had forced him to pick his burdens back up in some form or fashion.

"I didn't know, but it was a pretty safe bet. The world I live in, the one that your dream walking ability seems to be slowly but surely sucking you into, is a savage, lawless place. Anyone you encounter here, anyone who's more than just a normal human, is going to be looking for anything that they can to track you back to your physical body. It's reflexive. Humans are a stewardship to be protected—or cattle to be preyed upon, depending on who you're talking to—but anyone who's not a human, anyone who has the potential to be a threat of some kind or another, either has to be confirmed as an ally or eliminated."

"I'm no threat to anyone."

"Sure you are. Our dreams are the only place where most people really give into their subconscious desires. When you see someone here you see them as they truly are, you see them with all of the illusions stripped back, you encounter them at their most vulnerable. It's a subtle power, but it's incredibly powerful."

"So what should I do? Are you going to come riding to my rescue?"

It wasn't my imagination; he was looking more and more tired by the second.

"No. If that's the help that your power thought I could provide then it was sadly mistaken. I can't even rescue those who are the closest to me. I'm not even sure I have the power to protect myself through the storm I can see approaching on the horizon."

"What about if I told you where I am? Could you send someone to help me? Even just someone to help me disappear? I'm…"

He held up his hand abruptly, cutting me off before I could say anything else. "Don't tell me that. You're safer if I don't know. Not that I would hurt you myself, but I can't promise the same for my father. He looks at people and he doesn't see individuals, he sees weapons and tools, implements to be used up in his quest for more power and influence."

It was hard to get much clearer than that. His father was bad, really bad. That didn't necessarily mean that someone working against him was good, but it was a starting point.

"So your father can't be trusted, but what about someone I saw spying on him?"

He looked at me for several seconds. "You mean in the dream? Tell me about him."

"I don't know. Male, older, like forties or fifties. He looks like a Native American."

"He was spying on my father?"

"Yeah, we were at the top of a building looking down at your dad, but it was odd, like the ground was only a few feet away. Your dad started climbing the building to get to us and the Native American guy seemed like he was going to take my head off. He turned into some kind of giant wolf-man and nearly killed me."

"Was that the only time you saw him?"

"No, I somehow pulled him into one of my dreams. He tried to get me to tell him where I lived, and then he taught me a little bit about how dream walking worked, but when I asked him about your dad he shifted shapes again and tried to kill me. Neither experience particularly made me feel like he was someone I could trust. By the way, you've never even told me your name."

"My name is Alec."

"Okay, Alec, what do I do? What help can you provide me? I've come across two other even scarier people over the last couple of weeks. One of them knows what school I go to and he knows that I'm a cheerleader."

"Very little I'm afraid. The most I can do is tell you that I think you're dealing with Dream Stealer."

"Who's Dream Stealer and why do you think he's the Native American?"

"Kaleb, my father, is part of a group, a terrible group. Dream Stealer was also a member of that same group at one point, but he's since started working against them. Until tonight, until I met you, he was the only person I'd ever heard of who could interact with people during a dream. Not only that, he's a shape shifter, like me."

"Are there a lot of you?"

"Too many and not enough all at once. We're not entirely in control of ourselves. Mostly we do okay, but if we're injured—or threatened in some way—sometimes our inner beast takes over."

"So maybe he's more trustworthy than he appeared?"

Alec nodded. "Possibly. It's always possible though that you weren't actually dealing with Dream Stealer. I've never heard a reliable description of what Dream Stealer's physical body looks like, I'm not even positive that he's a man. Everyone talks as though he is, but by all accounts it is rare for anyone to interact with him in the flesh. He generally sticks to the dream where he's the most powerful and least exposed. His tactics are...disturbing though. He's done things that a few weeks ago I would have said would make him irredeemable. I'm not so sure now, but even so he's not someone to interact with lightly."

I'd been standing, looking down at him on the bench, but now I let myself drop down to sit next to him.

"You've given me more questions than you've answered for me. After talking to you I still don't know whether the Native American is this Dream Stealer you've told me about, and even if they are the same person, I still don't know whether or not I can actually trust him. Are you sure you don't want to just tell me what to do?"

Alec's smile was sad, somehow sadder than the situation seemed to call for. "Adri, I'm not qualified to tell anyone what to do right now. I'm not even qualified to be running my own life. In the last little while, I've found out that much of what I've always believed was nothing more than a convenient set of lies meant to keep me safely out of the way. People I thought I could trust have been deceiving me so they could do whatever it was they thought would benefit them the most."

"I'm sorry, that sounds pretty terrible."

"It is, but I just keep telling myself that it was the living in ignorance that was awful. Knowledge is power and sometimes even freedom. As much as it feels like the sky is falling now that I know, it's better this way."

I swallowed a couple of times. "If I choose wrong then I probably won't live long enough to correct my mistake. There is a decided chance that we'll never see each other again."

"That's true, but you don't necessarily have to choose right away, you don't even know that you'll ever see the Native American again. There are a lot of different ways that your life could go from here and not all of them are bad."

"You don't seem worried."

This smile was less sad, like he was still mourning the past, but the future wasn't as bleak as maybe it could have been.

"I'm not. I can't tell the future any more than you can, but I feel a profound connection to you. I can't believe that the universe would put us together for just these few moments and then make it so we never meet again. You'll choose the right course and I'll somehow make it out of the morass I'm currently mired in."

I knew that my smile was a bit hesitant, a bit forced, but I was smiling, which was more than I'd expected to be able to do a few minutes ago when I'd realized I was in someone else's dream again. Instead of fighting for my life, I'd found that missing piece of myself that I'd only recently realize was absent.

"Do you think we'll remember this dream when we wake up?"

He looked at me oddly. "Why wouldn't we?"

"I don't know why, but these dreams tend to fade away once I'm awake. It's like I'm two different people and the other person can't wrap her mind around what happens in the dream. I can remember basic stuff like the fact that I'm in danger or that someone helped me, but so much of the actual emotion is nothing more than vapor."

"Well then, I hope that we both buck the trend where this particular dream is concerned. I would hate to lose this connection with you, slight though it is, because my memory wasn't up to holding onto the full measure of what I'm feeling right now."

"It doesn't feel like a *slight* connection."

I wouldn't have said that he could look shy. Bashfulness had no place on that justifiably confident face, but there was no arguing with my eyes. He was unsure of himself, possibly even as unsure as I was.

"No, you're right, this isn't a trivial thing, but it feels like it could be even more, like it could be something truly epic and not in a way most people use it these days."

"I know. It's actually a little scary."

"Yes, scary, but wonderful and exciting in a way that I thought I'd lost the ability to feel. Little kids get excited about Santa Claus and Christmas. Adults just cautiously anticipate."

I smiled as he slid imperceptibly closer. "Santa Claus and Christmas, and birthdays and the Fourth of July. That's a pretty good description of what I'm feeling right now."

Alec moved in slowly. He took forever to cover the painfully small distance between us, but when his lips touched mine it felt like my heart was going to explode.

His kiss was soft and gentle, but there was a sense of controlled power to it, like I was doing something dangerous, like I might not survive if he relaxed his control for the briefest of instants. He pulled me closer, effortlessly sliding me across the bench with one arm as his other hand cradled the side of my face.

There was more heat to his touch now and I could feel the iron control that I was realizing was an integral part of him, start to fray. It was terrifying and exciting all at once. I was scared to death of what might happen if he ever really lost control, but at the same time I wanted to know all of him, even the dangerous, feral parts that he normally kept tightly locked away.

His teeth bit down on my bottom lip, not hard enough to draw blood, but hard enough to tell me that he was even closer than I'd realized to losing control.

I seemed to have forgotten how to breathe. I gasped for air, I needed it, needed to be able to talk, but I didn't know if I was going to tell him to stop or if I was going to beg him to just let go of the inhibitions that were the only thing ensuring my safety.

I opened my mouth to say something when I heard a howl that made my skin crawl. Alec was shaking as he drew back from me.

"Even here, even in my dreams it seems I can't be happy, can't be free of the demons that chase me out there."

Now there was more than one creature howling and Alec looked up at me with eyes that had gone a paler, colder shade of blue.

"Get out now if you're able to, Adri. What comes next won't be pretty."

I shook my head. "No, I want to stay. I can help you."

"It's my dream, remember? I can influence it more than you can. Besides, I'll fight better knowing that you're safe."

I meant to argue with him, but before I could really get started *something* stepped out from behind a large rock. My heart skipped a beat as I took in a beast that should only be able to exist in nightmares. It was tall, somewhere between seven and eight feet, darkly furred with a face that was too unfinished to describe other than that it seemed to have hints of both canine and feline characteristics.

Claws that were nearly as long as my forearm tipped its fingers, gleamed darkly in the moonlight, but it was the fangs that I couldn't seem to look away from. If madness had been made flesh and bone and then given teeth they would have looked like this, impossibly big but still somehow fitting in a mouth that was obviously designed for rending and tearing.

The creature seemed to be in no hurry and a second later I realized why as a second and a third of its kind stepped into view. Alec looked back at me with concern on his face.

"I'd hoped not to expose you to this, to the monster I carry inside of me."

Alec's transformation tore through him before anything else could be said and my breath caught as I saw what now occupied the space where he'd been standing. A second ago I would have said that the three monsters that were approaching us looked like the Native American when he was in his wolf-man form, but now that I had Alec's wolf-man shape to compare them to I realized how wrong I would have been. They were larger than he or the Native American had been and where the creatures were unfinished and bestial, Alec looked like someone had taken human intelligence and simply crafted a new home for it.

He looked back at me with the same ice-blue eyes he'd had a moment before, and then lunged towards the closest beast in an explosion of speed that I somehow knew I shouldn't be able to follow. The first creature tried to dodge out of Alec's way, but he materialized a large rock in the direction it was trying to move and then shoved his fist into its chest as it bounced off of the rock that hadn't been there a second before.

The second creature jumped Alec, crashing into his back before he could spin around after finishing off the first enemy. Claws ripped across

Alec's back, but rather than tearing through flesh in a spray of blood as I'd expected them to, they skittered off in a spray of sparks.

Alec tried to turn around to capitalize on the surprise he'd created by manifesting armor underneath his skin, but the second creature had hold of him and although its claws didn't seem to be making any headway on his flesh it had him effectively immobilized.

Alec's third enemy struck, and again the claws bounced off, but this time there was blood along with the sparks. The second creature bit down on Alec's shoulder with its fangs and even I could see that Alec was weakening. He could only manipulate the dream around him to a certain degree and the attacks he was dealing with were already pushing him beyond his capabilities.

I stepped forward, wanting to help, and then I remembered my certainty that I could be killed in the dream. Oddly enough, it wasn't my vulnerability that stopped me, it was the fear that my being here was imparting the same weakness to Alec. In a normal dream Alec might be defeated, but he'd wake the next morning unharmed.

I didn't know the limits of my power, but he'd said that he couldn't normally dream in this level of detail. If that meant that I'd sucked him more strongly into the dream then the most helpful thing I could do was simply flee as fast as I was able.

The two creatures had him on the ground now. There was more blood and his struggles seemed to be weakening, but I forced my worry for him to one side and focused on the real world. It was surprisingly easy to return to the feeling of cotton sheets on my bare arms. As I lapsed back into a normal, dreamless sleep I had two thoughts.

The first was to hope that he was okay, that he would survive, both the dream fight and whatever real-world conflict he'd said was so imminent. The second thought was to wonder if it had been so easy to come back to myself this time because part of me didn't believe any reality that included someone like him—especially someone like him who had such strong feelings for me—could possibly be real.

Chapter 23

The dream with Alec was still with me on Friday morning when my alarm pulled me awake. I reflexively hit the snooze button, but I didn't feel like going to sleep despite the fact that I was exhausted. I couldn't remember a time when I'd been more tired, but it was the kind of tired that wouldn't be solved by sleeping in an extra fifteen minutes.

I knew I was worn out from dream walking with Alec, but I hadn't expected for it to hit me this hard. Either Alec was somehow more resistant to my gift than the other people I'd encountered in the dream, or he was much further away than they'd been. There was a kind of dull ache behind my eyes that seemed to say that I'd pushed too hard and stretched something inside of my head that needed some time to recover still.

I was going to be feeling the aftereffects of my time with Alec for at least the next day or two, but I didn't regret the time we'd spent together. I now had a potential ally, one who said he couldn't do much for me, but who knew more about the world I was being dragged into than I did. One who somehow knew me without ever having met me. One who felt drawn to me in the same inexplicable way that I was drawn to him.

I stayed in bed thinking about Alec, wondering whether my leaving the dream had been enough to save him, until my alarm went off again. One thing was for certain, in a few days, once I'd given myself a chance to recover from this last excursion, I was going to try and reestablish contact with Alec. Maybe he was right and there wasn't much else he could do to help me, but I had more reasons to be with him than just the possibility of safety.

I got an unexpected call just before I walked out the door to go to school.

"Hello, this is Adri."

"Hi, Adri, it's Missy. I'm just calling to tell you to bring your light uniform to school with you today."

"I thought we always wore our dark uniforms to away games."

"Yes, usually, but there was some kind of screw-up somewhere so the team is wearing their light jerseys today."

"Okay, thanks, Missy."

I went back to my room and grabbed my light skirt and shell, but I left my other uniform in my duffle bag too. I knew I was being paranoid, but that didn't mean that I was necessarily wrong. I wasn't going to trust Missy any further than I absolutely had to.

I practically flew to school. Classes went by in a blur that was eerily similar to the way I'd lost time after I'd realized that Jackson wasn't interested in me. This was better though because I was still aware of what was going on around me—I just didn't care about all of the stupid, petty crap.

Without the constant distractions involved in trying to ignore the whispers all around me, I managed to catch up on most of the homework I'd missed out on earlier in the week. As focused as I was, I still remembered to keep an eye out for the rest of the squad. A lot of the girls just wore their uniforms all day on the day of a game, so I figured that was one way to settle the question of whether we were supposed to wear dark uniforms or light uniforms.

Not too surprisingly, it turned out that none of them were wearing their uniforms today, which pretty much confirmed that Missy was trying to screw with me and she had all of the other girls in on it. I made a mental note to ask Sheree or Tristan what they'd been told as far as what color of uniform to wear and then just continued on with my day.

I'd started to gain back a little bit of weight as a result of not dreaming for so many days, not enough for anyone to notice with my clothes on, but enough that I'd been feeling a little better about having to go to the doctor so that Miss Winters would stop worrying that I had some kind of eating disorder.

All of that progress had been washed away as a result of dream walking with Alec. It was interesting that I hadn't gone below my lowest weight, but I was right back to it. I loaded up with an extra slice of pizza at lunch, wondering the whole time if my gift was somehow self-regulating. It was like my body had known that I'd pushed it as far as I safely could, so it had stopped me from dream walking until I'd had a chance to build back up the physical reserves that it knew I was going to need in order to be able to dream walk again.

I ate until I couldn't eat anymore and wondered the entire time if I could solve my dream walking problem simply by keeping myself too skinny for my body to permit another midnight excursion. It was an interesting possibility, but one that came with some very real risks. I didn't want to think about what might happen if I was wrong and got sucked into an extended dream session when I didn't have enough body fat to supply the energy the dream required.

It was possible that I'd just snap out of the dream once I couldn't sustain the exertion required, but it was also possible that if someone was holding me in the dream like the Native American had tried to do, that my heart would simply stop beating.

Between thoughts about Alec, my classes, and worries about my weight, I forgot to track down Sheree and Tristan. By the time I realized my mistake I was already headed towards my last class. I told myself that it didn't matter one way or the other because I had both of my uniforms, but that didn't stop me from stewing over it for most of the next hour.

The locker room had its normal complement of girls from the last PE class of the day, but not a single other member of the squad, which was even more evidence that something fishy was going on. I wanted to scream over the fact that Missy and the others were still being so petty, but I just took a deep breath and told myself that the worst that would happen was that I'd show up to the school bus in the wrong uniform and have to change once we got to the game.

Either way, the most that Missy could accomplish at this point would be to tip Miss Winters off to the fact that she was still hazing me. I just needed to hold things together for a little bit longer. Alec had said that he couldn't protect me, but no matter how much danger he was in, I was pretty sure that I'd be better off with him than staying here.

In another few days I'd dream walk to him again and try to convince him of that fact. Once that happened I could leave Missy and Cindi behind and never worry about them again.

I paused midway through pulling my white skirt up as the full impact of what I was considering hit me. I was fully prepared to leave my family behind and go off to be with some guy I didn't really know and the only person I was going to miss was my dad.

There were so many problems with that idea that I didn't know where to start. For all I knew Alec had used some kind of metaphysical whammy on me to create such an instant bond. I didn't think that was the case, but that didn't mean I was right. The fact that my life was so bad, that I'd connected so poorly with everyone around me that I was only going to miss one person, was just as scary.

I'd been convinced all of this time that I wasn't the one with the problem, but what if I was wrong there too? Everyone else around me seemed to be able to make friends and have fun spending time with other people; I was the clear anomaly there.

I forced myself to continue getting dressed. Those were all worries that I was going to have to deal with sooner or later, but being stalked by the old man, the Native American, and maybe even the wax woman had to supersede everything else. If Alec could get me away to somewhere safe then I was going to accept his help.

I wasn't really surprised when I went out to the bus and saw that all of the other girls were in their dark blue uniforms. I wasn't surprised, but that didn't mean that I wasn't mad. I was actually super-pissed. The one redeeming thing about the whole situation was that they hadn't screwed Sheree over too.

Miss Winters was looking down at her clipboard when I walked up with Sheree only a couple of feet behind me.

"Adri, what are you doing? You know that we always wear dark colors to away games."

I tried to keep the anger off of my face, but I probably didn't succeed entirely. "I got a call from Missy this morning telling me that we were supposed to wear our light uniforms today."

"Are you sure that's what she said?"

"Yes, I'm positive. It's fine though. It sounded fishy so I went ahead and brought my dark uniform too."

I could see the relief in the way Miss Winters' shoulders relaxed. My having outsmarted Missy meant that Miss Winters wouldn't have to further escalate things with the rest of the team.

"Okay, I'll have to think about this, but at least you'll be able to change once we get there."

Miss Winters waved me into the bus and I took my usual spot towards the front, only a little away from where Miss Winters sat to split the boys and the girls up. Jackson hardly even looked at me as I walked past him, but it wasn't exactly unexpected and it hurt a lot less after meeting Alec the night before.

Missy walked forward as though wanting to talk to one of her spotters, but on her way back she stopped at my seat, resting one hand on the fake, brown plastic leather in front of me.

"It's too bad that you didn't remember to wear the right uniform, Adri."

"Yeah, if only someone hadn't told me that we were wearing the white ones today. Luckily I'm not as stupid as some people, so I brought both."

I zipped my duffle bag open just enough for her to see the dark blue fabric of my other uniform and then I gave her the kind of smirk that she usually bestowed upon me. She obviously wasn't happy, but she gave me a sugar-sweet look in return and then turned to Sheree who had just sat down across from me.

"Sheree, can you come sit in the back with us, please? Cindi and I need to talk to you about the routines we're going to use tonight. You know, flyer stuff."

"Shouldn't Adri be coming then?"

"No, Adri is just a backup and all three of us are here, so I'm sure her help won't be needed."

That last bit was said in the same tone as the rest, but she shot me a look that had enough poorly contained rage in it for me to see that she wasn't very happy at having her plan foiled. I wanted to stand up and punch her in the face, but I knew that would just backfire on me. Right now Miss Winters was on my side and I needed to keep it that way.

"I'm fine, Sheree. You should go back there and find out what's going on tonight. I'll just stay here and catch up on some homework or maybe I'll even take a nap."

I hadn't planned on saying that last bit, but as I said it I realized it was the truth. I'd been gamely going all day, but I was still suffering from the exhaustion inherent in dream walking for such a long time with Alec. I really would be happiest if I got a nap on the way to the game.

Besides, maybe this was the first step in Missy burying the hatchet with Sheree. I didn't want to lose my only friend on the team, but I wasn't selfish enough to think that it was okay for Sheree to be unhappy just so I could be a little less unhappy myself.

Sheree gave me a worried look, but allowed herself to be led back towards the rear of the bus. I watched the two of them sit down and then turned back towards the front of the bus myself and closed my eyes.

It must not have taken very long for the rocking motion of the bus to put me to sleep because it seemed like hardly any time at all passed before Miss Winters started chivying us all up and out of our seats.

"Come on, girls, we're a little behind schedule and this is a key game for our team. The Jaguars are favored to win state."

I'd been half worried that I'd end up dream walking during my nap, but that hadn't happened. Instead I'd slept so deeply that now I was groggy from being woken up. I checked to make sure that my backpack and duffle bag were both zipped up and then stood and followed the rest of the girls off of the bus.

"Adri, you need a locker room so that you can get changed. The girls' locker room is through those doors there and then on the far end of the gym on the right side. Hurry, please."

I nodded and started off in the direction she'd indicated. I found the girls' locker room without any problems and thankfully it was empty of girls from the other school when I arrived. I stripped off my white uniform and put on my blue uniform. The shell went on with no problem, but the skirt went over my hips too easily. For a second I worried that I'd somehow lost even more weight than I'd realized, but that couldn't be the case. My light uniform had fit just fine and both uniforms were the same size.

I let go of my skirt and watched as it instantly dropped down to my ankles. I stepped out of it and then picked it back up. The seam along the side had been cut. It had been fine the last time I'd worn it, I was even pretty sure that it had been fine when I'd put it into my bag this morning.

My mind spun as I tried to put the pieces together. Cindi had been pretty pissed at me the night of the party and she'd been in our room by herself for hours. She could have done it then, but that didn't fit very well with Missy's attempt to make me wear my white uniform today.

HUNTED

It didn't fit, but I couldn't think of any time today when my uniform hadn't been with me...any time *other* than while I'd been sleeping on the bus, sleeping after having shown Missy that I'd brought the correct uniform after all.

That fit perfectly. It was exactly like her. I could almost see her sitting on the bus trying not to giggle while she took scissors to my skirt. I had to give her credit too, she'd come up with her plan almost instantaneously, that had to be why she'd gotten Sheree to move back there with her. Once she had Sheree distracted then there hadn't been anything to stop her from sneaking up and taking my bag just long enough to do the damage.

I pulled my dark shell back off and slipped back into my white uniform. It only took a couple of minutes to find Miss Winters and the rest of the girls warming up on the visitors' side of the football field while the junior varsity players were doing their calisthenics.

"Adri, why are you still in that uniform? Did you have problems finding the locker room?"

I held up my skirt, making it easy for her to see that the seam had been cut. "I found it just fine, but sometime between when I woke up this morning and when I got off of the bus somebody destroyed my skirt."

I could see the wheels turning inside of her head.

"Do you think you know when it happened?"

I nodded. "I fell asleep on the bus, I'm pretty sure it happened then."

She looked at the pile of bags next to the bleachers where everyone else had put their stuff and then turned back to the rest of the squad. "Okay, I want everyone to stay where you are. Adri is going to keep an eye on all of you to make sure you don't try to ditch the evidence. While she does that, I'm going to search your bags so that I can figure out who ruined Adri's skirt. You can protest if you want and say that I'm violating your civil rights. That's fine, if you don't want me to search your bags I won't, but that will mean that you're off the team."

Some people moved around like they wanted to say something, but nobody did. Miss Winters gave them almost a full minute to protest and then walked over to their things and started opening up bags one at a time.

It took almost fifteen minutes for her to look through everyone's stuff, fifteen long, torturous minutes where it took all of my willpower not to turn and watch Miss Winters instead of watching the other girls, but finally Miss Winters called me over.

"I've checked all of the bags, Adri, and only one has scissors."

She said it in a low enough voice that I was pretty sure the other girls couldn't hear her, which I understood, but I didn't understand why she looked so unhappy.

"It was Missy, wasn't it?"

"No, Adri, it was Cindi. I'm sorry, I know this is going to make things bad at home, but I have to break this bullying ring."

"But Missy is the one who knew I had the other uniform, Missy's the one who got Sheree away so that there wouldn't be any witnesses when my skirt was ruined. Maybe she planted the scissors in Cindi's stuff."

Miss Winters shook her head. "I know this is hard to hear, but Cindi hasn't been acting like normal ever since you joined the team. I just found out tonight that she's failed three tests in the last two weeks."

"But that's my fau..."

I trailed off because the actual *number* of tests she'd failed finally sank in. Only one test could even remotely be construed as being my fault.

Miss Winters could obviously see that I was in shock. She patted me on the arm and then turned back to the other girls, holding Cindi's light-green bag up where everyone could see it.

"I don't enjoy doing this, but I can't let this kind of behavior go unpunished. Cindi, you're the only one who had scissors in your bag, you're the only one who could have done this. Do you have any explanation for your actions?"

Cindi had gone completely white, but she shook her head.

"Fine. You're suspended from the team effective immediately. You won't be cheering tonight and

Adri will be taking your place as the team's third flyer."

"You can't do that!"

Cindi looked like she was nearly ready to cry. Miss Winters' lips went into a tight, thin line.

"I just did. Frankly we would be having a similar conversation at some point if only because your grades are slipping so dramatically, but I'm giving you a chance to earn your way back onto the team because this is the first time I've had problems with you. Get your grades back up and then we can talk about next steps."

I thought Cindi was going to say something else, something that might prevent Miss Winters from ever being able to let her back on the team, but she didn't. Instead she just stalked off, disappearing around the corner of the Jaguars' school in just seconds.

"Does anyone else have anything they'd like to say?"

The rest of the team looked like they were in shock. I would have said that nobody on the whole squad had the guts to say anything after that kind of bombshell, but after only a couple of seconds Missy raised her hand.

"You said that Adri is going to perform with us still tonight? How is that possible? She doesn't have a matching uniform."

"I'm putting Adri in the front and center of each of the routines. It will look like we alternated the uniform colors on purpose and put everyone's focus on her. The same goes with the stunts, Adri will take the center position and you and Sheree will be on the sides in positions two and three."

Missy looked truly angry for the first time all night. She hadn't been mad when Cindi had been caught, hadn't been mad when Cindi was suspended from performing and practicing with us, but she was mad that I was going to be center stage for everything we did this game.

"With all due respect, Miss Winters, Adri isn't ready to be in the top spot. Just because she and her sister are having some kind of fight doesn't mean that she should be top dog around here."

"I'm not making her 'top dog'. I'm just making do as best I can given the fact that Adri isn't going to be able to wear the same uniform as everyone else."

"I think that you're punishing me for no good reason. I haven't done anything but you're bumping me out of the number one spot. When my mother hears about this she's going to convince the other members of the school board to fire you."

I half expected for Miss Winters to kick Missy off of the team then and there, but Sheree broke in before anything else could be said.

"It wasn't just Cindi who was involved in cutting up Adri's skirt. Missy was involved, she had to be."

"What do you mean, Sheree? Do you have some kind of proof that Missy helped Cindi?"

Miss Winters managed to keep her tone even. There wasn't anything in her manner that suggested just how badly she wanted Sheree to have some kind of hard evidence, but I was pretty sure everyone knew that was exactly what she was hoping for.

"No...I don't have any proof, but she wanted me away from Adri, that's the only explanation for her inviting me back to talk about our stunts for the game. I thought it was weird that she wanted to talk in the first place, but then once I got back there we didn't even talk. She and Cindi just whispered to each other for a couple of seconds and then Cindi disappeared."

Miss Winters closed her eyes for a couple of seconds and then shook her head. "That's not proof and I won't kick anyone off of the team without proof."

"But it's not fair! Missy is getting away with terrible things."

Before Sheree could say anything else Miss Winters held up her hand. "I won't kick a girl off of the team without proof, not even a girl who threatens me, but I still have full artistic control as far as who does what when it comes to our performances." She turned to me with such casualness that I knew she was putting on an act. "Adri, does what Sheree said match up with what you saw happen?"

I still felt numb inside, but nodded. That didn't seem to satisfy Miss Winters so I cleared my throat. "Yes. I mean I wasn't back there with them, but it was right after I showed Missy that I had my other uniform that she asked Sheree to come talk to her and Cindi. I remembered thinking it was odd at the time."

"I see. That isn't proof, but given everything that has happened, do you feel like you can trust Missy? Do you feel like you can work with her?"

"Honestly? No."

"What about you, Sheree?"

I'd never seen Sheree look so uncomfortable, but she shook her head. "No, she's doing terrible things. I don't trust her not to hurt Adri or me during our stunts."

I could tell that Miss Winters was still being very careful to keep the satisfaction out of her voice as she looked at Missy.

"There you have it, Missy. You've lost the trust of your fellow flyers, so it looks like we'll be going with just two flyers today until I can select and train replacements for you and Cindi."

I'd only thought that Missy was mad before. She was shaking now and her face had gone white.

"I'll kill you for this, for putting her above me!"

"You're off the team. There are some threats that I *have* to react to. Think very, very carefully about what you do next. I've got a dozen witnesses who just heard you and I can have a police report filed so fast your head will spin.

Any action you, or your mom, take at this point is going to look petty and retaliatory."

"This isn't over."

Even as she spit the words out at Miss Winters and me, Missy was turning and stalking away from the team.

"While I'm thinking about it, you'd probably better call your parents. You won't be riding home on the bus with us, so you'll need them to come and get you."

A few of the remaining girls looked like they were having a hard time breathing, but when Miss Winters gave us all one last chance to protest nobody took the opportunity. Satisfied that everyone was going to take her seriously, Miss Winters then proceeded to give us all our new assignments for each of our standard routines and cheers.

I kept thinking that I should be feeling something, but I seemed numb from the neck down and it didn't go away by the time the JV game started. Miss Winters had us starting out slow and easy, saving our big numbers for the second game so that we had a chance to get used to being down by two girls, but I could tell that I was doing better than normal even despite the simplicity of what we were doing.

I hit every mark exactly and my form was perfect the entire time. On another day I would have been excited, proud even of having done so well, but I just couldn't seem to muster up the emotional energy to feel anything.

We started stunting a few minutes before halftime and it was everything I remembered it being, just without the emotional thrill that I'd loved so much. I could feel my body prepare to take off by dumping adrenaline into my system, gravity clawed at me as I was launched upwards and then I experienced that timeless instant where I was perfectly weightless, but it was like it was happening to someone else.

Flying in front of a live crowd at a real game for the first time ever should have added to the intensity of the experience, but it was like some emotional conduit inside of me had been shattered.

The realization that I'd been robbed of my single favorite part of cheering started thawing out my insides. Instead of numb indifference, I started to feel a hot rage that demanded some kind of retribution against Missy and Cindi.

For a split second, if they'd been there and I'd had the strength to do so, I would have ripped them limb from limb, and then I suddenly realized what that would mean. I was distracted enough that I screwed up the landing, but Jackson caught me as effortlessly as always.

It took everything I had to stay there on the sidelines for two more minutes until the halftime horn sounded, but I forced myself to finish out the last few cheers with everyone else. I was thankful that it was an unseasonably warm night as I walked over to where Miss Winters was waiting for everyone. It was hot enough that the rest of the girls stopped off at our bags so that they could grab water bottles before coming over. It meant that I made it to Miss Winters before anyone else did.

"You're looking really good out there, Adri!"

"Thank you. Can we talk for a couple minutes before you talk to everyone else?"

She shook her head. "We've only got a few minutes before the other school will be done with their routine. I'm sorry, Adri, but there just isn't time. Let's talk once the game is over. I can give you as much time as you need then."

"Please, it's important and I promise that—I'll only take a minute."

She frowned for a moment and then looked past me at the rest of the squad. "Take a couple of minutes, girls. I'll be right back."

I followed her a few steps away from everyone else, took a deep breath and then just forced the words out.

"I'm quitting the team. I'm sorry, I know that I've made a complete mess of everything. It would have been better if I'd never joined in the first place, but I did, and now I'm just quitting right in the middle of everything which is terrible of me, but I can't cheer anymore."

Miss Winters' mouth opened and closed a couple of times. "Adri, you're a natural. You've picked everything up faster than I would have believed possible and you just keep getting better. At the rate you're improving, you might be able to get a cheerleading scholarship to college. It's a long shot because you started cheering so late, but you have all the right qualities so I think you could do it."

Tears started pooling in my eyes. It was so rarely that anyone other than my dad ever told me I was good at anything, and even he didn't have a lot to work with when it came to complimenting my talents.

"I...I really appreciate you saying that, Miss Winters, and I really am sorry, but I have to quit and sooner would be better than later."

"Can you at least tell me why?"

"I think I've been in shock ever since you suspended Cindi. I'm not saying that you did the wrong thing, I'm actually really impressed that you stuck to your guns like that, but none of that went down like I expected it to."

She smiled and patted me on the arm. "I'm not surprised that you're having a hard time processing everything. To have Cindi turn on you like that had to have been hard, but that just means that this is a terrible time to be making any kind of big decision."

"That's just the thing though. I started coming out of shock as we started the last few cheers and I realized just how much I hate Cindi and Missy. I hate them so much that it scares me. I could probably deal with hating Missy like that, but I don't want to hate my own sister that much."

Miss Winters had obviously been about to interrupt me, but my last comment shut her up faster than I would have believed possible.

"I love cheerleading. I never thought I would say that, but I do and somehow the fact that I've only loved it for a few weeks doesn't seem to matter to me, I still love it. I love it so much that I can't help but hate anyone who tries to stop me from continuing to cheer."

I suddenly had to bite back a laugh and I wasn't surprised that there was an edge of hysteria to it.

"It sounds pretty crazy to quit when I say that, but I was happy before cheerleading and I don't think Cindi knows how to be happy if she's not cheering. As much as I want to stay on the team, I can't if it means that Cindi is going to be unhappy. If I quit now then she won't have as much reason to resent me."

"Even with you out of the picture, it won't change anything as far as Missy and Cindi's punishments are concerned."

"I know, and I think that's probably for the best anyways. Missy is off of the team and Cindi will be suspended until she can get her grades back up, but you did say her punishment was only a suspension. She wants to be back on the team badly enough that I know she'll have her grades back where they are supposed to be in no time flat. Maybe then she can forgive me for everything that's happened."

"Will you be able to forgive her? There's a chance that this is just going to cause you to resent her and hate her more. Giving up something we want is never easy, Adri."

I nodded. "I know. It's a risk, but it's one I'm willing to run. I think the fact that it's my choice will make it a little easier than it would have been if they'd forced me to quit."

The tears that had been gathering a few seconds before chose that moment to break free and start coursing down my face. I tried to wipe them away without ruining the little bit of makeup that I was wearing, but I was pretty sure I failed. Miss Winters looked like she was on the point of tears too though so maybe it didn't matter that I was acting like a big baby.

"I can't stop you, Adri. Part of me really wishes that I could because I'm not so sure that Cindi is worthy of what you're doing for her, but I can't stop you. You're a good person and a great sister."

"Thanks, Miss Winters. I wish I could help out somehow. This is going to leave you three people short and regionals aren't that far away."

"It's okay, Winning regionals would be nice, but there are more important things in life than putting another trophy in the school's display case. I wish I could tell you that you'll always have a spot on my team if you change your mind, but that wouldn't be fair to whoever replaces you."

"I know. It's a nice gesture, but no matter what else happens I won't be coming back."

"Never say never, Adri, you might be surprised where your path takes you. For now, let's just say that if you change your mind I'll make you the first alternate on the squad so you'll have a place if anything happens to one of the other girls."

"Thanks, Miss Winters. Do you need me to help with the half-time performance? I guess it probably doesn't matter if I do one more routine…"

"No, if you're set on quitting the team then let's not prolong the agony. We'll make do without you."

She started to turn back to the other girls and then stopped and gave me a quick hug, which just made me want to cry even more, but I managed to keep it all inside. It was just cheerleading, it wasn't like someone was dying, but now that most of the shock was gone I *felt* like a part of my life, a part that I'd enjoyed and been good at, was dying.

I stood there for nearly a minute, forlornly watching Miss Winters explain to the rest of the team that I was quitting. I got a wide variety of looks from different girls, everything from sadness on the part of Sheree to a mixture of disbelief and satisfaction from most of the others. It was the looks of satisfaction that finally snapped me out of my funk enough to walk past them so I could get my things.

I walked away from the football field without looking back even though I didn't have any idea where I was going to go. I wandered for a couple of minutes before eventually finding myself inside the school and only a few steps from the girls' locker room.

It didn't feel right to still be wearing my uniform now that I wasn't part of the squad, so I went in for just long enough to change back into the shorts and shirt that I'd worn to school earlier in the day. Once I'd changed I just sat there on the hard, narrow bench that ran down the center of the aisle between the rows of lockers.

Both shells and the damaged skirt were in my duffle bag, but I laid my white skirt out across my lap and smoothed the material out flat against my legs. I knew I was going to miss being a cheerleader, but actually having taken the uniform off for the last time choked me up more than I expected it to. I probably would have stayed there for hours, but some atypical sliver of practicality finally worked its way to the forefront of my mind.

If I stayed too long then I'd definitely run into the cheerleaders from the other team and possibly even the girls from our school too. Besides, I needed to get back to the football field and see if I could find someone to give me a ride home. It was a long shot considering how much the rest of the school hated me, but I honestly wasn't sure what else to do. Now that I wasn't on the team it was possible that I wouldn't be able to get a ride home on the bus. Miss Winters probably wouldn't leave me stranded, but there wasn't any guarantee of that fact.

Either way, I didn't want to spend one moment longer than I had to with the rest of the squad and given that my mom and dad were still camping in the middle of nowhere for another day or two, it wasn't like I could just call them to come pick me up.

As I stood to go I thought that I heard someone else in the locker room, but when I called out nobody responded. I was pretty sure it had just been my mind playing tricks on me, but that didn't stop me from leaving at as fast a walk as I could manage. I'd had plenty of evidence that there were monsters out there and I wasn't eager to meet one in real life. Besides, given how much Missy probably hated me right now she was pretty high up there on the list of threats that I needed to avoid at all cost.

I made it back to the visitors' bleachers without running into Cindi, Missy, or anyone else who wanted to rip my arms off, and my heart started to sink at just how few people were there from our school. It was darkly funny that a crowd that had seemed huge when I'd considered performing in front of it was disappointingly small when it represented my only chance at making it home.

I started at the bottom row of people and worked my way from one side to the other, but not surprisingly most of the people who'd driven an hour and a half to come to the game were the popular kids who hung out with the cheerleaders or the football players. There were a few grownups here and there who weren't sitting with anyone my age, but I wasn't particularly excited at the prospect of hitching a ride home with random people I didn't know.

It took less than three minutes to realize that there wasn't anyone I both knew and trusted who was likely to help me out. I was nearly ready to despair when I remembered that Sheree's parents sometimes came to the games to watch her perform. It was a slim chance, but it was the best I'd been able to come up with, so I made my way to the very top of the bleachers, so that I'd have the best possible view of both the crowd below me and the cheerleaders off to the side, and sat down.

The junior varsity game had apparently finished up while I was in the locker room, which was odd considering that I hadn't thought I was in there for very long, but I wasn't going to complain. Anything which brought this night to a close sooner rather than later was okay in my book.

Jackson found me a few minutes before the first half concluded. "Hi, Adri. Do you mind if I sit here with you?"

"Wait, aren't you supposed to be down cheering?"

"Is that a no?"

I felt myself blushing, which was just as embarrassing as always, but also somehow a relief. It was nice to know that I was still capable of feeling something other than anger or sadness. Given just how often I'd been embarrassed lately it was almost like being back to normal.

"No, you can sit here. I guess I'm just surprised."

He smiled and sat down next to me. "We're down to just one flyer, which means that we only need a third as many spotters as normal. Miss Winters is using a couple of the other guys to try and fill in the formations for some of the easier stuff, but mostly us guys don't know any of the routines beyond just spotting."

"Oh, I guess that makes sense. I'm sorry, I didn't mean to make it so that you couldn't help out tonight."

"Don't worry about that. Honestly it's going to be nice to be able to just sit here and watch a game without any distractions. That's half the reason I tried out for the squad, you know, just so I had a reason to come to the games."

"Because of your mom? She sounds crazy strict."

"Yeah, that's probably one of the bigger understatements ever made. Your parents seem pretty cool though."

"Right, they are the coolest for the twenty minutes every day when they aren't yelling at each other."

"Ouch, you did mention problems at home. I figured it was just friction between you and Cindi now that you were both on the team."

I sighed. "Was it that obvious to everyone? Was I the only person who didn't realize just how pissed she was at me?"

"No, probably not. I kind of have an advantage over most people, what with hanging around cheerleaders most of the day and all. They talk a lot when you aren't around and it's been more and more obvious that Cindi isn't liking you being on the team as much as she expected to."

"It sucks. The only reason that I even joined the team in the first place was to spend more time with Cindi. I thought maybe it would help us be closer, but instead it's pretty much ruined things between us."

Jackson patted my knee. "Don't worry about it. Things seem like they are irreparable right now but they'll work out."

"What if they don't?"

"You didn't mean for things to go bad, and you've done everything you can to make them better. Cindi will eventually see that and forgive you."

"I don't know, she can be pretty stubborn. What if she doesn't ever get past it?"

"Then she's not worth the worry. I know you care about her, but that only goes so far. If she can't do her part then there's no way for things to work out, and killing yourself trying to make up for her lack of interest is just a good way to get screwed over."

"Wow, that's pretty profound. When did you get so insightful?"

"It's all that time hanging out with you cheerleaders."

I rolled my eyes at him. It was a pretty lame joke, but it had brought a smile to my face, which bought him a lot of points. It was irrefutable proof that I really hadn't lost the ability to feel good. It was also the perfect segue into telling him that I didn't care that he wasn't interested in me. Normally I never could have done that, but knowing that Alec was out there waiting for me made it a lot easier, and I really did want to try to keep Jackson as a friend for as long as I could.

"Right. About all of that time spent hanging out with cheerleaders, it seems like it's really one cheerleader in particular..."

He went stiff, but I held my hand up in an effort to placate him. "It's no big deal, really. That's the only reason that I'm bringing it up. I didn't want you to think that I was jealous or anything. You have been a good friend to me, and you helped me out a lot, especially when I first made the squad."

"I got the impression a few days ago that you really didn't like the fact that I was spending so much time with Wendy."

My face started heating up, but it was too late to back out of the conversation gracefully.

"I didn't—not at first—because I thought for a while there that you were interested in me, but I'd rather us continue to be friends and not drive you away because you think I'm crazy jealous of the fact that you want to date Missy's best friend."

Jackson pursed his lips and then sighed. "You probably don't even realize that what you said is exactly what a girl who isn't really over the idea of dating a boy would say, do you?"

"Okay, I didn't think of it in those terms. I do actually know that girls do that, I watch TV after all, but I just didn't look at things that way because all I was thinking about was the fact that I want to continue to be your friend. Besides, that's not the kind of behavior you'd expect out of a cheerleader anyways."

"I'll give you that. Alpha females like Missy would never do something like that. They'd expect the guy to come to chase them, even if they had to manipulate him into doing it in the first place. But you're hardly an alpha female, Adri. Don't get me wrong, you're hot enough to be one, but you just don't think the same way that Missy and the others do. Heck, even Cindi doesn't think like that and she's been moving in those circles for years longer than you have."

"Fine, you're right, I'm not that kind of girl, but I really wasn't trying to keep you as an option for later. You've proved your point and you get extra kudos for comparing Missy to a dog in your argument."

That earned me a chuckle. "Okay, so maybe that wasn't the most diplomatic way to explain things, but it's true. You should try thinking about it that way sometime. Humans really aren't that different from a pack of wolves. Everyone likes to think otherwise, and it's true that some of the rough edges have been worn away by a few thousand years of civilization, but the fundamental drives and urges are all the same. That's why high school sucks so bad. Society tells us all that everyone is equal, but we're not, and telling a bunch of kids they are just confuses things while the pecking order is sorted out."

"Riveting. You must be a real hit at parties. So are we cool now?"

It was more sarcastic than was typical for me, which probably didn't help my case when it came to convincing him that everything was fine.

"I don't know, Adri, are we? You didn't really ever provide any kind of convincing proof that my suspicions are wrong."

"Fine. The truth is that I met someone else."

The words just kind of came out of my mouth without me having consciously decided to say them and I immediately wished I could take them back.

"That's exactly the kind of thing you'd say if I was right, Adri."

Now I was starting to get mad and given how much residual anger I still had floating around inside of my head from earlier, that was a dangerous thing.

"What do you want me to say, Jackson? Every valid reason for a girl to lose interest in a boy has been pulled out and polished up by some desperate girl at some point, so no matter what I tell you there's still going to be that niggling little suspicion that it's just a lie to throw you off the scent."

Apparently more of my anger leaked through into my voice than I'd realized, because Jackson leaned away from me and put his hands up in mock surrender.

"I'm sorry if I'm being too brutal, Adri, it's just that I've been in this exact situation a few times before and it never ends well. You have to understand that there haven't been any rumors or anything to back up what you just told me. Cindi has been pretty pissed that you're hitting on Tristan, only you're not, but the fact that she thinks you're available enough to chase Tristan is a pretty good indication that you don't have some other guy you're chasing. You don't have a car of your own, so it's not like you're driving somewhere without her realizing it."

"And everyone in school would start talking as soon as I hung out with anyone there."

"Right, and I'm with you at all of our practices and games, so it's not like you're seeing someone on the down-low there either."

"You're right, there's absolutely no reason for you or anyone else to believe me."

"But you're sticking to your guns, it's the truth? There really is some guy that you've got your eye on?"

"Yeah, there is."

"So where does he live, what is his name?"

I opened my mouth to answer him, to at least give him Alec's name, but I suddenly remembered just how much work I'd gone to in order to remain anonymous in the dream. Alec hadn't said anything before we'd been interrupted, but I was pretty sure that he didn't want to be publically tied to all of the crazy supernatural stuff that was trying to seep into my life.

"I...I don't actually know where he's from, and I'm not sure that he'd be very happy if I told people his name."

Jackson's expression had taken on a hard edge. "So what am I supposed to believe? Is this some kind of weird internet chat room thing?"

His partial apology from earlier had gone a long ways towards calming me down, but this last question reignited my anger to a white-hot living entity.

"I saw him in..." I caught myself just barely in the nick of time, but it left me without anything convincing to say. "You know what, just forget about it. I'm being stupid, I just thought that after everything terrible that it's brought...I mean everything terrible that's happened. Never mind, just forget I said anything."

I stood to leave, but Jackson grabbed my wrist. His grip wasn't painful, but he was so strong that I was practically handcuffed to him. He pulled me around so that I was looking at him.

"I'm sorry, Adri, that wasn't fair of me. Everyone needs a *dream*."

My stomach dropped like I'd just been thrown out of a plane without any parachute. The warning from the girl at the first away game played back inside of my head. She'd warned me that someone dangerous was close to me, but I'd always assumed it was Tristan. I'd been wrong though. Something about how Jackson said the word 'dream' told me that he knew more than he should. His voice had even gone slightly different. It had still mostly been Jackson's voice, but it had also been uncannily similar to the voice that had haunted my dreams ever since the sunflowers had been sent to our bus.

I tried to control my breathing, tried to pretend like his statement hadn't rattled me, but I *was* rattled. It was all I could do to muster a response to him.

"I don't understand what you mean. If you're implying that my dream is to still catch you then you're wrong, but either way I'm done with this conversation."

I tried again to walk away, but he still hadn't let go of me. I debated screaming. If I made a big enough scene then I would almost certainly be guaranteed a ride home and I was probably going to be safer in a crowd than by myself, but I didn't actually *know* that. If Jackson really was the old man somehow then there was no telling what he was capable of and the last thing I wanted to do was get people killed.

Besides, there was always a chance that my effort to pretend that nothing was wrong had been successful enough to leave him with at least a little doubt as to whether or not I was the cheerleader he was looking for. It was doubtful, but I didn't know what else to do.

"I didn't mean to make you mad, Adri. Sometimes I get too cynical where all of this stuff is concerned, but it's good that you haven't gotten that way yet. You're right, I should give people the benefit of the doubt more than I do. Just because I'm not a romantic doesn't mean that I should try to deprive everyone else around me of those kinds of dreams."

"Fine, apology accepted."

He hadn't actually apologized, but it wasn't like I believed his explanation either. He was obviously just making stuff up to explain away his comment from a second before. He still hadn't let go of my wrist yet and I didn't know how much more stress my heart could take.

"Let me make it up to you, Adri. I'll call my mom and she can come get us. I know you well enough to know that you don't want to ride the bus back. Miss Winters might agree to let you come with us, but you're not going to want to deal with all of the gossip and knowing looks from the rest of the team."

Did his mom know what he was? Had he always been different, or had he developed some kind of unique ability at some point recently? If he really was the old man, then she almost certainly had to know.

It didn't matter either way though because I couldn't allow myself to end up alone in a car with the two of them. He still hadn't let go of me, it was almost like he was a different person entirely right then.

"You're hurting me, Jackson, that's hardly the way to make anything up to me."

"I'm sorry, you're right."

He loosened his grip enough for me to slide my hand free, but he didn't exactly let go and I got the feeling that he was savoring the feel of my skin against his as I freed myself.

"So what do you say? I'll call my mom and we can ditch this place?"

"No, I don't think so, not after your big speech about how you're worried that I'm secretly in love with you. You apologized, but that doesn't mean that you really believe me. I'll get home another way. I think it's best if we don't see as much of each other for a while. Maybe then you'll believe that I only wanted to be friends."

He wanted to call my bluff, I could see it in his eyes, but anything he did right now would be witnessed by at least a couple hundred people. He let me back away without saying anything else, but we both knew that it was only a matter of time before I'd be by myself.

I wanted to run down the bleachers as fast as I could, but I knew that would just put me in even more danger. I needed an escape that provided the illusion that I didn't realize just how much danger I was in. If he thought I was about to leave town he'd move sooner than he would otherwise. I needed him to remain complacent and sure of himself if I was going to have even a sliver of a chance of getting somewhere safe, of making a run to wherever Alec was.

I managed to get down to the ground without cracking from the stress and fear I could feel ratcheting tighter and tighter inside of me and then was faced with walking the length of the bleachers with hundreds of eyes on me.

A few minutes ago it had seemed smart to sit as far away from our cheerleaders as I could get, but now I wasn't sure that I'd be able to make it to Sheree and the others without betraying just how scared I was. It took nearly everything I had to force myself to take one slow step after another. I could feel Jackson's eyes on me and my shoulders kept trying to knot up.

I could see Sheree now; she was on the far end of everyone else, an impossible distance away from me. My legs were weak now and my backpack and duffle bag were dragging at my arms. I started to fall, but a pair of strong arms caught me before I traveled more than an inch or two towards the ground.

"Adri, you look terrible. What's going on? Where did Cindi and Missy go?"

Tristan's voice was full of concern and I grabbed onto it like the lifeline it just might be.

"I'm off the team. It's hard to explain, but I need a way home. I'm…I'm scared."

I said that last bit in a whisper while looking away from him. I was afraid to meet his eyes and see the mockery in them, but he reached up and gently turned my chin until I didn't have a choice but to look at him.

"You're serious, aren't you? This isn't some kind of joke or anything, you're actually scared for your life. Do you need to leave right now?"

He responded in a whisper, for which I was profoundly grateful. I couldn't manage a response other than a shaky nod.

"Okay, my phone is over there, do you have yours handy?"

Now that the anger was gone I felt shocky and numb again. I handed him my phone without thinking about what I was doing. As Tristan started dialing I noticed his coach headed in our direction.

"Hey, Mathews, how about you stop talking to the skirt and get your head back in the game before I bench you."

"Just a sec, Coach. Trust me, taking care of this will help me keep my head in the game."

His coach, a massive guy who looked like he'd probably played on the line back in his glory days, was obviously not very happy about the fact that Tristan was blowing off the game to talk to me, but apparently he felt like he could only push his star quarterback so far.

"I don't want to get you in trouble."

Tristan waved my concern away. "The defense is doing their thing, my watching isn't going to make much of a difference. Besides, the worst that could happen will be that he'll bench me for a couple of games which would just mean that we'd lose. He's not going to do that without a lot more reason than this."

Tristan put the phone back up to his ear—apparently he'd remembered the number and it was dialing.

"Hey, Brad, I need a favor. Yeah, I know it's the middle of the game, but did you drive? Okay, do you have room for one more person? Great, that's even better. Tell Sally that I'm sorry, but I need you guys to leave right now. Yeah, do you know Adri Paige? Right, she'll meet you on the far edge of the bleachers in like two minutes. Thanks, man, I owe you."

Tristan's smile was worried as he handed my phone back to me. "That's the best I can do right now. Brad's a stand-up guy and his girlfriend Sally is actually pretty nice. They'll get you home right now so that you don't have to be worried anymore."

I tried to put on a brave face, tried not to let him see just how terrifying the thought of sitting home alone was right now, but he could tell something was wrong.

"Oh, crap. Your parents are still gone, aren't they? Do you want to just go to my house instead?"

"Yeah, they are gone until Sunday, but I shouldn't get you anymore involved. It's...well, it's not safe."

Tristan closed his eyes for a second and when he opened them the arrogant teenage quarterback had disappeared and been replaced with someone serious, someone who *felt* dependable in every way.

"If you tell me that you need me to blow off this game, I'll do it. It's going to suck, but I'll do it. What do you need? My parents are out of town too. You and I could go up to the cabin my parents bought last month. We'd be safe there; nobody at school even knows where it is. Dad bought it using one of his corporate fronts to keep it quiet, so there's probably a grand total of six people in the entire state who even know how to link it to us."

I desperately wanted to take him up on his offer, but I knew just how big a price he might end up having to pay if he left with me right now. He'd be off the team and he'd probably have to move to another school if he wanted to play next year. It might cost him a college scholarship, maybe even a future as a professional athlete.

"No, I can't ask you to leave right now, but maybe you could come get me as soon as you get back from the game."

My insides were quivering at the thought of spending even that much time alone, but I willed my face to keep that secret, to do what I asked for at least once tonight. It was a calculated risk, but Jackson would be riding back on the bus so he wouldn't be home any sooner than Tristan would be.

"You're sure?"

"Yeah, it's the best compromise, just hurry every chance you get. Here are my keys, just in case. I'll let myself in with the spare one that we've got hidden outside."

"Right, no overtime. I'll see you soon."

"Thanks, Tristan. I misjudged you."

A hint of his normal humor and cockiness crept back onto his face.

"It's easy to do. I like to keep people guessing a little."

HUNTED

I leaned in and gave him a kiss on the cheek and then turned and headed towards where he'd told Brad to meet me. Tristan had just bought me some time, but I wasn't under any illusions when it came to my safety. I wasn't going to be safe until I'd found someone bigger and scarier than Jackson, someone who could go toe to toe with all of the other supernatural creatures out there.

I needed Alec.

Chapter 24

I'd never met Brad before, but he turned out to be a six-one giant who looked like he belonged out on the offensive line keeping the other team away from Tristan. Apparently my look of surprise wasn't anything new for him.

"I know, right? I actually played football for half of a season my freshman year. I took a really hard hit during one of my games and tore my rotator cuff. My mom freaked out and still won't let me play."

"I'm sorry to pull you away from the game, it's just…"

I wasn't actually sure how to explain the craziness I'd just been through, at least not without sounding like a complete head case, but he just shrugged.

"It's not a problem. If Tristan likes you then most of the rumors floating around school can't be true. Besides, we all know he's just going to throw four more touchdowns and destroy the other team."

Sally turned out to be exactly the kind of girl you'd expect a football player to date. She was tiny like Sheree was tiny. She wasn't just short, she also had the kind of super-small frame that meant she'd look skinny even if she was ten or fifteen pounds overweight. She wasn't overweight at all though, so she just looked like she was made out of plastic like some kind of perfect blonde Barbie doll.

She didn't say much, but she smiled at me and seemed to actually mean it, which was more than I normally expected to get out of girls who looked that good. I was just as skinny now, but I still kind of felt like most of the really attractive girls looked at me and figured I was too far beneath them to bother getting to know.

Almost before I knew it we were in Brad's blue Pathfinder and headed home. He made a couple of valiant attempts at carrying on a conversation with me, and I really did try to reciprocate, but things just kept petering out after a minute or two.

We were both making a legitimate effort, but the fact of the matter was that we just didn't have very much in common and I was having a hard time focusing on anything other than the fact that Jackson was going to come for me as soon as the buses got back into town.

"...can't believe that you've managed to resist Tristan's charms for so long. I think this is some kind of record."

I looked up and realized that Sally had decided to help draw me out.

"I can't really take full credit there. My sister has wanted to date him for a couple of months now and he didn't exactly make a good impression by telling me that he didn't care whether she got hurt as long as he got what he wanted."

Brad winced a little. "I knew that was going to bite him in the butt."

Sally punched him in the arm. "You're a complete jerk. I still think I gave him the right advice. Maybe he screwed up the execution, but he needs to stop just dating whomever chases him or he'll continue to have one bad relationship after another with girls who like him more than he likes them. He needs to tap into his inner jerk a little more or he's never going to be happy."

Brad shrugged as he changed lanes to pass a red Miata. "I don't know, I still think he just needs to go somewhere new and make a fresh start. He's tried to keep things low-key here, but there's a couple of girls on the cheerleading team that I'm pretty sure have figured out who his dad really is. Even if they haven't, he suspects the same thing, which means every time they look at him he thinks they are seeing dollar signs."

I felt my eyebrows start to creep up in astonishment. I'd always figured that Tristan's family was rich, or at least moderately well-off. You didn't buy vacation cabins without at least bringing home somewhat big bucks, but Brad and Sally seemed to be hinting at lifestyles-of-the-rich-and-famous kind of wealth.

"Just how rich is Tristan?"

The two of them looked at each other for a couple of seconds and then Sally sighed. "Tristan said he was going to take you to his cabin, right?"

"Yeah, he invited me there a couple of weeks ago and I turned him down. I think that's where we're going tonight though."

"Okay, don't tell him I told you this or he'll be mad, but it's not like you wouldn't have figured it out for yourself as soon as you saw their new place."

"You've seen it? I thought he told me that nobody else had been there yet."

It was silly of me to ask the question. I was interrupting her in her response as to just how wealthy Tristan was, but it was almost like I didn't really want to know even though I'd been the one to ask.

"We haven't been there, but he showed us pictures that they shot when they went up there the first time to check it out. It's ridiculous, in a good but still over-the-top way. Are you sure you really want to know this?"

"Yeah, it's always best to know what you're getting into."

"The truth is I don't know, but I'm pretty sure that they are billionaires by now. His dad is pioneering that new technology to project images from your phone onto another flat surface. He's some kind of super-genius. Everyone is saying that the technology is still a year or two away from mass production, but Tristan said his dad cracked the power consumption problem and figured out how to fit it all into a small enough footprint to make it viable."

Brad changed radio stations without turning it up and then jumped in with his two cents. "It's all pretty much way over my head too, but Tristan said that it's one of the key steps in turning our phones into real mobile computing platforms. It's crazy stuff, like all you need is your phone and a desk. You'll put your phone down, it will project a keyboard onto the desk and then his dad's invention will project a display onto the wall at eye level."

"So you just sit down and type? No more desktops, no more laptops?"

"Yeah, pretty much. The other tech companies are going wild over it. He's got money pouring into his company already in advance orders and licensing agreements like you wouldn't believe."

It was almost too crazy to contemplate.

"Why is he going to our school instead of some snotty private school?"

HUNTED

Sally looked at Brad like she didn't know the answer either and was curious to see what he'd say.

"His dad offered to put him in any school he wanted, including some that have wicked good football teams, but he wasn't interested. I think Tristan figured that it would just paint a bigger target on him because people would know he had to be rich in order to be going there. Here he's stayed pretty incognito up until now. He's really a pretty good guy when you get right down to it."

Sally snorted, but even that was a delicate sound. I wouldn't have said that there was such a thing as a ladylike snort, but if there was, she managed it.

"He's almost too good if you ask me. You've only managed to ever even get him drunk once and he still only had like two beers."

"Yeah, he can be a bummer at parties sometimes, but I can't really blame him. A girl like Missy or Wendy is totally not above getting him drunk and sleeping with him just to get pregnant so she can get her hands on some of his dad's money."

"So why did he give in and let you get him drunk that one time then if he's held strong up until now?"

I managed to make the question sound casual, but the truth was it was anything but. I knew when he'd gotten drunk, it had been for Cindi's party, and Sally was right—he hadn't really been drunk, more like he'd just had enough to take the edge off.

Sally suddenly went bright red. Interesting. I would have said that nothing could throw her off like that. Brad frowned at her. "Now you've done it. She wasn't supposed to find out about that."

"Find out about what?"

"Brad's right, I wasn't supposed to say anything, but Tristan isn't nearly as self-confident as he seems. He hates parties. Really, any group bigger than four or five makes him uncomfortable. He doesn't usually go to that kind of stuff and when he does, he always feels like he just stands there and looks like an idiot. So...Brad convinced him to have a couple of beers as a way of relaxing a little and being more himself around you. Did it work?"

"I...well, I'm not sure, not really. He was more aggressive, he pretty much backed me into a corner of the room so that I didn't have any choice but to listen to him. Then he told me that we should date because I needed someone to help me navigate the social waters now that I was a cheerleader and that he needed someone who was cute but not as...witchy as the other girls."

Sally turned an even darker shade of red and Brad's smile spread from ear to ear. "Only he didn't say 'witchy', did he? You can thank my sometimes big-mouthed girlfriend for that. He was pretty much quoting her directly."

"Well, it's true. Adri was in over her head, and Tristan needs a nice girl, but he should get a nice girl who's also attractive. Can you imagine the inferiority complex an ugly girl would have if she dated him for very long? Not only is he gorgeous, but once she realized that he was rich enough to buy a small country she'd start expecting that he was going to cheat on her because she couldn't compete with the kinds of girls who would constantly be throwing themselves at him."

Brad's sigh was pretty eloquent. "Give the guy some credit. He doesn't just care about looks."

"I know, but most girls aren't going to think like that. We automatically think that we're not pretty enough or smart enough or skinny enough to be with a guy like Tristan. Besides, you have to admit it would still be a temptation for him."

I opened my mouth, but Brad interjected a dose of humor into the conversation. "You know, I'm starting to feel like a poor substitute for Tristan. If you keep talking like that, I'll tell him to just date you and I'll go find someone else to date who's happy to settle for me instead of shooting for the proverbial moon."

Sally hit Brad in the arm, harder than before, but still probably not hard enough to leave bruises or anything.

"You know I'd rather be with you than Tristan. He's rich and gorgeous, but you're pretty hot yourself and you're way more fun than he is because you don't take yourself so seriously all of the time."

The rest of the drive went by quickly. Sally and Brad still carried the conversation, but things weren't as strained as they'd been before. I'd started out the trip just hoping that I'd make it home without anything bad happening along the way. I hadn't expected to find out that Tristan was an even better guy than I'd realized.

It didn't really change the big picture at all. Alec still completed me in ways that Tristan never could, and I didn't want to destroy Cindi's hopes by dating someone she had her heart set on, but now I felt a lot worse about some of the things I'd said to Tristan along the way.

Chapter 25

By the time that Brad and Sally dropped me off I was starting to wonder if Tristan had used some kind of code during the brief phone call when he'd asked Brad to take me home. I'd been listening to the entire conversation, Tristan's half at least, and I knew he hadn't said anything outright about me being scared, but Brad was awfully willing to stay with me until Tristan got back in town.

All I could figure was that Brad was just more perceptive than most guys, but luckily he still bought my assurances that I'd be fine. Even so, he and Sally waited until I'd grabbed the spare key and let myself inside the house before they backed out of the driveway and drove away.

I watched them go as I locked the front door and then I walked around the house double-checking that every single door and window was closed and secured. It only took a couple of minutes to confirm that I was as safe as I was going to get, at which point I started to calm down a little.

I was home, the doors were locked, I had my phone so I could always call 911 if I needed to and then just hope that the police made it to my house before Jackson kidnapped me or killed me, or whatever it was he was planning on doing.

Apparently I'd been running on pure adrenaline because as soon as I sat down a crushing, bone-deep exhaustion swept through me. I couldn't ever remember being so tired at any other point in my life, but something pulled at me, refusing to let me go to sleep. I realized what was missing just before the last of my strength poured out of me.

I needed to warn Cindi. If Jackson was really the old man, then he'd know that I'd turn myself in to save Cindi. I had to keep her safe if I was going to be safe myself.

Cindi still didn't have a phone, but it was a good bet that she and Missy had gotten together by now. Calling Missy's phone number was the last thing I really wanted to do—even if Cindi was with her I was going to get an earful before I'd possibly be able to get my message out—but I had to at least try.

Missy's number was still in my call history. I dialed it and waited as it rang twice, at which point I was sent to voicemail.

"This is Missy, but then you already know that, don't you? You know the drill."

I waited for the beep and then let the words just tumble out of my mouth in an effort to get them all out before I lost my battle with sleep.

"Missy, if you have any way to get ahold of Cindi please tell her to be careful and to stay away from Jackson. I'll explain later. Look, I know you hate me right now, but I didn't start all of this. Please just tell Cindi if you can."

A huge yawn forced its way past my lips as I struggled to get the last word or two out. I blindly stabbed the disconnect button. I didn't remember lying down, but I was already on the couch in the living room. I had a moment to be grateful that I'd gone ahead and cleaned it up earlier that morning, and then sleep claimed me.

I realized my mistake as soon as I saw my new surroundings. I'd fallen asleep and let myself start dream walking. I immediately tried to shift so that I was transparent similar to what the Native American had done the last time I'd seen him, but my skin simply turned gray for a heartbeat or two before lapsing back to its normal color.

If I'd been in my own dream I'd have been able to accomplish the transformation and even more, but even here I should have been able to at least change my own appearance. Changing myself was always the easiest thing to accomplish. The fact that I couldn't manage even the slightest change right now couldn't be good. It had to either be because I was too tired still after my dream walk with Alec, or because I was inside the dream of someone whose mind was even more disciplined than the old man's had been.

I needed to get out, get back to my own dream, but I already knew from past experience that I was hit-and-miss when it came to that. I looked around at my surroundings, trying to find somewhere to hide, and my heart sank.

I was standing in the middle of a huge plain of uneven black glass. It looked like the glass had been there for a long time, because it was cracked in some places and I could see where the cracks had ground against each other like miniature fault lines in the Earth's crust.

I took a tentative step forward and shards of glass crunched underneath my feet. Thankfully I'd come into the dream wearing sneakers, but that was the only thing about my appearance that was helpful. I was dressed back in my cheerleading uniform, the dark blue one that Cindi and Missy had destroyed, and I was uncomfortably close to being just as skinny here in the dream as I actually was right now in real life.

I touched my cheeks with my fingers and they felt exactly like they did each night when I washed my face. I was out of time and I knew it. I finally saw a bigger crack in the ground a hundred yards or so away and took a step towards it, thinking it would provide at least a little concealment while I tried to rip myself free of this nightmare.

HUNTED

Ribbons of agony lit up in my foot. I looked down and saw that my sneakers had disappeared, leaving the bottom of my foot to be savaged by the razor-edged shards of glass I'd just stepped on. My lunch started to come back up at the thought of walking across that distance without shoes, but I couldn't think of any other option.

I took another step and was watching this time as my shoe disappeared. Knowing it was coming just made the pain worse, but I gritted my teeth and forced myself to take yet another step. I looked down again and the sight of the bright-red, bloody footprints I was leaving behind nearly pushed me over the edge. I had to close my eyes for a second and focus just on my breathing and even then I still almost threw up.

With my eyes closed it was easier to ignore what was happening to my feet. The pain was just signals traveling along damaged nerves, it didn't mean anything, wouldn't mean anything once I was awake again. I'd completely ruined my nails in that one dream and just had to deal with a little bit of phantom pain the next day. As long as I didn't die here I'd be okay, and I was pretty sure it would take a while to bleed to death from the lacerations on my feet.

Keeping my eyes closed helped me endure the pain, but a few steps later I tripped and fell. I tried to catch myself with my hands, but remembered at the last second what that would do to them and jerked them back out of the way.

I landed on my right side with enough force to knock the wind out of me and then rolled over onto my back.

More blood soaked through my uniform from the new cuts on my shoulder and side and I suddenly realized that the pain was going to make it even harder than normal to leave this dream and get back to reality.

I tried to roll back to my feet, only I couldn't because someone had put their foot on my throat. It was the wax lady. There was no way that she should have been able to follow me like that without me realizing she'd been there, but somehow she'd done it. She'd watched while I tried to make it to safety, possibly she'd even been the reason my shoes had disappeared, and she'd obviously enjoyed it based on the cruel smile that was the only part of her face that wasn't melted into a featureless blob.

"I almost couldn't believe it when he called to tell me that it was you all along, Adri Paige. You have no idea how much effort I've expended over the last few weeks trying to find you. He practically worked himself into a frenzy tonight after realizing the way that you'd fooled him for so long. They both did, and they hardly ever see eye to eye anymore."

Acting with no more feeling than a normal person would squish a bug, the wax lady stomped down on my stomach hard enough to knock the wind out of me.

"My name is Pamela, but you will address me as Master."

My diaphragm had unclenched enough for me to breathe again and I even managed to talk. "How do you know that I'm really Adri? I can change my shape inside the dream, you know."

She kicked me in the kidney, but there still wasn't any rancor in it yet, it was like she was disciplining a dog. "Oh, I'm quite positive that it's you, Adri. I'm sitting outside your house hidden in some bushes and I'm only partly dreaming. A portion of my mind is here with you, but the other half is watching this little scene unfold from inside of your mind. Nothing you do can surprise me at this point and the fear coursing through your system over the last few minutes has amply proved that you're the prey I've been hunting."

She looked at me once again, surveying my bloody clothes and damaged feet before nodding to herself.

"I believe it's time to conduct the rest of this interview face to face."

A chill ran up my back and came to rest somewhere at the base of my neck. She was talking about breaking into my house and if she really was right outside like she'd said, then there was no way that anyone could get there to save me before she made it inside.

It was crazy, I wasn't at any less of a disadvantage here than I was fighting against her in the real world, but as she closed her eyes to concentrate I kicked her in the stomach. There wasn't much power behind it, but the blow caught her completely by surprise and I was profoundly grateful for how much more flexible I was after a few weeks of cheerleading.

Normally I would have said it would be impossible for me to kick someone while lying on the ground like that, but adrenaline gave me the extra push I needed and I doubled her up enough that she collapsed to the ground, taking gashes of her own against the unforgiving glass in the process.

I half turned to run away in the hope that doing so would allow me to escape back to the real world, but before I'd even taken my first step I realized that was the wrong thing to be doing. I needed to keep her here in the dream for as long as possible. It was unlikely it would make any difference in the end, but there was a very slight chance that if I could keep her busy for long enough Tristan would arrive at my house before she could come get me.

It put Tristan in all kinds of danger, but I had to at least try. Maybe she wasn't as scary as some of the other supernatural creatures out there, maybe her abilities didn't include the kind of increased speed and strength that the Native American had demonstrated.

I turned back towards her and as I stepped forward I kicked her as hard as I could in the stomach. This time it wasn't a cheerleader kick that was thrown primarily from the hip, this time I kicked her like I would have kicked a soccer ball and the force of the impact knocked her over onto her left side.

I'd obviously knocked the wind out of her, but as I hauled back for another kick, this one to her face, her hands blurred forward so that they were between us. She caught my kick, still moving faster than I'd ever seen anyone else move before, and dumped me on the ground.

I was completely unprepared, so I hit hard enough that I saw stars, but I tried to get back to my feet as quickly as possible. Being trapped on the ground was the worst possible place to be when it came to a fight like this, but even before I'd stopped sliding across the glass she jumped on top of me, trapping me against the ground with her weight.

"You've got more fight in you than I expected. That's good. It means that the next few months and years are going to be a lot more unpleasant for you than they otherwise would have been, but I've found that people with spirit tend to make the best slaves once I've finally managed to break their will."

We were both incredibly bloody by now and she had a stream of blood dripping down into one eye, but it didn't seem to bother her, at least not much. She blew at it, kind of like you'd do to clear a stray hair that was tickling the side of your nose, but she didn't release my hands to wipe it away like I would have been tempted to do.

"I owe you a slight debt of gratitude. Just now I was ready to come get you in the flesh, but that would have been a mistake, a lost opportunity if you will. I'll be punishing you quite a lot for the next little while and those kinds of things will take a lot out of your poor human body. Here I can punish you over and over again and I suspect that you'll be just fine tomorrow morning. It's a rare advantage that I hadn't fully appreciated up until now."

The smile, absent for the few seconds when I'd been resisting her more or less effectively, was back now and she moved one hand to my shoulder and pushed. The glass beneath me had already been cutting into every part of my back, but she applied pressure in just the right way to slide my flesh across the ground and shred it even more.

"Normally bleeding someone out like this is much more work."

I was out of ideas. At least here inside of her own dream she was faster and stronger than me. I was completely at her mercy. In the real world I could hope for Tristan to come help me, or maybe for a nosier-than-average neighbor to see her skulking in the bushes and call the cops, but here there wasn't anyone who could help me.

Even as I thought it, I realized that it wasn't exactly the truth. I'd encountered exactly three other people while dream walking who had been supernatural in some way or another. I was pretty sure that Jackson was the old man and that he was working for her somehow, but the Native American had demonstrated as much control over the dream as either of the other two and he'd been the only one actually willing to teach me anything about how to survive here.

Alec's words rang through my mind, but at the end of the day he didn't know whether the Native American—Dream Stealer—could be trusted any more than I did. There was a chance that I'd simply be exchanging one devil for another, but I knew deep down in my bones that I wasn't going to get away from the wax lady on my own. I was going to try to escape via fleeing to my own dream, but if that didn't work then I was going to do whatever I could to bring Dream Stealer to me.

Fire raced up my right leg as she rubbed it against the ground, but I closed my eyes and told myself once again that it wasn't real pain, that I was going to wake up with nothing more than some faint aches from all of this.

I struggled to assemble a coherent vision of the real world. I imagined the feel of the couch cushions on my back, I remembered the slight smell of stale beer that Cindi had never come home to clean up, and most of all I tried to bask in the feeling of being home, of being safe and secure. I wrapped my mental arms around all of those feelings and sensations in an attempt to hold them steady, and *pushed* with all of my might.

The harder I pushed the more my anchors seemed to flicker and disintegrate. I might have been able to make it work without smell and touch, but it was the feeling of security that disappeared the quickest. Deep down I knew that I wasn't any safer in my home than I was here and that was robbing me of the certainty I needed to make an escape work.

The wax lady wasn't holding me here with metaphysical mojo that I couldn't counter, but it turned out that she didn't need to. She'd created a reality inside this dream that harmonized with my circumstances in the real world in a way that made it impossible for me to escape.

"Don't try to retreat back into yourself; I need you to fully experience this."

The pain, which had faded to a dull but persistent roar, suddenly surged back up to the top of my mind. Even worse, it was joined by fresh agony as something sliced into my stomach. I opened my eyes to find that she'd grown claws on the end of each of her fingers and was using them to make a red ruin of my midsection.

My body tried to curl up in an involuntary motion meant to protect me from further damage, but she simply stabbed me in the shoulders as she pinned me back to the ground.

The world around me flickered as I fought to hold onto consciousness. I couldn't afford to delay anymore. I'd done it once before, but even so, the odds of me being able to replicate what

I'd done the last time I'd seen Dream Stealer were slim.

I remembered how he'd made me feel, the mixed fear and hope that he'd represented almost from the first time I'd seen him. I remembered how sure of himself he'd seemed, and I willed him to appear behind the wax lady.

Even if I was capable of reproducing my earlier feat, everything still all depended on him being asleep in the first place. I knew I was probably doomed, but I reached for him and strength drained from my body in a torrent that I couldn't sustain for more than a second or two. It was like a million tiny, invisible threads had sprouted from every square inch of my body and gone streaking away at impossible speeds. I could feel them lengthening, unspooling from my body and taking something vital with them, but as terrifying as that was, now that the process had started I wasn't sure I could stop it even if I was willing to give up my last chance at survival.

One of the threads found something or someone and more strength poured into it as the thread thickened, turning from something no thicker than spider silk into a massive steel cable that was impossibly strong.

My heart was fluttering now, as if my body couldn't sustain everything I was trying to do, but the other threads were dissolving back into my body and I felt my pulse stabilize somewhat as I reabsorbed some of the strength they'd robbed me of earlier.

The tiny threads were all gone, leaving just the massive cable and whatever it had made contact with across a distance that was simultaneously nothing at all and the most impossible distance imaginable. The cable jerked in my mental hands as whoever I had caught started to struggle in an attempt to free themselves.

I almost lost my grip on it, but I managed to hold onto it by the slimmest of margins and then I *pulled* with every ounce of strength remaining to me. What I was doing was impossible and I could feel the universe itself fighting my efforts, but I'd done it once before and I refused to give up and accept the fate the wax lady had planned for me.

The far end of my cable whipped through space at speeds I couldn't really comprehend, but the distance it had to cross was likewise immeasurable and the journey seemed to take hours inside of my own mind. Now that the cable was moving, its speed started to accelerate at an exponential rate as I greedily sucked the slack back into my center and reclaimed yet more of the strength that I'd expended to get this far.

I'd built an incredible amount of momentum up by this point. It wasn't real momentum, but on the metaphysical realm it felt like a thousand-ton wrecking ball moving towards me at millions of miles per second. I would have said that nothing could stop my efforts now, but just before my cable had returned completely to me I felt it hit something that I couldn't explain.

I'd just pulled the irresistible force into the immovable object and I knew in that instant that I'd failed, only somehow the object I'd captured and pulled all of this distance had just enough momentum. The immovable object lost.

It seemed as though a bleeding hole was ripped into the universe. I tried to close my eyes against the sudden flare of light, but they were already closed, it was just so bright that the light was shining through my eyelids.

Something ripped the wax lady off of my hips and I heard her hit the ground a dozen feet away.

"It seems that you've decided to trust me."

I was still blinking away spots from my vision. An odd, person-shaped cutout in my vision seemed to indicate that the wax lady's body had shielded me from the worst of the light, but I could see just well enough to make out the bestial wolf-man shape that Dream Stealer and Alec both shared.

"I didn't have any choice. She figured out who I was and tracked me back to my home. She said that she's just outside of my window and that she has tendrils of thought inside of my mind."

"*Vampire.*"

I'd never known that a single word could contain such loathing and menace, but this time the rage wasn't directed at me. Dream Stealer stalked towards the wax lady, towards the vampire, and I could feel the same invisible wind blowing towards her that he'd used to trap me inside of the dream the first time we'd run into each other.

She couldn't leave, but that didn't mean that she couldn't fight. The vampire jumped at Dream Stealer in a blur of motion that I couldn't follow, but it seemed like he slid out of the way. One second they were each in their respective corners and in the next they'd swapped places and were both bleeding from slashes that hadn't been there before they'd started moving.

The vampire attacked again and once more all I saw was an unidentifiable blur as the two of them clashed. I knew that there probably wasn't much I could do to help in this particular fight, but I'd never be sure given the fact that I was simply too slow to be able to even tell what was going on.

I needed to be able to follow the fight, needed it in a way that I'd never needed anything else before. I looked around, hoping for some kind of inspiration, and realized that the ground had lost some of its definition. It was still an uneven plain of jagged black glass, but it no longer had loose slivers of glass scattered across everything.

It was a definite sign that the wax lady was distracted and most of her concentration was being spent on the fight. It was still a long shot, but I fixed the idea of her being slower than me in my mind and threw in a healthy dose of just how superior that would make me feel before pushing to try and force my version of reality to manifest.

I knew I needed confidence in my ability to make it happen if I was going to be successful, but I didn't actually expect it to work. I was weakest when trying to change another person. On some level I knew my efforts were doomed from the start, but as I pushed my version of reality I felt something catch and start pulling strength from me.

I opened my eyes, expecting to find that the vampire was moving more slowly, but instead found myself face to face with her.

"Nice try, Adri."

Even as she said it her hand, claws already glistening with blood on them, shot towards my chest.

I seemed to have forever in which to respond, but it wasn't that my efforts had worked, it was simply the natural side effect of so much adrenaline hitting my system.

Dream Stealer was headed towards us in a desperate bid to save me, but she'd somehow managed to outmaneuver him enough that he was still a couple of seconds away. I tried to throw myself to one side, but I was moving even slower than she was.

Without any other options, I grabbed hold of that strange catch I'd felt when trying to slow her down a second ago and pushed even harder. I would have said that I didn't have any significant reserves of strength left, but somehow I found an extra store that I hadn't known existed and poured it into my latest visualization.

I'd never felt any kind of active resistance to this kind of thing before. Previously my efforts had either been enough to enforce my will or they hadn't been. There wasn't any middle ground and the threshold, even when I hadn't been able to sense it, had always seemed a fixed thing.

That wasn't the case here. Instead I felt like I was pushing against a large pane of glass that had a vast body of water behind it, pushing from the other side to try and crush me. There wasn't any way I could defeat the vast pool of power I felt opposing me, but somehow most of its force was directed elsewhere.

I hadn't closed my eyes. I wanted to, but I refused to give up while there was even the slightest chance that I might survive. Because my eyes were open I was able to see as the ground opened up in front of Dream Stealer in a clear bid to trap him in a dark chasm.

Dream Stealer leaped into the air with a speed and grace that no normal person could have matched, but the chasm suddenly widened, growing at a rate that made it obvious to me that there wouldn't be any kind of safe landing for him by the time he landed. I felt what I could only call a ripple and suddenly the chasm stopped growing as quickly. It didn't stop, Dream Stealer apparently wasn't strong enough—at least not inside of the wax lady's dream—to stop the ground from moving altogether, but he'd slowed it enough that it seemed like he might have a chance of landing safely on the other side.

It was going to be a close thing and for a split second I considered redirecting my efforts and trying to help slow the movement of the ground, but I was too selfish to throw away my own chance of survival. I pushed even harder, trying to slow the fist coming towards me down to something I could dodge.

The force pushing against me trembled slightly and then the ground sped back up. It was obvious that Dream Stealer was going to die, but two things happened in that instant that changed everything.

Dream Stealer's arms suddenly grew impossibly long, so long that he was able to reach down and stick his claws into crevices in the ground. I realized that it no longer mattered how fast the ground moved now because he'd be able to guide himself safely down, but only a fraction of my attention was on him because the force pressing down on me shattered.

I wrapped my whole being into the push to create my own version of reality inside of the dream as I felt the catch tear. Earlier I'd torn a hole in the universe to bring Dream Stealer to me. This time it was my own mind that was tearing.

A red-hot icepick of fire stabbed deep inside of my mind at the same time that the vampire screamed and grabbed her head with both hands. The tips of her claws sank into her skull, but she didn't seem to notice. I couldn't blame her. I shouldn't have been able to notice myself, but a tiny sliver of consciousness had torn itself free of the rest of my mind. Separate from the pain that had me on my knees with tears streaming down my face, it was able to dispassionately watch as the woman who had nearly killed me looked up with eyes that looked like something out of a horror movie.

The whites of her eyes had gone a dark red, like she'd had massive hemorrhaging inside of her eyes, but it didn't seem to interfere with her vision. She lunged forward again with her claws extended in an attempt to rip my throat out, but I effortlessly sidestepped her and raked my fingernails across the side of her face.

She wasn't any faster than me, but that didn't mean that she wasn't a better fighter. She spun around and sprang at me again, and this time as I dodged to the side I tripped and fell down. I tried to roll to the side, but I could tell I wasn't going to make it. Her claws slashed down towards my unprotected body, but a split second before they tore into me, Dream Stealer grabbed her from behind and whipped her through the air.

"What did you do?"

The pain had receded slightly and I found that I could talk.

"I'm not sure. I was trying to slow her down so that I could help you, but I think maybe I pushed too hard. It feels like someone ripped my head open."

"You didn't slow her down, you sped yourself up somehow. That shouldn't be possible."

The wax lady was impaled on his claws, but that didn't stop her from thrashing about in an effort to get at him. Her claws had already torn nasty gashes all up and down his arms, but she couldn't reach his head and neck, so he was safe for the moment.

"It's only a matter of time now before she gets away, at which point you'll be in danger once again. Based on your accent I relocated to Minnesota a couple of days ago. I only hope that I'm close enough to make it to you before she shakes off the effects of the dream and comes after you. Do you trust me enough to tell me where you live?"

The old terror was back, but I managed a nod and then gave him my address. I was placing my life in his hands, but I didn't know what else to do. If the wax lady, if an honest-to-goodness vampire, was about to break into my house then I'd be dead without some kind of equally scary supernatural protector.

"How far away is that from the St. Paul Hilton?"

"Ah...I think only ten or fifteen minutes depending on traffic. At night maybe as little as eight or nine minutes."

He grimaced. I wouldn't have thought his wolf-man face was capable of that kind of expression, but it apparently was.

"It will be close. I've seen people take longer than that to regain their feet, but I've also seen some take less time."

I started to tell him that I'd find a hiding place inside my house, but I stopped mid-sentence as I realized that the invisible wind he'd used previously to keep her inside of the dream was practically gone. I'd forgotten that he was capable of pinning her here like that and simply taken him at his word. It was a clear sign of treachery and I started backing away from him while I desperately tried to come up with a way out of the mess I'd just created by giving him my address.

"What are you doing, Adri?"

He'd seen my slow backwards motion, but his question didn't seem menacing so much as curious.

"You're letting her go when you could keep her here. You were working with her the whole time, weren't you? This was all a ploy to get my address."

"What...oh, I see what you mean. No, Adri, I'm not letting her go, I have no choice in the matter. I can pin someone here against their will when they are healthy, but at a certain point when they are injured their mind rips them away from me despite my best efforts. It's a kind of natural survival mechanism. Maybe if I could suck them into my dream like you do rather than always having to face them inside of their own dream things would be different, but only a very, very weak-minded individual could possibly be killed inside of their own dream. A child maybe, but not a vampire and especially not one old enough to have manifested the kind of mentalist abilities this one has shown so far."

It was all just words without any proof and he knew it as well as I did. I'd been positive that I could be killed inside of the dream.

After a second the unseen wind picked back up.

"I shouldn't be doing this, Adri. It's burning up energy I'm going to need later, but for your sake, to keep your trust I'll actively try to pin her here as long as I can. You can feel my efforts, correct?"

I nodded. I still didn't know enough about how dream walking worked to be absolutely sure that he couldn't let her go while still making me think he was holding her there, but I didn't have any way of staying away from him if he wanted to hurt me.

"Maybe she was just bluffing about her powers. Maybe she's weaker than you think, maybe you'll actually be able to kill her here in the dream before she can get away."

He shook his head. "Can't you see the tendrils of power linking the two of you?"

I started to tell him that I couldn't, but it was like his mentioning them somehow made them easier to see. He was right, there were black threads running back and forth between us. I tried to break one of them, but I was just too tired and my head hurt too much to push very hard at all. I'd been too scared earlier to really think about the fact that she was inside of my mind, but I suddenly felt like throwing up.

The wax lady had mostly gone still, but now she thrashed around again in an attempt to further shred Dream Stealer's arms. Apparently even his massive wolf-man body had its limits because he shifted her around, tearing new holes in her side and back as he got her repositioned to where she couldn't continue to hurt him. The new wounds drew a gasp of pain from her and I saw her flicker and start to go insubstantial.

The wind doubled and then doubled again as Dream Stealer tried to keep her from fleeing to safety. She'd gone pale from blood loss, but I could tell that she was going to get away before she died. I'd always thought of myself as being fairly pacifist, but I suddenly wanted her dead and the desire was so strong that it pushed me to action despite the continuing pain in my head.

I didn't know exactly what Dream Stealer was doing to keep her here, but I knew what had worked so far when it came to enforcing my will onto a dream. She was trying to flee the dream, trying to disappear, so I visualized the opposite. I imagined her here in the dream with us more fully. It was hard to describe what I was after, but it was a bit like the first time I'd increased the detail in the grass.

I created a living, three-dimensional model of her, instilled it with all of the revulsion and hatred I felt for her, and then pushed my reality into existence.

The pain was even more intense than before, but I couldn't tell if it was just the result of what I'd done earlier or if I'd torn something else inside of my mind. I was down on my knees again without any recollection of having fallen. Tears pooled in my eyes, but there was something wrong there, tears weren't supposed to make it this hard to see.

I absently wiped the tears out of my eyes, and nearly threw up again when my hand came away red and bloody. I heard screaming and only then realized that it was me, but before I could shut my mouth the vampire dangling from Dream Stealer's claws flickered again and all hell seemed to break loose.

She flickered, but this time she didn't become less substantial, she became *more*.

Another crack opened up in the ground, pitching Dream Stealer forward as he jumped for safer ground. The earthquake that had accompanied the new rift knocked me down and

I felt new slivers of glass digging into my palms. It took me a split second to understand why that surprised me. All of the loose glass had disappeared during the first part of the fight as Dream Stealer had forced the wax lady to focus on him more so than on maintaining our environment.

She was practically bled out, nearing dream death if not real death. She shouldn't have been able to strengthen the detail inside the dream, but this was even worse than that. The razor-edged shards weren't just back, they'd multiplied a dozen times over.

I tried to warn Dream Stealer that we were in trouble, but a hurricane whipped up between one heartbeat and the next. The winds would have been bad enough all by themselves, but they were sufficiently violent enough to pick up some of the black slivers and I whipped my arm up over my eyes as my clothes started to shred off of my body.

It had to be my efforts at holding her here that had given her such power. I started to let go, started to relax the corner of my mind that was screaming in pain, but a deep voice made it to me over the howl of the wind.

"No, Adri. Push harder!"

It went against every instinct I'd been born with, but it was too late to stop trusting Dream Stealer now. The world went white behind my eyelids as I threw everything I had left into making my vision of reality even more complete. I felt another micro-tear inside of my mind and for an instant it almost seemed like something was trying to claw its way inside of my skull with me.

A second later, the wind died down as if it had never been. Dream Stealer pulled himself back up to his feet and crossed the distance between us in a halting limp. The vampire—the corpse—was still dangling from his claws, but now my eyes refused to focus on it. My mind was trying to protect me from seeing what he'd done by refusing to make sense of the glimpse I'd seen before turning away.

"She's dead."

I swallowed a couple of times. "I know. I guess this means she'll be coming for me."

"No, Adri, she's truly dead. Look at the ground. It's disappearing."

I carefully turned even further away from him and then opened my eyes. He was right, although I wouldn't have described it quite that way. The ground right where we were standing was losing its substantiality and the plain had already started shrinking. A minute ago it had stretched off farther than the eye could see; now it simply faded away to nothing less than a hundred yards away from us.

"I don't understand."

"It shouldn't do this. When someone leaves the dream they are the first thing to go. Usually I get kicked out of the dream so quickly that I don't even see them leave, but sometimes their mind leaves the dream up for a second or two without them in it. This is completely backwards. Her mind can't sustain the dream anymore. It's thrown everything into trying to keep her whole. She's dead, or at least dying. Once she's completely gone we'll probably still get snapped back to our bodies, but we won."

"I'm safe?"

He nodded. "None of this should be even remotely possible, but yes, she's no longer a threat."

A wave of relief crashed through me. I knew that later I'd start second-guessing what I'd done, start worrying about the fact that I'd helped kill her, but right now I was just glad to have survived. I started to thank Dream Stealer for his help, but was cut off when the dream flickered around me.

"Did you see that? Is that supposed to happen?"

"Did I see what?"

"Everything flickered. Like someone had turned off the light here in the dream."

He'd shifted back down into human form and I noticed that much of the damage from his fight with the vampire and the flying shards of glass seemed to have been healed in the process. My question brought a frown to his face.

"Is there someone else in the house with you? It sounds like you're being woken up against your will."

My stomach dropped. In all of the terror and adrenaline of the fight I'd forgotten about Jackson, forgotten that he'd be heading over to my house as soon as he got back from the game. I didn't know how much more time I had, but it couldn't be long.

"I think there's another vampire. They were working together and he's the one who finally figured out my real identity."

"Hold on. Try not to let him get you into a vehicle. I can track the two of you as long as there is a scent trail, I'll be there as soon as..."

I didn't catch the rest of what he said because I was ripped away from the dream and back into the waking world.

Chapter 26

Jackson looked down at me impassively. "I'm impressed, Adri. I wouldn't have thought you capable of killing Pamela like that. How did you manage it?"

I debated my response, discarding several ideas before deciding that my best bet was just to cooperate as much as possible. I didn't want him to know about Dream Stealer, but everything else was fair game if it would keep him talking and buy more time for the cavalry to arrive.

"It's not supposed to be possible. I'm not even really positive how I did it or if I could do it again, but I managed to pull her so strongly into the dream that she couldn't flee when her dream body died."

"Hmm, interesting. That means that you're an even better weapon than she originally thought you would be. We've spent weeks looking for you, you know. She knew you were somehow special when the two of you ran into each other that first time. She's a mentalist, so she was able to pick up bits and pieces from your mind, mostly that you'd been developing this incredible dream power but that you didn't fully understand how to control it. It's really too bad she didn't get your identity then."

I swallowed nervously despite my best efforts. "She could have if she hadn't killed me. I mean she didn't really kill me, but she choked me and when I passed out in the dream I came back to myself here in the real world."

Jackson nodded. "We figured as much. We didn't know for sure, but we suspected that you had to be fairly close by. Most psychic powers don't work very well over extreme distances. When there weren't any cheerleader deaths in the news over the next couple of days we were pretty sure you'd survived."

I slowly sat up. "Then when I met you in the dream you knew that I was still alive and you knew I was on the team with you."

Jackson snorted softly as though laughing at a joke that only he understood. "I suppose you're right in a way. The truth is that it was me, but it also wasn't me. You actually met Alan in that dream, he's the part of me that couldn't…deal with what Pamela demanded of her minions. She split the two of us up early on when I proved harder to break than she anticipated."

"Wait, you mean like split personalities?"

"Yes, exactly, only there's more bleedthrough between the two identities than you'd normally see in your typical textbook case. I'm actually quite fond of Alan. He's weak and completely useless outside of his particular area of expertise, but he makes it a lot easier to deal with you humans. I find it quite fatiguing trying to maintain a facade of normality, so I spend much of the day taking cues from him."

"How does he feel about you?"

I couldn't actually identify anything different about Jackson's smile than normal, but there was an edge to it that made my skin crawl.

"Oh, he positively loathes me. And rightly so. I've done things with our body that he never would have agreed to. Then again, I would have never said that Pamela would be able to recruit him to help track you down. I wonder what she promised him, he's been awfully quiet where that particular bit of information is concerned. Probably something ridiculous like getting rid of me altogether. We both know Pamela would never have done that, but he does refuse to give up hope."

"I thought he couldn't hide anything from you."

"No, things bleed through, but not everything and Pamela can temporarily shut down one personality if she wants to keep something a secret. That's really the heart of the problem that you've left me with, Adri. Jackson and Alan functioned solely because Pamela continued to tinker with our shared mind. With her gone, I'm not really sure what will happen. Likely the two personalities will try to reintegrate."

"Isn't that a good thing? Wouldn't you like to be free?"

"Alan would certainly say so, but it's not a good thing for me because I like...working for Pamela. I'm exactly what she intended me to be. Don't be fooled into thinking that I'm all of the bad and Alan is all of the good. The truth is that I'm all of the attributes Pamela thought were useful and he's everything she didn't want. Normally vampires scheme nonstop looking for a way to be free of their master. Alan certainly does, but I've never seen the point."

"Because you love her?"

"Hardly. No, because the weak will always serve the strong. As much as I might prefer for it to be otherwise, I am weak. Given enough years for my powers to grow, Jackson could eventually become strong enough to become a vampire elder, but Alan wouldn't last five minutes without Jackson's help. I'm weak because Alan makes me weak and you've made it so that eventually Alan will assume partial control over me."

"I'm sorry."

Jackson waved my words away. "Your regret or lack thereof makes no difference. That's the thing you never quite understood. Jackson expressed interest in you because Pamela ordered it, but when you didn't react more strongly to the sunflowers that Alan told us to send to all of the cheerleaders, Jackson moved on to Wendy. It was simply orders. Your feelings never entered into the equation in any manner other than as a possible vulnerability to be exploited."

Listening to him made my skin crawl and not just because of the way that he'd convinced me he was interested in me.

"Is there a third person in there too? Is there someone else besides just Jackson and Alan?"

I'd caught him by surprise for the first time all night, maybe the first time ever. He tried to hide it, but his face had been so dead and expressionless that even a slight change was as good as if he'd gasped.

"You know, I'd never even considered the possibility. I suspect that particular blind spot was created intentionally by Pamela. Possibly that is how she's managed to keep the two of us in such a static balance of power for so long. It explains so much."

He'd turned his back on me, but I was under no illusions when it came to my ability to escape. If he was even half as fast as what Pamela had been inside of the dream then nothing I could possibly do would allow me a big enough head start to get away from him.

A flash of movement from the front door caught my eye, but I forced myself not to move. If it was Tristan or Dream Stealer then I couldn't risk alerting Jackson to their presence and if it wasn't them then it didn't matter who or what was out there. Instead I tried to regain Jackson's attention.

"What are you going to do with me?"

"Yeah, back to the problem at hand. I don't actually know. You represent an astonishing weapon by any measure, but you're equally a liability to whoever tries to master you. The fact that you were able to kill Pamela while she was dreaming means that you'd almost certainly be able to kill me in the same fashion and locking you up would do absolutely nothing to prevent my demise."

He was tapping the side of his face as he looked at me, but the thing that struck me the hardest was the fact that his face wasn't the expressionless, dead thing it had been a few seconds ago.

"I'm talking to Jackson again, aren't I?"

"Of course. Alan...and the other one aren't qualified to deal with vampire politics and frankly they are both a little nervous at the idea of reintegration. They don't want to know everything that I've done over the last few decades."

"How old are you?"

"Old enough to be your grandfather, which still makes me little more than a child compared to most of the vampires who served Pamela before we were run out of Atlanta. I thought that bowing and scraping to them for all those years was the most miserable existence possible, but it doesn't have anything over on being forced to pretend that I'm still a teenager."

"You could drug me."

Jackson smiled. "There's the spirit. I like that you're a problem-solver. You're right, if drugging you ensures that you sleep without being able to get inside of my head then that would be one way to make sure that you were safe. The problem is that I won't know whether or not the drugs are working until you make your first attempt at killing me. Do you already know that certain drugs don't work on you, Adri?"

I couldn't get over how genuine his smile looked, especially considering the fact that I was pretty sure he didn't actually feel emotions.

"How did you learn how to pretend to be normal so well when you don't actually feel any of the same emotions?"

"I actually do feel some of the same emotions, but mostly I've just been practicing for longer than you've been alive. You still haven't answered my question though."

I licked my lips. I knew it was a bad visual cue, a sign that I might be lying, but I couldn't help myself. The next couple of seconds were going to decide my fate one way or another.

"I don't know. I've never tried it. I wish I would have thought of it because then I could have stayed drugged as a way of ensuring that I didn't run into you or Pamela again."

"Indeed. I almost believe you, Adri. You paint a tempting picture. If you can be controlled then it would mean that I could take you to another vampire elder in return for leniency. I'd have to select another mentalist, a fairly powerful one, and I'd have to hurry. There's no telling how long I have before integration starts happening. It could actually work."

I'd been concentrating on looking at Jackson, so as not to tip him off to the fact that Tristan was creeping towards him, but I'd still been able to see that Tristan had a shiny aluminum bat in one hand, which short of a gun was probably the best equalizer he could have brought with him.

Tristan made it almost to within striking range without being caught. He was a natural athlete and he had some pretty powerful incentive to be quiet. If the floor hadn't creaked he might have even been able to take Jackson down, but instead of his blow taking Jackson in the head, the vampire spun around and got an arm up, deflecting the bat away even as his arm crumpled from the force of the blow.

For a split second, I thought Tristan still had a chance. Jackson seemed to be moving quickly, but not that much more quickly than a normal human. It wasn't until Jackson hit Tristan in the stomach with his uninjured left arm that I realized Jackson wasn't moving slower than expected, I was just somehow still able to process what was going on around me extra fast, just like in the dream.

Jackson's blow hadn't seemed particularly quick or powerful, but it sent Tristan crashing back towards the living room wall in painful slow motion even as it pulled a scream out of me. My scream seemed to go on for forever, but eventually I had to take a breath. Only the scream didn't go away as I sucked air back into my oxygen-starved lungs.

It wasn't until Jackson took two quick steps back towards the front door and backhanded Cindi that I realized there were actually four of us in the room. Cindi crumpled to the ground, her scream dying away instantly as her head hit the ground. For one heart-wrenching second I thought he'd killed her, but then I saw that her eyes were fluttering and she started groaning and trying to pull herself back to her feet.

"Really, Adri? If you were going to call for reinforcements you should at least have gotten the police. Tristan and Cindi are just going to end up as more collateral damage."

Tristan had been gasping for air, but he gamely grabbed the baseball bat up from off the floor and tried to pick himself back up off of the ground. Jackson was obviously keeping an eye on things though because he once again hit Tristan with his uninjured hand, this time in the side of the head, and then he held his hand out and the bat flew through the air towards him without any visible force propelling it.

"You actually did manage to take me by surprise, Tristan. If I'd had even a fraction of a second more time to react I would have just stopped the bat in the air using my telekinetic gifts. I really am sorry to do this, believe it or not, I'm actually a pretty big fan of your work on the field."

Jackson slammed the bat down on Tristan's lower leg and I heard both bones in his right leg snap. Tristan screamed, but that didn't mask the sound of his other leg breaking as Jackson lifted the bat again and slammed it down on Tristan's left leg.

Cindi was crawling towards Tristan, sobbing his name softly. My altered perceptions gave me enough time to notice trivialities like the fact that her favorite blue purse was still dangling from her left shoulder, dragging along the floor as she crawled.

Jackson turned back to me and sighed. "As much as I'd like to take a chance on you, Adri, I just don't think I can. You have this alarming way of convincing people to help you almost in spite of themselves. You're going to have to die."

Cindi's voice was calm, without even the slightest trace of the hysteria I'd been expecting.

"You'll have to go through me first."

Jackson turned, bat raised to strike, and got a face full of pepper spray.

Cindi had pulled the tiny black cylinder out of her purse and fired from the ground in one smooth motion that told me she'd practiced this dozens of times already. Her aim was true and although Jackson didn't scream, he let out a hiss of pain that told me that the unnatural strength and vitality of a vampire wasn't completely proof against the burning pain in his eyes. He brought his bat up again, doubtlessly intending on incapacitating Cindi like he'd incapacitated Tristan, and I threw myself off of the couch.

I was moving in slow motion just like Cindi and Tristan had been, which proved that my altered time sense hadn't done anything to break the rest of the laws of physics, but I did the best I could with what I had.

Jackson was still moving faster than I was, but he'd brought the bat way up over his head, which meant that it still had a long distance to travel. I was pretty sure that I could make it to him before he hit Cindi, but I wasn't under any kind of illusion that I was strong enough to actually stop the bat, so I kicked the back of his knee, the front one that had all of his weight on it.

He went down with another hiss of pain as his broken arm hit the ground, but he kept ahold of the bat and before I could step forward to try and kick him in the head something hit me from the side hard enough to knock me to the ground. I caught the barest glimpse of it as I fell and realized that Jackson had launched the ugly, gray, stone idol that my mom had picked up on her trip down to South America before she and my dad got married.

At first I thought the shooting pain in my arm was from how hard I'd hit the ground, but then I realized it was the wrong arm for that. I was pretty sure my left arm was broken, but I levered myself up into a sitting position as Jackson slowly walked towards me, involuntary tears still streaming down his face.

"You had a good run, Adri. Honestly I never would have expected a mere human to last this long."

Jackson raised the bat one last time, but the crash of breaking glass interrupted his swing. It was dark enough that at first I wasn't sure what I was seeing. It looked like a piece of the night had detached itself from the rest of the darkness and thrown itself at Jackson, but just before it collided with him it shifted from a shape with four legs to one with two.

Dream Stealer shed his wolf form and tackled Jackson with his towering wolf-man form despite a glancing blow to his side from the bat. Dream Stealer didn't move with the kind of speed and strength that I'd remembered from the fight against Pamela, and Jackson still displayed the same kind of unnatural strength and vitality that had kept Pamela going long after she should have died, but with one arm broken and Dream

Stealer's bigger, heavier body pinning him to the floor there wasn't much he could do to resist.

It only took a couple of seconds for Dream Stealer to impale both of Jackson's legs with the long talons that seemed to be standard issue for guys like him and Alec. Once that happened, Jackson had even less leverage and Dream Stealer was easily able to pin Jackson's uninjured shoulder to the floor and execute him.

I wasn't prepared for all of the blood. It wasn't any more than I'd seen in the dream, but I'd known that wasn't real. This time I did throw up, or least my body tried to throw up, there wasn't actually anything left in my stomach.

Once I was done, Cindi helped me back up to a sitting position. Dream Stealer had changed back to his human form and was checking Tristan for a concussion.

"He'll be okay once his legs heal, but we're all going to need to talk about what happened."

Chapter 27

Nearly every single part of my body hurt. Dream Stealer—he'd told me I could call him Taggart—said that it wasn't normal for the mind to induce phantom pain in the body like this after a dream, but apparently that was one more side effect of the different way that my power worked.

My arm hurt of course, and would be hurting for a while, although when it came to broken bones I'd come out quite a ways ahead of Tristan. In addition, every single square inch of my skin felt like it had been peeled off with a cheese grater, and I had a couple of different spots in my stomach and chest where I felt stabbing pains every time I moved.

I vaguely remembered being stabbed in that general area, so I suspected it was going to take the longest to return to feeling normal. All in all, I couldn't think of a time when I'd felt more beat up, but I would have gone through twice as much physical pain if it had meant that I would be able to forgo the emotional and mental anguish I was currently trying to deal with.

Dream Stealer—Taggart—had loaded Tristan, Cindi and me into Tristan's car and then driven us to one of the worst parts of Minneapolis. Apparently there really were doctors willing to cast broken bones and not ask questions.

Taggart not only knew how to get in touch with the city's underground, he also seemed to have the ridiculous amounts of money required to buy his way in to see pretty much whoever he needed to talk to. While Tristan was being taken care of, I'd given Taggart the spare house key and he'd promised to have someone repair the damage from our fight before my parents returned home on Sunday.

Normally I would have asked about the cost of arranging all of that, but the doctor had injected me with something to dull the pain while I waited for my turn and I was more than a little out of it. As a consequence, I didn't remember much of what happened for the next few hours, but I'd woken Saturday afternoon and found myself in one of the largest hotel suites I'd ever seen.

I panicked for a second until I saw Tristan on the bed in the room across from mine and Cindi asleep on a black leather couch that had been positioned so that it was equidistant between the two of us. Getting out of bed with only one working arm was more difficult than I'd expected it to be. It wasn't that it wasn't doable or anything, but I was realizing that I used my left arm for a lot more than I'd ever realized.

I made enough noise getting out of bed to wake up Cindi. She quietly pulled Tristan's door closed and then came into my room so we could talk. Taggart had filled her in on nearly everything and the parts he hadn't known about she'd guessed correctly.

She said she was sorry for being so jealous at how easy cheering had come for me, and I said I was sorry for not having told her about the fact that I was sharing people's dreams. We cried a little and hugged a lot, and when everything was said and done things felt better between us than they had in a really long time.

I was surprised at just how calmly she was taking everything. If I'd been in her place I would probably have run away screaming that none of what I was being told was possible. I guess it's hard to argue with your own eyes though and she'd seen Taggart shift forms and seen Jackson move objects around with his mind.

While Tristan and I had been unconscious, Cindi and Taggart had come up with a plan to explain Tristan's injuries. Taggart had backed Tristan's car into another automobile and then had fake police and hospital reports created indicating that Tristan had been between the two cars when they'd impacted.

I wasn't sure how well it would hold up, but then again I would have said it was impossible to fake police reports on such short notice and in a town that was obviously not Taggart's normal base of operation.

The cover story included the fact that Tristan had been knocked unconscious and that his identification had been inside of his car, which explained why his parents hadn't been called immediately. There were a bunch of other details that helped flesh everything out, but that was the basics of what they'd come up with.

There had been a lot of debate around what exactly my parents were going to hear. In the end, it was both harder and easier than I expected it to be. The only thing that everyone had agreed on was that Cindi shouldn't mention vampires or shape shifters.

Watching Cindi walk away, pushing Tristan in his wheelchair, nearly made me change my mind, but I knew I had to go through with my decision, if for no other reason than it was the best way to keep everyone that I cared about safe.

Taggart had been trying to give me space and time to deal with things in my own way, but I could tell that he was getting impatient. He walked over as I looked down at the blocky gray burner phone he'd given me more than an hour earlier.

"I'm sorry, Adri, but if you don't make your call now I'm going to have to arrange for another vehicle."

Tears started to come, but I choked down the urge to break into tears. I'd already done enough crying to last a year.

"Tell me again why this is the best option. It feels like pretty much the same thing that would have happened if Pamela and Jackson had gotten their hands on me."

"I'm not going to be torturing you for starters. I'm also not going to make you do anything you don't want to do."

"I'm still leaving my family, maybe never to see them again, and I'm still going to be turned into a weapon."

"I can't change the realities of the situation, Adri. You can choose to stay with your family if you wish, but you will be exposing them to some degree of danger."

I started to laugh and then forced myself to stop. I was a stiff breeze from being pushed over into complete hysteria. If I got started laughing I'd almost certainly end up in tears within a few minutes.

"And you don't know how much danger they'd be in?"

"No, there's no way to tell, not without knowing who Pamela and Jackson might have told about their suspicions. Even if they just told another vampire back in Atlanta that they'd found someone who was potentially a powerful weapon then all of the evidence would point to you. It ultimately doesn't matter how well I hide the bodies, there is too much physical evidence between Tristan's legs and your arms. It all points to the two of you having been involved in Pamela and Jackson's deaths. At least it would for anyone who knows just how unlikely they were to just disappear—for anyone who knows that they were vampires."

Taggart looked away from me for several seconds and then shrugged. "As for the other, you're already a weapon. You've been a weapon almost from the first day that your power awoke, you just didn't know it. I'm giving you a chance to be your own weapon. Trust me, it's much better to chart your own course than it is to simply be unleashed on targets not of your own choosing at another's command."

I nodded. "I know. Intellectually I'm on board with everything you just said, but my heart hasn't signed on fully yet."

"I understand. Take as long as you need to. I'll go see about arranging another car."

"No, I'll make the call now. If nothing else, I need to save Cindi from the interrogation she's currently suffering through."

I dialed my dad's number. I half expected it to go through to voicemail since he wouldn't recognize the number, but it was his work phone and he rarely let a call to it go unanswered, even when in the middle of a family crisis.

"This is John."

"Daddy."

I tried, but for a second I couldn't get anything else out.

"Daddy, it's me, Adri."

"Adri, where are you? I'm on my way to get you right now."

"No, you can't come. The letter Cindi just gave you is more for the police than anything else. You'll need it to explain why I left, but I meant it when I said I couldn't come back home, at least not for a long time."

"I don't understand, sweetie. Was it something we did? Your mom and I had a lot of really good talks while we were away. I'm sorry we left the two of you home alone, but things are going to be better, you'll see. Just come home."

"I'm sorry, I can't do that. I want to more than anything, but I can't. It's not safe, not for you guys or me, either one."

"Are you being held against your will?"

"No, this is my choice. I...well, things happened. I'm not safe to be around right now. I need time to learn how to...control things. I'm sorry, Dad. I wish I'd been able to stay and say goodbye in person, but I was afraid that you wouldn't let me go."

"I don't care what happened, Adri, we can deal with it. Please just come home."

"I love you, Daddy."

Something in my voice convinced him. I would have said it was impossible, but apparently he knew me better than even I'd realized. He knew that I wouldn't be doing this if I thought there was even the slightest possibility of any other course working for all of us.

"I love you too, Adri. If you ever change your mind we'll be here waiting. I don't care how dangerous you think you are, it doesn't matter what you're involved in, if you come home we'll be here for you and we'll deal with whatever it is."

"I know. Thanks. For that and for everything. I'm sorry I wasn't a better daughter."

I could hear the tears he was fighting off, they came through in the way his voice thickened and quivered.

"You don't have anything to be sorry about. You were everything I could have ever hoped for. I'll miss you."

"I know. I'll miss you too, Dad."

"Your mom wants to talk to you. I'm sorry, I'd put you on speaker but this damn phone hasn't worked right for months."

"Adri, is it really you?"

She'd been crying. I could hear it in her voice.

"Yeah, Mom, it's me. I'm sorry I made you guys worry."

"You're not coming home are you?"

"No, at least not for a really long time."

There was silence for several seconds and then a shaky sigh. "I'm sorry that I made your last few weeks at home so difficult. Your dad and

I are going to work things out. If you do decide to come back home, things will be different."

"That's good, Mom. I think more than anything else that's what I want, for you guys to take care of each other and Cindi."

"You were always too selfless for your own good. I'm sorry that I didn't spend more time with you and take you shopping like I did your sister. I guess I was always just a little jealous of the bond your dad has with you."

"It's okay, Mom. Don't be too hard on Cindi. You guys probably already realize that there is a lot she isn't telling you, but it's for your own safety."

There was a quiet thump as though the phone had been set down, and then I heard the sound of distant crying. Dad picked up the phone a second later.

"As much as I'd like for you to stay on with us for hours, I suspect that you need to be moving. Do you want to talk to Cindi before you hang up?"

"Yes, please."

"I'll go get her."

I heard Dad knocking on our...on Cindi's bedroom door a few seconds later.

"It's Adri. She doesn't have much time but wanted to talk to you. I'll leave so you have some privacy."

"Hi, sis."

"Hi, Cindi. Are Mom and Dad punishing you too much?"

She hesitated for a heartbeat. "No, not too bad. When you look at everything that happened, everything that I did, they are probably letting me off easy."

"This isn't your fault, Cindi."

"Are you sure about that? Maybe if I'd been a decent enough sister for you to tell me what was going on, then Jackson never would have figured out that it was you he'd run into in his dreams."

"You can't think like that. Besides, it was really only a matter of time until someone found out about me. Don't think about all of that though. Get your grades back up, get back on the team, and enjoy the next few years."

She didn't say anything for several seconds. "I'm not sure I'm going to rejoin the team. There doesn't seem to be much point. I mostly joined because I thought it would make it easier to finally find a boyfriend. That didn't work out very well."

I'd thought we were past this, but I couldn't let our final conversation end on a sour note. "I'm really sorry about Tristan, Cindi. I promise that I never consciously did anything to lead him on."

"I know. We actually talked for a couple of hours this morning. He told me the rest of his side of the story. Kind of funny to know now that I would have had a better chance with him if I hadn't joined the cheerleading squad. I guess that's good though. Teams and clubs help segregate people out so that likeminded people are all together. Having a cheer squad means that all of the self-centered, spoiled brats are all in one place so that guys like Tristan can avoid them more easily."

Now I was angry. "Stop that. Don't let them define who you are. Miss Winters isn't like that and I don't think you are either, at least not deep down. Give Tristan some time and maybe he'll come around. He saw you stand up to Jackson just like I did. Not a lot of girls would have the guts to come running into the house like that and then hit a vampire with pepper spray."

"No, he's pretty head over heels for you still, Adri. It's okay, I don't begrudge you having won his heart."

"Cindi, I'm...well, I'm not coming back, not for a long time, maybe never. I don't want him to sit there and pine for me. It wouldn't be fair to him, especially not considering that there's someone else I'm interested in."

"Yeah, he told me you'd said that to him too."

"It's the truth. Just give him time, Cindi. He's a lot better guy than I ever realized, and the two of you have a bond now that he doesn't share with anyone else in the school. If you honestly, in your heart of hearts, don't want him then that's fine, but otherwise it would make me really happy to know that the two of you eventually got together."

It was obvious by the silence that she wasn't ready to agree to anything yet, but I figured that was a good sign. If she was still conflicted then it meant that she did still want Tristan. Eventually that desire would trump her regret over having treated me like crap for the last few weeks.

"Adri...will you at least call us from time to time?"

"I'll try. I don't know what the future will bring or what Taggart will decide is too dangerous, but I'll really try to keep in touch."

Taggart was walking back over to me and I could tell by his manner that our ride was almost here.

"I'm sorry, Cindi, but it looks like I'm going to have to go. I love you. Tell Mom and Dad that I love them too."

"I love you too, Adri. Be careful out there."

She hung up before anything else could be said, but I'd heard the tears in her voice, so I knew it wasn't out of spite.

A black SUV pulled up as Taggart took the burner phone from my hands and wiped it down with a white handkerchief. A couple of rough-looking guys got out and handed Taggart the keys to the SUV.

"You two know your job?"

The taller guy, the one with the chin piercing, nodded. "Yeah, we take your car back the way we came. The rest of our payment is waiting for us in Marshal."

Less than a minute later all of our things had been moved to the SUV and Taggart had dropped my burner phone on the side of the road.

As we drove away I knew two things. First, leaving my family was the hardest thing I'd ever done, but in a way I was glad that I was leaving them rather than the other way around. With all the crap that had happened it was still nice to know that they were back there waiting for me to return to them someday.

Second, as soon as I had a chance to recover from the last few days, as soon as I put five or six pounds back on, I was going to start trying to contact Alec again. Nothing short of death was going to stop me from finding him.

Acknowledgements

Once again, this book wouldn't have ever seen the light of day. My editors, RJ Locksley and Amy Jirsa-Smith, did great work cleaning up typos and mixed metaphors. Once they had finished pummeling Hunted into shape, it went out to my beta readers who helped make sure that I didn't introduce too many new errors while fixing the issues that RJ and Amy identified. In no particular order my beta readers are: Mom, Dad, Shalese, Matthew, Mark VanderDoes, Mimi VanderDoes, Kim Allred, Chris Beijk, Janine Anderson, Janelle Gordinier, and Heather Tucker. Thank you all for your assistance!

A big thanks to Brittany Gale who was kind enough to read through Hunted and make sure that I didn't go too wrong when it comes to life as a cheerleader—thanks, Brittany.

My wife, Katie, continues to be the glue that holds the Murray household together. She is the first person to see each new book, she provides great feedback as to what does and doesn't work with the plot, and then she pitches in to do my covers around all of the other responsibilities that she has. Thanks, Katie.

About the Author

Dean Murray is a prolific author with more than thirty titles across multiple pen names and more than half a million copies of his work currently in circulation.

Dean started reading seriously in the second grade due to a competition and has spent most of the subsequent three decades lost in other people's worlds.

Things worsened, or improved depending on your point of view, when he first started experimenting with writing while finishing up his accounting degree.

These days Dean has a wonderful wife and two lovely daughters to keep him rather more grounded, but the idea of bringing others along with him as he meets interesting new people in universes nobody else has ever seen tends to drag him back to his computer on a fairly regular basis.

Keep up to speed on Dean's latest projects at www.DeanWrites.com.

Torn

Shape shifter Alec Graves has spent nearly a decade trying to keep his family from being drawn into open warfare with a larger pack. The new girl at school shouldn't matter, but the more he gets to know her, the more mysterious she becomes. Worse, she seems to know things she shouldn't about his shadowy world.

Is she an unfortunate victim or bait designed to draw him into a fatal misstep? If she's a victim, then he's running out of time to save her. If she's bait, then his attraction to her will pull him into a fight that'll cost him everything.

The Greater Darkenss

Dean writing as Eldon Murphy

Something powerful is stirring in the darkness. Something so ancient that even creatures who've been alive for hundreds of years have long since discounted this new threat as nothing more than myth.

Normal humans will be caught in the crossfire, but then that's always the way of things. Geoffrey has no memory of his past life or any idea how to survive in the violent, dangerous world in which he's trapped. Despite his best efforts, he's about to find himself in the middle of a conflict that threatens to sweep away everything, and everyone he's been fighting so hard to protect.

Frozen Prospects

The invitation to join the secretive Guadel should have been the fulfillment of dreams Va'del didn't even realize he had. When his sponsors are killed in an ambush a short time later, he instead finds his probationary status revoked, and becomes a pawn between various factions inside the Guadel ruling body.

Jain's never known any life but that of a Guadel in training. She'd thought herself reconciled to the idea of a loveless marriage for the good of her people, but meeting Va'del changes everything. Their growing attraction flies against hundreds of years of precedent, but as wide-spread attacks threaten their world, the Guadel have no choice but to use even Jain and Va'del in their fight for survival.

CHET

Whispers From the Past

By Larry Murray

Meet Charles Tucker, he has spent nearly 30 years living in denial, trying desperately to hide from his past and the events that shattered his heart beyond any possibility of healing. He can't let anyone close, for doing so would open him up to being hurt again, and there's no way he could survive another wounding.

Meet the Saunders family, new to the neighborhood and teetering on the verge of bankruptcy. Mark, the father, talks a good story but is that all he is? His plan could hold the key to reversing his family's financial misfortunes, or it could wipe out everyone involved.

Meet Chet, a battered old '64 Chevy pickup that was there on the night Charles' life imploded. For nearly three decades, he has been locked away in an old barn, safely out of sight if not completely out of mind. For 29 years Charles has blamed the old pickup for the destruction of his life, now he's about to find that the vehicle that destroyed his life might be the key to his healing and a journey of unexpected miracles.

www.ingramcontent.com/pod-product-compliance
Lightning Source LLC
Chambersburg PA
CBHW020634020726
47494CB00001B/191